THE GIRL FROM BLIND RIVER

THE GIRL FROM BLIND RIVER

A NOVEL

GALE MASSEY

CROOKED
LANE

NEW YORK

Copyright © 2018 by Gale Massey.

Published in the United States by Crooked Lane Books, an imprint of The Quick Brown Fox & Company LLC.

Crooked Lane Books and its logo are trademarks of The Quick Brown Fox & Company LLC.

Library of Congress Catalog-in-Publication data available upon request.

ISBN (hardcover): 978-1-68331-640-4
ISBN (ePub): 978-1-68331-641-1
ISBN (ePDF): 978-1-68331-642-8

Cover design by Melanie Sun.

Printed in the United States.

www.crookedlanebooks.com

Crooked Lane Books
34 West 27th St., 10th Floor
New York, NY 10001

First Edition: July 2018

10 9 8 7 6 5 4 3 2 1

For Lyra

1

Jamie shielded her eyes from a gust of wind blowing down the street and crossed the dirt yard in front of her uncle's trailer. A beagle huddled against the night air in the back of a pickup lifted its head and whined, but Jamie had nothing to feed it. Halfway up the porch steps, she heard the men inside, grabbed the mail that no one had bothered to collect for the last few days, and opened the door.

The air inside was thick with smoke and the smell of beer and whiskey. The wind from outside lifted her uncle's ball cap, but he caught it and said, "Shut that door before everything goes flying."

He sat at the head of the kitchen table with five of his buddies, most of them still wearing blue work shirts from their shifts at the fertilizer plant south of town. Every Friday night, these men clocked out at five o'clock sharp and drove to her Uncle Loyal's place for a night of booze and poker. Years ago she'd vowed never to become some good old boy's wife sitting around a duplex waiting for her life to turn out like her own mother's had. Not when she was so good at poker and not when other nineteen-year-olds were already playing the professional circuit. She had almost enough money to go pro, and pretty soon her little brother would be big enough to handle himself alone with their uncle.

Loyal tossed an empty pizza box on the floor and peeked at his hole cards, a bottle of Jack Daniels parked near his elbow. His best buddy, the county judge, sat to his left looking somewhat out of place in this group with his neatly trimmed gray hair and red sweater, but his presence explained the Cadillac parked alongside the pickups outside. The sight of him made her bristle; Keating was the one who'd decided Jamie and Toby would live with their uncle while their mother spent those eight years in prison, but he rarely came around to this side of town.

Toby belched and wiped his mouth, avoiding the welt that ran the length of his cheekbone. His eyelids sloped just short of shut as he guzzled the dregs of a beer, crushed the can with his fist, and threw it toward the garbage. An empty shot glass was his card marker and he was down to his last chip, which he tossed into the pot. "I'm all in," he slurred.

A few beers and a little whiskey and Toby was trashed enough to make a stupid bet. He was always the first player to go broke. Jamie searched the remaining pizza boxes until she found a piece of crust and chewed it while she watched the hand play out.

Loyal called the boy's bet and huffed when Toby flipped over a two/three.

"Whatever." Toby tripped when he stood and the table rocked beneath his weight.

"Get him out of here, Jamie." Loyal pushed the boy away.

It seemed Toby might push back or take a swing at his uncle, but his face went slack with the effort to stay upright and he lurched toward the dark hallway. Judge Keating grabbed one of his arms and helped Jamie steer him down the hall to the back room.

Toby passed out facedown on his cot, stinking of boyhood and pepperoni.

"I hear he can be a handful," Keating said.

She expected him to drop Toby on the cot and leave, but he just stood there. The room was too tight to have a grown man standing in it. Jamie turned on the lamp. Clothes and school books were scattered on the floor, and with their two cots there wasn't much room to navigate. Keating hovered near the doorway as though his being in this cramped room was natural. It wasn't and she wished he'd leave. It was nobody's business how they lived. He looked around the room and she could feel him judging every detail, the torn curtains, grimy plywood floor, the old thin mattresses sunk low in the middle.

"You two share this room?"

"Yeah." He knew how they lived and she took it as a put-down. She picked up a pair of jeans and folded them, giving him a look that meant it was time for him to go.

But Keating lingered. He pointed at the Army

recruitment poster hanging on the wall over Toby's bed. A uniformed soldier standing in front of a U.S. flag. "I wanted to join the Army when I was his age, too," he said. "Guns and tanks. Boys like to dream about powerful things like that."

Jamie hated that poster, those eyes always staring at her, but Toby was crazy for anything Army. "He's going to military camp for the summer."

"That private school upstate? You got money for that?"

It was a stupid question. They never had that kind of money and this man standing in her room with his brand-new L.L.Bean sweater knew it. The back of her neck got hot. "They let two kids in for free last year."

"Hardship case, huh? I got an old friend there. I could give him a call. I doubt he'll get in without a decent reference."

Keating stepped closer to her. She flinched before she realized he was just turning to leave.

"It's only a phone call." He hesitated at the dresser by the door and picked up a framed photograph of her and Toby with their mother from ten years ago. "Huh," he said. "He looks like his dad."

"You knew him?" It always shocked her to realize there were people in town who had known her father when he'd been dead half her life.

"Of course. Knew both your parents in high school, decades ago. And you look a lot like your mother."

People who knew Phoebe Elders were always saying that, and it bothered Jamie. She saw herself as different and cringed at the notion that fate was handed down through family DNA.

He touched a finger to the photo. The gesture was intimate and wrong for someone outside the family. Jamie grabbed at the frame, accidentally jabbing a fingernail into the back of his hand. He winced and dropped the frame.

She stepped backward. "Sorry." She picked the frame up off the floor. There was a crack in the glass, but she could fix it with a little tape.

Keating loomed in the doorway, rubbing his hand. "It's nothing."

Toby, thick-headed with sleep, muttered something that sounded like, "Nah, man," and rolled over.

She held the photograph to her chest. "Sometimes he talks in his sleep."

"That camp might teach him a few things, maybe keep him out of county detention—and from that last social services report, I'd say that's where he's headed."

Wind slammed across the open field out back and shook the trailer on its foundation. Jamie tried to think of a comeback but got caught up worrying about that social services report. Six months to his eighteenth birthday and then they'd both be out of the system.

"That camp works out, you can pay me back some-day," he said as he left the room. He disappeared down the hallway and Jamie shut the door, wishing it had a deadbolt. It didn't sit well, being indebted to anyone even in this small way. Debts and favors were exactly how Blind River kept its hold on people.

She sat on her cot up against the wall, pulled her laptop out of her backpack, and powered it up. Its rumble and grind suggested yet another failing battery, but she was able to get online and log into her bank account to check if the transfer from her latest winnings had been deposited. It hadn't. She logged into the poker site and checked the date of her withdrawal. Seven days had passed. A few days was normal, but she would need a new computer any moment now, and every day that the money didn't show up added to the worry that something had gone wrong. If the transfer didn't come by morning, she'd have to figure another way to get online, because every day she wasn't making money meant one more day in this town. The windowpane over her bed rattled in the wind, and she pulled a blanket around her shoulders.

Through the thin walls of the trailer she heard the men in the outer room, their voices low and rhythmic as they grumbled and traded chips, complained about running low on beer, and convinced Loyal to crack open another bottle of whiskey. Footsteps thudded down the hallway, and Jamie thought about pushing her cot against the door. A minute later the toilet flushed. The footsteps stopped outside her door, and she held her breath until her uncle called out something muffled and angry and the footsteps trudged back up the hall.

She flipped through the day's mail, stopping at an envelope with the official seal of the family services department. The social worker had just visited them and they weren't due to see her again for months. It still floored her how Ms. Jilkins could appear on any given day and demand an explanation for the smallest infraction. The envelope was addressed to her uncle, but she tore it open anyway. Just as she suspected, Jilkins had ordered another meeting to discuss Toby, this time with the high school principal on Monday afternoon. Jamie would have bet anything that Keating had been copied privately. She wanted to rip the letter in half. Instead she folded it and stuck it inside her backpack until she could think it through.

She closed her laptop and yellow haze from the streetlight filled the room, shining on the Army poster. Toby refused to take it down, claiming he could put up whatever he wanted on the one wall that belonged to him. She turned away from the poster. She hated that face constantly staring out from that wall. Outside a truck backfired and she peeked through the curtain—just a neighbor off to the graveyard shift at the plant. Toby snored loudly, but Jamie would be awake until the men left. She might at least get some practice.

She went to the kitchen and poured a glass of milk. They were a bunch of hacks, no skill or finesse, but they were happy to let her deal and pushed their chairs around so she could have the spot closest to the center of the table. She didn't look at anyone, knowing they were eyeing her.

"How do we know there's nothing up her sleeve?" Keating asked, only half teasing. She waited for her uncle's cue.

"Pull your sleeves up, girl," Loyal said.

She made a show of it, pushing the sleeves of her sweater up to her elbows and turning her palms up, then down. "All good?"

They grumbled okay.

She gathered the cards from the last hand, still face up. Jacks over aces. She flipped the aces over. The cards were old and worn and felt like feathers on her fingertips. Some were split along the sides, bent at the corners, or rolled so they wouldn't lie flat on the table. She gathered them quickly, shuffled them twice, and sent the hole cards flying.

"Wait a minute." Lenny Chiles, the youngest guy there, sat opposite Loyal at the other end of the table. "What's up with these cards?"

She held the deck in her left hand and waited for Loyal. This was his game, his home, his rules, and Lenny was about to get schooled by a man with a quick temper.

"We're in the middle of a hand, Lenny." Keating held out his palm as though they were in a courtroom.

Lenny tossed one of his hole cards to the center of the table. "That one's marked."

The card sat in the middle of the table, a tiny smear on its upper right corner. Jamie cut her eyes toward Loyal and saw what any of them could see if they looked—red in the corner of his thumbnail. She squelched a smile. Loyal was lousy at cards but decent at marking them. Chew a nail past the quick and smear a corner with blood. It was late and these men were unpredictable when they were tanked on whiskey and beer. The mark was so obvious she was surprised a fight hadn't already broken out.

Loyal shrugged. "We're all hardworking men. Everybody's got cuts."

Keating said, "Let's be gentlemen here."

Lenny reached out and flipped the card over. The ace of hearts. "But that blood on your thumb only made its way to the corner of this ace?"

Loyal seemed twice the size of Lenny when he stood over the table. "You got a problem? Say what you mean or get out."

"I'm just saying it's kinda funny. Maybe we should get our money back."

"This isn't my style," Keating said. "I think this game is over." He stood, picked up his coat, and slipped out the front door.

The men were alert now. They pushed back from the table as Loyal walked around them, grabbed Lenny, and pushed him into the wall. "You don't get your money back just by calling foul. We been playing with these same cards all night."

"Long enough for someone to mark 'em good."

"You're losing and now you want your money back so you're making up some shit?"

Jamie was trapped between the table and the kitchen counter. She crouched low in her chair, ready to slide under the table if they came to blows. This guy was an idiot challenging her uncle in his own home in front of others. Lenny's head snapped backward before Jamie realized Loyal had decked him on the chin. His knees buckled briefly and his eyes rolled skyward. The wall shook from the thud of his body, but he caught himself from falling.

Loyal rubbed his fingers. "You just went half a round with my fist and bought yourself a fifty-dollar story." He went to the front door and threw it open. "Get him out of here."

The men grabbed their jackets and headed out, chuckling at Lenny but pulling him along behind them.

Dogs barked and jumped up at the chain-link fences. Doors slammed, engines roared. Loyal turned the lights out and sat on the couch, his shotgun across his lap. Jamie sat on the opposite end. She fingered a burn hole that had been there forever, waiting. It grew quiet again. An orange glow flared briefly in the dark as Loyal lit his last cigarette of the night. He was waiting, and because she knew that, she waited, too.

A diesel engine sounded from a block away. Headlights careened across the walls as a truck returned and rounded the corner. A single gunshot cracked the silence and Jamie dropped to the floor. There was a small explosion and a short burst of falling glass as the streetlight went out. Someone laughed maniacally in the distance. She covered her head expecting a second shot, hoping it wouldn't come through the window, but the truck's engine faded into the wind. Her hands shook like they did when she got scared. She couldn't help it and tucked them between her legs.

"That asshole," Loyal said, glancing at her sideways.

"You calling it in?" she asked, knowing he wouldn't want to. He hated cops, and besides, outside the city limits of Blind River, they never came. Maybe for a dead body but not for random gunfire or a shot-out streetlight.

"No. I hated that fucking light anyway." He headed

down the short hallway to his room. "Get some sleep. I got a run for you in the morning," he said, and shut the door.

*   *   *

Jamie spent the rest of the night caught between half-dreams and worry. The wind slammed against the trailer. The night shift came home and the day shift cranked their engines. In the morning, harsh light lifted across the field behind the trailer and lit their room. The fuzz on Toby's cheek glistened in it, and for a moment he seemed younger than his seventeen years. The welt on his cheek was red and a knuckle on his right hand was split. His mouth hinged open on a jaw loose with sleep, his breath reeking with booze. He was at that age when his bones were growing fast and elongating his face, and nothing much could wake him from a hangover on a Saturday morning. The phone in the outer room rang as Jamie lay unmoving beneath her blanket and waited for her uncle to answer it. The sulfur from his match drifted in under the door. He picked up the phone and mumbled hello. She listened.

"All right," he said loud enough for her to hear him through the wall. He slammed the phone down and thudded up the hallway. Jamie swung her legs off the cot and pulled a sweater over her head. Loyal opened the door, pointed a knuckle at her, and ran a hand through his sandy gray hair. He'd slept in his clothes again, jeans and a tan flannel shirt, probably with the shotgun across his chest. Her laptop sat on the floor near the door. He pushed it toward her with his foot. "Come out here."

She pulled on her jeans, threw her blanket over Toby, and picked up the laptop.

It was colder in the kitchen. A draft seeped through the floorboards, cutting the smell of dirty ashtrays, stale beer, and mildewed carpet. Sunlight slanted hard at the window over the sink. "What's up?" she asked.

Loyal shook another cigarette from a soft pack and lit it without taking his bleary eyes off her. "A big game. Tonight. Keating's place. He wants you to deal. Pays a hundred bucks."

She unplugged the toaster, plugged in the laptop, and cringed at the memory of last night—Keating encroaching on the space where she slept. "Who's going to be there?"

"No one you know."

Her dark hair fell over her forehead and she pushed it behind her ears. "You going?"

"Yeah." He went off toward the bathroom, calling over his shoulder, "Put some coffee on."

She pushed the power button on her laptop and listened to its whine and rumble. When the screen stayed black, she got the sinking feeling that it wasn't just the battery, that the laptop was shot.

The remnants of last night's game were scattered across the table—cigarette butts, empty bottles. She dropped the empties in a paper sack, rinsed the ashtrays, propped the back door open with the garbage can. Snowfall spotted the hill out back and bent the morning light at sharp angles. Wind swept through the trailer and cut the smell of last night's smoke. A dried-up plant sat in the window-sill begging for water, but when she turned the faucet on, the water was icy and she guessed the pilot light had blown out again. She splashed some on her face anyway, cupped and drank it, grabbed a dish towel and rubbed her cheeks till she felt the blood come up. What she needed was a hot shower and some clean clothes and time to think about whether or not it was smart to go any-where near a man as powerful as Keating and how profit-able it might be if she did. From what she could tell, a friendship with him had worked out pretty good for her uncle.

The toilet flushed and Loyal thudded up the hall. He sat down hard at the table, rubbing the back of his head. "Shut that fucking door and bring me the cash bag."

She pulled the door closed and got him the bag and the bottle of aspirin they kept on the windowsill. The bottle was nearly empty. He leaned back in his chair and scratched his week-old scruff, but it was Saturday and by supper that beard would be gone. "You get this one right, you hear? Take your cues from Keating and don't fuck it up." He started stacking bills in denominations of twen-ties on down.

Toby came into the kitchen, his hair flat from sleep, stains from last night's pizza on his T-shirt. "What's going on?"

"Nothing. I got a gig tonight is all." Jamie flinched at his breath and hoped he wasn't still drunk enough to start something.

He looked at Loyal. "Why not me?"

"I need someone with a poker face."

"I got a poker face."

"No, you don't," Loyal said. "She's a thousand times better than you and besides, she's a girl."

"So what?"

"Boy," Loyal said, dropping his hands on the table impatiently, "you get caught and bones get broken."

"She gets caught and they don't?"

Jamie tore open a box of Pop-Tarts. "I don't get caught."

"Shut up," Toby said. He poked at her computer's power button. "Piece of crap."

"Don't touch it." She threw him a Pop-Tart and lowered her tone for Loyal. "Can I get the money up front?" What she really wanted was a little cash and a little downtime so she could figure out how to get her computer fixed.

"You get paid *after* you do the job," he said, but he pulled a couple of fives from one of the stacks and shoved them toward her. "That's a loan. You pay me back tonight."

It was more than she'd expected, but then he said, "Wear some makeup or something. Give them something to stare at besides your hands."

She pushed the money into her pocket.

"And don't show up looking like a dyke."

Loyal lit a cigarette and started adding up the stacks of bills. She turned to walk down the hall and he said, "And do something with your hair."

Goddamn. It made her want to scream, but she'd learned early on to sidestep his hangovers.

Toby followed her to their room. "Who's going to be

there?" He yanked off last night's T-shirt and threw it on the floor.

"Probably some rich guys from out of town." She knotted her hair into a ponytail and sorted through some clothes she kept in the box beneath her cot for another pair of jeans and her favorite black sweater. She jammed all of it into her backpack. "How about you wash some clothes today?"

He rubbed his scalp. "No. My head hurts too bad."

"Buy a new bottle of aspirin, okay?" She handed him five dollars.

"What I need is a beer."

"Damn it, Toby." She got the letter from Jilkins out of her backpack and waved it in his face. "Look at this. Jilkins called a meeting with the principal on Monday. Stop drinking until she's out of our hair."

"Jilkins? What's she going to do?" He found a camo T-shirt beneath his bed and sniffed the armpits. "Send me off? To where?"

"She finds you drunk, she'll throw your ass in juvie or rehab. And you can kiss that Army camp good-bye. Keating might be able to get you into that camp. Said he knows someone there. Maybe you could keep straight for a while. Prove you're worth it."

"Maybe." He pulled the T-shirt over his head.

"What do you mean, maybe?"

"Maybe you just want to get rid of me for the summer."

It was frustrating. One day he was all for it; the next all he wanted was to lie around all summer smoking blunts and playing video games. "You told Jilkins you wanted to go."

"So what? I tell her what she wants to hear."

"She asked for Loyal to come to the meeting, too."

Jilkins never fazed him like she did Jamie. They'd been nine and ten years old when their mother was sentenced to prison and Jilkins was assigned to their case as a social worker. When she showed up the first time, Jamie had thought the woman intended to take them to county juvenile housing, a low building with barred windows surrounded by a barbed-wire fence out on the county highway where boys and girls were separated no matter if they were family. But Jilkins had just inspected the trailer—the rooms, the kitchen, and the small bathroom, her nose turned up in an air of loathing—and explained that she knew a married couple with a two-story house who were looking for a boy and girl to adopt; she just needed time to work out the details. But a month later Keating granted their uncle court-supervised guardianship, and the married couple with the big house was never mentioned again. Jilkins came around every few months to inspect the trailer and write her reports, but nothing much had changed over the years—until recently, when Toby had discovered he could get pretty much anything he wanted with his fists. Jilkins had started coming around more often then.

Toby shifted his eyes toward the door. "Did you tell him?"

"No. He didn't see the letter. I'll go and say he sent me instead."

"Then what's the big deal?" He picked at something crusty on his sleeve.

Jamie grabbed his shirt and pulled his face close to hers. "I'm asking you to keep it together for a few days. Can you just do that? And stay away from Loyal until he feels better."

He pushed her hand away. "I hate him. He orders me around. Last week he made me wax his new truck, the whole damn thing. It took all afternoon."

"He takes care of you, though, doesn't he? Bought you boots last month."

"Only because my old ones finally fell apart. He just keeps us fed and clothed to keep the state out of his hair. I'm working my own deal." He pulled a sheet of paper from under his pillow and unfolded it. "Check it out."

She took it from him. He'd drawn a grid and filled in the top and side with numbers. It looked just like the ones Loyal ran for NBA and NFL games. He'd already sold most of the squares.

"When did you start this?"

"Last week. It's for the Trojans game tomorrow night. Made enough to buy Mom something nice for her birthday."

Their mom, Phoebe, had been out of prison for almost a year now. When her sentence was finished, the parole board had allowed her to return to Blind River because her children were there. That and because the women's group at the Methodist church had set her up with a job at the diner on Main and some garage apartment off a rat-infested alley behind the town's strip of storefronts. Phoebe had never lost visitation rights but was barely able to make ends meet, so it had been decided that the kids would stay with Loyal. Toby often went to the diner for supper, and sometimes Jamie followed him there and watched the two of them through the plate-glass windows. They always laughed and it amazed her. How could they have anything to laugh about? Once, Jamie went inside and sat at the counter and let the woman serve her a bowl of soup and a cup of coffee, but they'd barely been able to look each other in the eye. Prison had left her mother smaller somehow, even though she seemed heavier and her skin had turned gray, as though the colorless concrete walls of the institution had left a permanent stain.

"I sold most of it. Two bucks a pop."

"Then give me back that five." She fastened the straps of her backpack. "And keep that out of school, okay? They'll bust you hard for that shit."

"Doubt it." He studied the five-dollar bill. "Coach bought ten boxes. You're not the only one got it going on, you know."

"Never said I was."

He flattened the bill against the windowpane and squinted at it. "Do you think I could copy this on the library's printer?"

"Don't be stupid. It would cost more than five dollars in ink alone." She grabbed the bill from him.

He picked up a length of rope. It seemed as if he learned a new knot every week. She put her jacket on and watched as he slipped a hangman's knot over his head and pretended to choke. He was such a child sometimes.

"You better put that back in Loyal's truck."

"He doesn't even know it's missing."

"He goes to tie something down and he'll know it's gone. And clean up around here, will you? Put your stuff under the bed or something." She swung her backpack over her shoulder, the weight of it knocking her into the wall. She balanced and straightened.

"Where you going?"

"The computer store, then over to Angel's house for a shower. I'm going to take her some stuff and I haven't seen the baby for a month."

"Does Billy have weed?" Toby asked.

"I doubt it. Angel laid down the law about that shit." She pushed through the narrow hallway to the front room.

He picked up his boots and hopped down the hall behind her, yanking them on. "I'm coming with you."

Loyal sat on the front porch steps, finishing last night's bottle of whiskey. She squeezed past him and his dank breath, sucked the clean air into her lungs. He tossed a small brown paper package at her.

She caught it against her chest.

"That's added up to the dollar. Take it straight to Jack."

It was sealed with tape and heavy. She tested its weight in her hand and figured it had to be twice as much as the one from last week.

"He calls me if that seal's broke."

"I *know* the routine." She stuffed the package into her pocket and walked into the yard.

He came off the steps quicker than she thought he was capable of and caught her by the arm. "Cut the attitude, girl. And don't be late tonight."

She steadied her eyes on his chest, aware that Toby was standing in the doorway, that he'd fly out the door at Loyal if he raised his hand and then she'd be stuck here the rest of the day keeping them from killing each other. But the moment smoothed out when Loyal loosened his grip and cupped her chin, almost affectionately. "Be there by eight," he said, and turned her toward the road. He wheeled back to Toby. "You're not going anywhere until you change the oil on the Ford."

Across the street in a vacant lot, the high branches of a winter-bare sycamore scratched at the pale sky. In the distance a semi worked its way up the highway, the whine of its engine snaking its way through the pines, reminding her of the time when she was twelve and she'd convinced Toby to get on a Greyhound bus with her and run off to Florida, a place she'd heard was always warm and where you could eat oranges right off the trees. She'd never known such freedom as she felt when riding in those high-backed seats with Toby curled up next to her sleeping with his head on her shoulder. But at midnight they hit a roadblock of red and blue flashing lights, bouncing against the bus window. They hadn't even made it to the state line. A state trooper locked them in the back of the cruiser and she'd stared at the metal security mesh bolted across the back of the front seat, unable to breathe and enduring knifelike spasms in her lungs. Toby peed his pants. They'd crawled to the floorboard and huddled there, spines back to back, the entire ride home.

She could walk to the highway right now, stick out her thumb, and catch a ride. She had enough of Loyal's money in her pocket right now to head out on her own. Toby was almost old enough to take care of himself. Almost, but not quite, so she aimed her boots down the narrow blacktop that led to town and bent her body into the wind.

CHAPTER

2

THE ROAD TO town was lined with jagged pines. Jamie tucked her hair inside her skullcap, buttoned her jacket against the cold gray dawn, and walked with her head forward, hands deep in her pockets. Her phone buzzed from inside her backpack and she ignored it in exchange for a few minutes to think. The town of Blind River was a twenty-minute walk down a narrow two-lane. Weeds bent to the ground by morning frost sloped along the embankment to black ditches, thick with mud and smelling of the runoff from the fertilizer plant upstream. Ice-slicked grass crunched under her boots, and she was careful to keep at least one foot on the blacktop. The down jacket and backpack gave some bulk to her figure so that anyone coming around the curve could see her and swerve. Still, she kept close to the shoulder until the road flattened on a bend where the town's only 7-Eleven had been built.

The low building, its windows plastered with neon beer signs and lottery posters, sat square in the middle of a gravel parking lot just off the road in a notched-out patch of woods. Between the ads, Jamie could see the vacant checkout counter, and she walked toward the smell of burning weed at the back of the store.

Myers had the door propped open with the mop bucket. He leaned against the jamb, staring at a folded newspaper—the crossword puzzle, she guessed, by the pencil behind his ear and the confusion on his face.

She had worked for him three months in the kind of dead-end job designed to keep people from ever improving their lives. After taxes she got a hundred and eighty-seven dollars and sixty cents a week for opening the store and keeping the coffee pots full and the breakfast burritos hot, unless she got docked for forgetting to mop the floors after the early rush. Myers had always found a reason to dock her paycheck, and when she'd shown up late three shifts in a row, he'd fired her. The hardworking people of this town needed their daily packs of smokes and giant Styrofoam cups of coffee at six in the morning, not seven. Her uncle kept a more fluid schedule. On days like today, when he was too hungover to get out of the house, he paid her fifty bucks to collect money from a few of his gambling machines scattered around town.

At the sound of a car coming off the highway, Myers pinched the ember off the blunt, crushed it under his shoe, and went inside. Jamie slipped into the storage room through the back door and grabbed what she thought Angel might need—a box of tampons, some cheese, and a package of salami—and crammed it all into her back-pack. In the front of the store the cash register slammed shut and the chimes over the door clanged. She had about five seconds before Myers would shuffle back to the storage room. She grabbed a quart of milk, headed out the back door, and kicked the mop bucket over. He threw the door open and yelled, "Goddamnit!" but she'd already made it up the path that cut through the woods. She crested the hill knowing he'd never leave the store long enough to chase her down, and chances were he hadn't seen enough of her backside to make an official accusation. She stopped behind a tree to catch her breath. She heard the bucket bang against the wall and the back door slam shut. By the time she got to the other side of the woods, the sun was high and ghostly behind frigid white clouds.

The path ended at the alley between the computer store and the old strip mall turned satellite community college. She walked around to the front of the store and went to the help desk. A few students were ahead of her. She took a number and bought a Coke from the vending machine. A long-haired petite girl sat reading against the wall in a corner by the window.

College. She'd bombed her classes worse than anything in her life. Now just seeing a textbook made her stomach turn. Never able to keep up, she'd studied late every night, read the assigned chapters twice, gone to sleep at three in the morning feeling like a loser because the words didn't make sense. Woken up feeling that same way. Her adviser hinted at a transfer to the tech program; maybe she'd be better at food service or welding. Then her grades came in. She'd flunked out in one semester. When Loyal had found out, he'd screamed at her until she agreed to sign up and try again in the winter. Like he gave a damn about college. It didn't make sense. He'd never cared about her grades or what subjects she took. The college put her on probation and reinstated the grant that covered tuition and books for kids living below the poverty level, but it didn't matter. After three weeks she was so far behind she stopped going to class. The only thing that made her feel better about that was not having to face midterms.

That had been two months ago. The only person who knew was her uncle's business partner, Jack DelMar, the guy who ran the check-cashing store on Main Street. He'd said not to worry about college, that he'd done the same thing twenty years earlier and it hadn't hurt him at all. He let her hang out in his back office and she'd kept it from Loyal since, left the house at the same time each morning and came home late each night. Wasn't his business anyway.

After a week of pretending to be at school and poking around on the Internet, she'd found an online poker site. Right away she saw she was better than most players. And it was all legit. No sleight of hand, no marked cards. Every time she cashed, it was due to knowing the odds, playing her position on the board, and calculating the perfect timing of a bluff. She was good even without cheating and the rising balance on her account proved it. A one-dollar tournament could pay a hundred bucks if enough players signed up. After one month she was winning a little money nearly every day, putting her average at about five percent. She knew from the chat rooms that the best players averaged ten percent. *This is the future*, she thought, *and I'm in on the ground floor*. Every day her brain expanded. She could see a hand developing and knew immediately how much to bet or when to fold. If she'd had a faster laptop, she'd have been able to play four or five tournaments at once and really rake it in. She was getting close. Last week she'd won her first twenty-dollar tournament and it had paid big. Almost six thousand dollars. If her transfer had come through since last night, she'd be able to buy the new laptop today.

She sipped the Coke and tried to power up her laptop. She got nothing but a blank screen.

The girl reading by the window closed her book and stretched her arms over her head with swanlike grace. Jamie figured the girl had understood every single word of that book and instantly hated everything about her— the highlights in her hair, the pink fingernail polish, the clearly above-average reading comprehension.

When the tech desk called her number, the news was as she'd expected. The battery was ruined and that wasn't all. Her computer was so outdated the batteries had been discontinued. She'd hoped to give it to Toby, but he'd been such a tool lately and he'd probably just use it to watch porn anyway.

The model she needed was twenty-six hundred dollars. It was a lot, but she needed it if she was going to get serious. She'd heard of players tucked up in their parents' attic playing three or four days in a row, making tens of thousands. It would pay for itself in a week, probably less, and then she'd work on saving enough to get to Florida. She'd never waited more than five days for a transfer, so it would definitely come through today. It probably already had. She gave the techie guy a thumbs-up and he unboxed the new laptop.

It took him an hour to get everything off her old hard drive and load it onto the new laptop. While she waited, she bought another Coke and practiced with a deck of cards. When she flipped over a queen, she remembered what her mother had used to say whenever the queen of spades appeared: "The Luck of the Odds." She'd said it so often that Jamie had begun to imagine a little family with round sad faces like queens and jacks. The Odds family. A lucky family. A boy and girl that she would draw in the margins of her homework because homework was hard but drawing this family pulled her into a quiet space inside her head. She drew them until she got in trouble and her teacher started subtracting points from her grade. But that didn't stop her. She drew them in study hall, and later in detention, and only stopped when a guidance counselor insisted that the reason she drew the little people was because there were problems at home she needed to talk about.

Sitting in the café now, she tried to stick an ace from the bottom of the deck, but her concentration was off and her fingers were clumsy. The cards didn't distract her from what she'd have to do if the transfer hadn't come through. She touched the jacket pocket holding her uncle's envelope, guessing at the amount of cash the south route usually brought in. Five or six thousand at least.

The techie guy brought the laptop to the checkout line, where a tall good-looking dude ran the cash register. The bill was over twenty-nine hundred dollars with tax, so she waived the extra fee for a service contract. She'd use her debit card and hope the balance would get covered by the little credit attached to the account. If that didn't work, she'd have to go with the backup plan.

She swiped her card.

It failed.

"That happens," the good-looking dude said.

"Huh," she said. She tapped her card on the counter and thought it through one more time, even though she'd already decided. There was a window here, probably a good forty-eight hours before Loyal would know something was off with the deposit. Besides, Loyal hadn't gotten where he was today without taking chances, skirting the rules, floating money from one account to another. If she never took a chance, she'd never get out of Blind River. What were her choices anyway? Every day she wasn't playing online she was losing money. According to what she'd learned in the poker chat room, transfers could take up to ten days, though she'd never had to wait that long. Chances were it would come through this afternoon and she'd skate through unnoticed. She pulled out the envelope, shook her head at what she was about to do, and slit the tape with her fingernail.

"It's okay," she said. "I have cash."

CHAPTER

3

A BAND OF clouds rolled in from the west as Jamie
headed up Main Street. She passed the hospital
and police station and the parking lot at the courthouse.
By the time she got through town to Angel's neighborhood, the cold had seeped through her jacket and she was
shivering. The sky squatted low over the ramshackle bunga-
lows, their roof gutters bulging with soggy leaves and black-
ened icicles. Jamie turned the corner at Sikes Avenue and
saw Billy Wages, red-nosed and bubbled in a stadium
jacket, sitting in a lawn chair in the yard of their rental
unit, feet propped on a cooler, bobbing his head to music
from a boombox.

"Jamie!" he hollered, and spread his arms wide. Not
for a hug. They didn't hug. It was a two-handed wave that
indicated Billy was already deep into his Saturday morning six-pack of Molson's.

"What are you doing out here?" she asked. "It's fucking cold."

"I'm just minding my own business. Chilling in my fucking yard, man." He waved his hand at his tiny kingdom of dead winter grass.

"Whatever makes you happy," Jamie said.

"And I am happy," he said, staring into space and drawing out his words. "Always happy to see my wife's best friend come nosing around my house."

She thought about making a peace offering of the salami, but that was Angel's favorite food. "Where is she?"

"Inside. Says the music's too loud for the baby. I say, whatever." He reached down and cranked the volume louder. The bass pulsed and he nodded with the rhythm. This was what people did in Blind River for entertainment. Kids snuck off to the woods to get high, and then when they became adults, they sat in their yards in the snow and ice and drank beer.

She stepped around him and the extension cord snaking off the front porch.

Inside, the place smelled of used burp pads and soiled diapers. Angel paced at the window with Tucker asleep on her shoulder. Her bleached-out hair hung in her face and her eyes were ringed with the dark bags of a sleep-deprived mom. A blue vein ran just beneath the pale skin of her jaw.

"If I put him down, he wakes up and bawls."

Jamie dropped her things and said, "Give him to me." The baby's eyes flicked open briefly as she took him. She cupped his head and held him upright against her chest.

"It's going to be a long day if he doesn't slow down," Angel said, looking out the window toward the front yard. "He doesn't help much, especially in the middle of the night."

"He's a big baby," Jamie said.

"You're telling me." Angel peered through the blinds at Billy.

"I mean Tucker. He seems big for three months." She nodded toward her backpack. "There's some stuff in there for you."

Angel grabbed it and flopped on the couch, fishing through it and tossing the packages on the coffee table. She laughed. "Nice assortment."

"Just some essentials."

"Small, high-priced items. Overpriced tampons. Very efficient."

The baby was alert and active now, holding his head up and looking around the room. Jamie liked the weight of him in her arms, like a warm overfed cat.

"What's up? Shouldn't you be studying or something?"

"I need a shower and our water heater's out again." Jamie sat down in the rocker and pushed. The baby kicked his feet as if to go faster.

"How's school?" Angel stretched out and pushed a pillow under her head.

Reflexively, Jamie checked Angel's face for sarcasm, but she knew better. Angel wasn't mean when it came to Jamie. "It's not the same as high school. Harder than I expected."

"So you cut back. Take some easier classes."

"Nope. I'm out."

"Just like that?"

"Exactly like that. You don't flunk out two semesters in a row and get to stay in."

"Huh." She pushed Jamie with her foot. "I always thought you were the smart one."

"Doesn't look that way." Jamie bent her head toward the baby's head, remembering hearing something about pheromones that caused adults to respond positively to a newborn. This one smelled like rotten milk.

"There's something more, isn't there?" Angel narrowed her eyes. "What?"

Jamie hesitated, then smiled. "I took money from Loyal."

"So what?"

"He doesn't know. I'm waiting on a transfer and needed a loan, so I took it from this morning's deposit."

"What the fuck? Jamie's gone rogue! This is the best part of my whole week!"

"Shut up. I needed a new laptop. It's in that bag."

"Seriously? You just took his money?"

"I, you know, borrowed it. Just until my transfer comes through. He'll never know."

"That's awesome, but you got balls to fool with that man's bankroll."

"I know." It was a little unnerving to say it out loud.

"Doesn't he have partners? It's not all his money, is it?"

Jamie cut her eyes at the window. She hadn't thought that part through. "Yeah, he has partners."

"That judge, right?"

"Listen, you can't tell anyone, especially Billy."

"Okay, but those aren't the kind of guys you want to

fuck with. They don't play by anybody else's rules. Cops are in their back pocket."

Jamie rubbed her eyes, wishing she'd gotten better sleep. "It doesn't matter. I'm making my own money now. I'll pay it back before they find out."

"What? How? With that online shit?"

"Yeah," she said, though she didn't quite believe it herself. "Maybe enough to hit the road."

"You're making that much? Damn. If you're so hot to get out of town, my aunt needs someone to house-sit at her condo in Fort Lauderdale. She's asking around, but you'd have to deal with her pack of Chihuahuas." Angel stuffed a pillow under her knees and lit a joint.

"When?"

"Next month. But you can't fuck around with it. Her sitter just bailed and she's going to Italy with some travel group. Let me know soon, but be careful what you wish for." She waved smoke from her face and pointed toward the front yard. "All I ever thought I wanted was to marry that guy, and look how that turned out." She said this inside a yawn and laid her arm over her eyes.

The bass from the boombox came through the walls, low and dull, and the baby fell back asleep in Jamie's arms. She slipped him onto the couch beside Angel, threw a blanket over them both, and went to the bathroom to start the hot water. While the tub filled, she smoked the rest of Angel's joint, breathing deeply of the mix of smoke and steam. She soaked her neck and shoulders, scrubbed her nails and feet, wondered how long it had been since she'd felt this warm or this clean—but thinking about that new computer and playing five, maybe six, games at once made her antsy. She got out of the tub as soon as the water cooled.

She wiped a circle in the mirror, checked her face, thought about some eyeliner but changed her mind. It was always the eyes that caught her off guard—her mother's eyes—and made her turn from her own reflection.

Someone banged on the bathroom door, and Jamie threw on a sweater and her clean jeans. She opened the door to Billy glaring at her. She smelled his beer breath and squeezed by him in the doorway.

In the kitchen, Angel and the baby were up. Tucker was in his bouncy lounger on top of the table.

"You hanging out here today?" Angel asked while she tried to get the baby to eat some mashed orange food. Not much of it got past his fists.

Jamie sat down and towel-dried her hair. "Just for a little while. I'm dealing a game at Judge Keating's house tonight."

"What's that like? A bunch of guys getting plastered? Be careful. You got mace in your pack?"

"Always." Jamie pulled on her socks.

"You know what? You should go to that school where you get certified to deal in a casino. Those babes make real coin. That's a career."

Jamie combed through a tangle while she powered up the new laptop. It didn't make a pained sound like the old one, just a nice blingy noise when it was ready to use. "Forget dealing. I want the big time."

"You think you can make that much online? Staring at a computer for hours?"

"Yeah. Online is all legit. None of these fools marking cards and bending corners. And when I get a big enough bankroll, I'm going to hit the professional poker circuit in South Florida."

"But computer work? How much fun is that? You should go to Mimawa. They always need pretty young dealers."

She'd heard the stories about Mimawa from some guys at school. Almost every weekend a bunch of them drove up to Mimawa. Stole their parents' debit cards, boozed it up, went a little crazy. Almost always some fool lucked out and won a little bit of money. It sounded like fun but she'd never gone, never had enough money to blow. And then she'd learned about online poker.

"It isn't like computer work. It's a blast."

"It can't be as much fun as a casino. And you, Jamie Elders, are lucky. If I had any cash, I'd float you to play at one of those high-stakes tables. Ever think about that?"

"Might be a fun night for me and Jack."

Angel's eyes widened. "Jack at the check store? Jack your uncle's business partner? The guy with the floppy brown hair and dreamy eyes? Jack who is married and twice your age? See how casually you slipped that in? How long's that been going on?"

"A month or so." Jamie tied her hair up. "You could come, too. We could party."

"Party at Mimawa? I got a kid, Jamie. I stay home to get drunk."

"Jeez. When was the last time you got out? It's not like you're chained here. Where's the old Angel, the one that crowds parted for? There was never a boy in town willing to mix it up with Crazy A."

Angel made like a prize fighter and they both laughed, remembering the time in third grade when she'd pounded a boy on the playground until blood ran out his nose, all on account of the boy sticking his hand down her pants. By high school, the story had grown to mythic status: one of the boy's eyes had popped loose during the fight, his right ear had been cut off, and both were reattached in emergency surgery. Since then, nobody had messed with "Crazy A," and the badass rep had saved them both a few times.

"Times change," Angel said. She wiped the muck off the baby's face and put the spoon down. "So, you and Jack, huh? Does his wife know?"

"I don't know what she knows." Jamie punched a button on the laptop and got nothing. "What's up with your Wi-Fi?"

"It's out. But about Jack, what did he tell you?"

"He said they're through. Doesn't matter anyway. It's just a thing."

"Come on, Jamie. Husbands always say their marriage is over when they have the chance to bang someone else. Billy probably says that to chicks all the time."

Billy came out of the bathroom, red-eyed and wobbly, and dropped into a kitchen chair. "Smells good in here." He pulled his sweatshirt up over his belly and scratched. The prize catch of the Blind River Varsity football team, Angel's first choice over every other guy in town. Billy, the guy you didn't want to cross, the guy who never forgot an insult, the guy who'd five years after middle school found his seventh-grade science teacher's house and poured a jug of bleach into his gas can for having failed him.

Angel handed the spoon to Billy. "Feed him and I'll make you some coffee."

"Deal," he said, and zoomed the spoon around making plane noises while Tucker batted away his hand. Billy licked the spoon. "Jesus, that's disgusting. Why do you feed him that shit?"

"Babies need nutrition," Jamie said. She packed up the laptop.

Billy rolled his eyes at her. "Thanks, Einstein. Why are you even here?" he asked, only half playful. "Don't you have class or something?"

"I'm just visiting, man." Jamie spread her hands across the table face up, mimicking him.

He didn't laugh but shook out a Winston and stuck it in his mouth.

"No, seriously. The water heater at Loyal's was out. I might have used all yours."

Her phone buzzed inside her backpack.

"You should get that," Angel said. "It keeps going off."

She dug it out of the side pocket. Jack had called twice and texted five times wanting to know where the hell she was.

"Damn, I gotta go," she said, and tied up her boots.

4

WHEN JAMIE WALKED through the front door of the check-cashing store, Jack ignored her until he finished counting out cash for a customer. She stood shivering in the corner until they left. Once the store was clear, he shut the cash register and put up the back-in-five sign. Then he pulled her into his small office in the back.

"I've been calling you for an hour. My cash drawer is almost empty. I was going to have to send folks to the bank, and you know that's not how I make money."

She knew that. Cashing payday checks with a twenty-percent fee and laundering her uncle's money for a neat ten percent was how Jack DelMar made money.

His laptop sat opened up on his desk, glowing in the dark room. She flipped on the overhead light.

"Sorry," she said, and tossed her backpack on the ratty futon. "I ran an errand and then stopped by Angel's. I'm only an hour late."

"You're two hours late, but that's not the real problem. You haven't been online today, have you?"

"No, my computer died. What's going on?"

He pointed to his laptop. "You won't believe it."

She sat down and tried to understand the logo on the screen. It was an official-looking government seal, and that never meant anything good. "What is that?"

He leaned over her shoulder and pointed. "Look at the URL. That was Poker Stars, but it's been shut down."

"Uh, no. That can't be right." She refreshed the screen, opened a new window, typed in another address, and watched as the same seal appeared. Poker Stars, Mega Chips. The same government seal was displayed on every site. Her hands were still freezing but sweat pricked at the back of her neck. "What the hell? I have six thousand dollars in there."

"Had. You *had* six thousand dollars in there. They shut the whole thing down."

Oh, fuck, no. Her eyes started jumping around the screen. "What? They can't do that."

"They're the U.S. Justice Department, Jamie. They can do anything they want. They can crawl through that laptop and take your entire checking account if they want to."

"But it's my money. I won it." She pulled off her stocking cap.

"Why didn't you transfer it? You should know better than to leave that much money out there."

"Don't talk to me like I'm a child. I transferred it the same day I won it, over a week ago. I've been waiting for it to come through."

"Bastards. Those sites probably knew this was coming down and stopped paying out."

"Shit." She dropped her head to the desk. "He's going to kill me."

"Who?"

She pulled Loyal's packet out of her pocket and tossed it on the desk.

He picked it up and peeled back the broken seal. "Oh, man, are you kidding me?"

She had refolded the envelope neatly, but the tape was slit and the folds didn't match the size of the bundle inside. It was obvious that some of the money was gone.

"Ten percent of that was mine." His voice seemed distant.

She closed her eyes. Her mind raced with panicky half-thoughts. The back of her uncle's hand. Three thousand dollars. Eight hours. She opened her eyes again. "What am I going to do?"

He thumbed through the bills. "You better get it back and you better be quick about it. There's two thousand here."

Her hands trembled as she dug out the receipt for the computer and read the fine print. "God damn. Electronics sales are nonrefundable."

"I can't believe you."

"He'll kill me if he finds out."

"He won't kill you," he said unconvincingly. "It depends on how Keating takes it. They split the rest. You know that, right? And they pay rent on all the sites in the middle of the month."

Fuck. She hadn't figured that in. She logged into her bank account, fumbling with the password. "Maybe the transfer came through before they shut it down."

He dropped to the futon and shook a cigarette from his pack. "It was all over the news. They shut it down at midnight last night. I checked."

She got the account called up and saw she was overdrawn. "Can you cover it for me?" She immediately regretting asking and added, "I mean, I can work it off."

"I know a guy who'd pay a couple hundred for a video of a naked girl doing it."

He could be such an ass. "Really? I'm fucked and you bring that up?" But even as she spoke, an idea began to take shape. There was only one way to make that much cash in a single day, and it wasn't by blowing him.

"Suit yourself." He held the cigarette between his teeth.

This is what it feels like, she thought, when there aren't any good options and the walls start closing in. This is when you make a move or die standing in the same pathetic town where you were born. Loyal knew exactly how much cash was in that packet. She thought through the options again.

"I'm going to Mimawa."

"Mimawa? That's your solution? You're whacked."

She stood up and threw her backpack onto her shoulder. "You got another idea, I'm listening."

"You're just a kid. You've never even been inside a casino."

"But I know poker." She picked up the remaining

cash and stuffed it back in the envelope. "Tell my uncle I never showed up today."

"No." He blew smoke out the side of his mouth. "It's a bad idea."

"You know I'm good and you know I'm on a roll."

He studied her hard, shook his head.

"You can come and watch or you can stay here by yourself, but I'm doing this, with or without you."

He was silent.

"If everything goes well, we can get a room." It wasn't exactly a lie. If she won fast enough, they could get a room for a few hours.

He smiled and picked up his car keys.

5

JAMIE STARTED THE engine of Jack's Taurus to let it warm and crawled over to the passenger's seat while he locked up the store. Her fingers were freezing but her gloves had gone missing days ago. She stuck her hands in her armpits and thought about the odds of beginner's luck. *It could happen. It's a long shot, but it only takes one lucky streak.* One big hand under the right circumstances could turn everything around.

Mimawa was one hour away. Close enough to be back before nightfall if they got in and out quick. Thinking about the possibility of losing Loyal's money, she almost changed her mind, but then, as the lights in Jack's store went out and he came running through the sleet, a little adrenaline kicked in. *You got to be in it to win it.* Despite the odds, she had to try her luck.

They took the county road south to loop around town and avoid the traffic at the caution light out by the

Walmart. A mile from the interstate they passed a series of neon billboards, brilliant and crackling with electricity. It tingled weirdly on her face and she rubbed her cheeks. "Do you feel that?"

"Yeah. Takes some juice to light that much neon. That buzz is why the cows won't graze over there." He turned onto the ramp for the interstate. Rain drizzled against the intermittent headlights of oncoming traffic, wipers cutting through the ice thickening on the windshield. "When we get there, I might play some roulette. See if my numbers hit. You know, just get the feel of the place."

"I thought you'd been there."

"It's been a while."

"What numbers do you play?"

"When's your birthday?"

They were so new they didn't even know each other's birthdays yet. "Seven-ten."

"Then that's what I'm playing." He wedged his cold fingers under her left leg and she shivered from the unexpected chill. "Sorry," he said. "I left my gloves at home this morning."

Home. She thought about that word for a moment, then dismissed it. They spent what nights they had together sleeping on the futon in his office, and once, a motel. He hogged the bed so much that at times she almost preferred her cot at the trailer. But Jack had been good to her and now he was trying to help her out of this mess. Secrets like this kept lovers close. Still, her stomach turned every time she thought about having slit open that envelope.

She wished she hadn't eaten that salami at Angel's.

She dug through her backpack hoping to find some crackers, anything to settle her stomach.

"You got your ID, right?" He gave her a pseudo-daddy look and she huffed. "And watch yourself, okay? At the casino."

"I can take care of myself."

"I'm not joking," he said. "Keep your drink covered and don't let anyone near it. Guys will slip something in your drink just to get an advantage at the table. Be careful."

"Okay, I hear you," she said. "I grew up around Loyal's crowd. Those guys spend entire weekends blitzed out on crack and weed. I got this." She wanted to reassure him, needed the reassurance herself. In home games she got away with a lot of tricks, but in a place like Mimawa there'd be cameras and floor bosses, people watching her hands all the time.

He squeezed her leg. "Maybe we should check in, you know, get a room for a few hours."

"Only if things go well and there's time. Otherwise, I've got to get back for a game at Keating's."

Jack turned in his seat. "You're playing a house game at Judge Keating's?"

"No, I'm dealing it." She didn't look at him but stared out the windshield, hoping he'd put his eyes back on the road.

"Huh. He pay you for that?"

"Yeah, a hundred bucks and the winner usually tips something."

"You dealing legit?"

"Depends." She didn't really want to discuss it. "How far to the casino?"

"Not far," he said. "You can be hard to read sometimes."

"No harder than anyone else. It's called a poker face." They passed a car in the right lane and water sprayed the windshield, hitting her door. They skidded a little and she held her breath until they were clear.

"You're getting in a little deep, you know? Your uncle runs a business that might not be suited for a girl."

"I've been around it most of my life. I know how things work. You get the money from my uncle, right? And get it in the bank without anyone noticing? What's the big deal?" She was crossing a line here, but he'd brought it up and Loyal was so secretive about his business that she wondered if Jack really knew any more than she did.

"It's a lot more than that, but you don't need details."

"Sounds complicated," she said, hoping he'd continue. Sometimes when she played dumb, he'd brag a little and she'd find out some new detail.

She'd grown up driving around the county with her uncle and Toby, hanging out in the truck while Loyal went inside a store or pub and cleared a machine of cash. Running his routes with him was how she'd learned to drive in the sleet and ice, learned how to take a sharp curve at the top of a rise. She'd been to each location, knew exactly how big his operation was: as wide as the county and then some. Big enough nobody talked about it and profitable enough to pay cops to look the other way.

"People get to gamble, win now and then. Makes them

feel good. Everybody gets a cut, everybody keeps their mouth shut," he said. "But cops can be tricky. New ones come along, old ones get promoted. They get uppity for no good reason and decide not to play along."

They skidded sideways when they hit a puddle and she decided to drop it and let him concentrate on driving. She worried about the tread on his tires, but she fought the urge to mention it, focusing instead on the droplets of water smearing the windshield, the rhythm of the wipers, the lightning off in the distance. After thirty miles of interstate, they hit a second cluster of neon billboards, the drizzle catching in the light like gems, and then there was the exit for the casino.

The landscape was clear-cut to the point of desolation, as though a bomb had detonated and wiped out trees in every direction for a mile. Inside the gates, though, it was all gloss and shine. Even the rain looked pricey. In the rainy afternoon light, the marquee and its spot-lit fountain glowed like a landing strip. The valet, smiling in his yellow slicker, motioned them to the curb, but Jack waved him off and headed to the five-story parking garage in the back.

Jamie caught her reflection in the window and wished she'd gone with more eyeliner and a different top. She brushed a stray hair off her shoulder, thinking how Angel would be appalled at her for wearing a sweater to a casino. Her hair glistened in the reflection when she swooshed it out from behind her ears and she reminded herself that she wasn't so plain, that she could be pleasing with a little more effort.

Inside the foyer, Jack put on his sunglasses and pulled his hoodie over his head. The entrance was high and wide with an overblown elegance of marble floors, wood paneling, and brass lamps, attendants in jackets and ties, a chandelier reflecting like firecrackers in Jack's glasses. Closer to the slot machines, the ceiling dropped low and the carpet got thick, but it wasn't enough to soften the seizure-inducing strobe lights or drown out the pings and bells and a mechanical voice screaming, "Wheel! Of! Fortune!"

The place was full of wealthy people flaunting their privilege, middle-aged couples on spending sprees and second honeymoons, and losers—the ones on the down and out and pushing their luck: an old woman chain-smoking and camped out in front of a slot machine, an unshaved man wedged in a corner and seemingly asleep. Gambling was a community affair. Lots of people lost so a few could win. Almost everybody left a little closer to broke. The roulette tables were full, so she and Jack walked past the cash cage toward the back. A cover band was set up by the bar and they might have been playing "Hotel California," but over the din of the crowd, it was hard to tell.

The poker room was tucked in the back of the casino with a velvet rope at the perimeter that kept spectators at a distance from the tables, a security measure to minimize collusion. She knew the story. Players working in teams; a spotter across the room with a cell phone at waist level snapping pictures of an opponent's hole cards and relaying them to their partner with hand signals.

"God, I miss this. I used to play here sometimes. Watch me and you'll get the hang of it," Jack said, and took a seat at a Texas Hold'em table near the front. He tugged his hoodie low over his eyes. Jamie knew his tough-guy look wouldn't intimidate the half-drunk rednecks who'd been waiting all day for him to show up with his big fat wallet, but he'd brought her here and that meant they were a team. She owed him a little loyalty, so she stood on the rail and watched as he bought in for two hundred dollars.

The cards went flying, and the action opened with Jack. He peeked at his two hole cards and bet twenty. Two players called his bet.

The dealer laid out the flop, the first three community cards, and the beginnings of what might amount to a ten-high straight. Jack raised the pot by thirty and the two players stayed with him. The fourth card was a king and Jack bet forty more chips. The first guy folded but the guy to his right scratched his nose and tensed his jaw, the snake tattoo on his neck twitching as he squelched a smile and called Jack's bet.

The dealer turned the last card. The action was on Jack and he bet another forty. Mr. Itchy Nose raised it to a hundred. Jack called the bet and turned over his pocket kings, clearly convinced he had the best hand.

Itchy Nose smiled big now and showed the straight he'd caught on the flop. Jack had lost his whole stack in one play. "Fucking hell." He knocked his chair over when he pushed away from the table.

Shit. This is no way to start the night.

"What was that?" Jamie asked when he got to the sideline.

"Asshole. Who fucking plays a straight like that?" He yanked his sunglasses off. Sweat was thickening on his forehead and a vein pulsed wickedly at his throat. He was angrier than Jamie had ever seen him, but he'd played it all wrong and she couldn't keep from saying so.

"You should've seen that coming," she said. "He had you all the way."

"Fucker played a seven/eight against my kings. He just got lucky."

"He didn't get lucky; he played it perfectly. He didn't raise the pot because he had the nuts and he wanted to keep you in the hand. Playing it slow like that guaranteed he'd take all of your chips."

"What are you talking about?" He took off his sunglasses and rubbed the bridge of his nose. "No one folds three kings."

"You should have. It was a bad call. He trapped you and you didn't even think twice." Jamie knew she should shut up, but it had been so obvious. "Plus his jaw muscles popped out when you made that bet. He scratched his nose so you wouldn't see him smile."

Jack pointed at her with his sunglasses. "So how would you have played it?"

"You bet a hundred and he reraises? You got to look at the board and see he was working a straight. You got to fold that. You got to know right there you're beat. Fold it and walk away."

Jack shrugged. "What if he's bluffing?"

"If he was bluffing he would've raised the flop. He was trapping all the way."

Jack unzipped his hoodie and glared at Itchy Nose. "So, how do you know this shit?"

"Mom taught me."

"That right?" Jack pulled out the envelope and gave her a hundred-dollar bill. "You think you can beat that guy?"

Instantly, she wished she hadn't mentioned her mom, the ex-felon. No one needed to know about her and how, when other moms were teaching their daughters to bake, Phoebe was showing Jamie how to peel an ace off the bottom of a deck. They used to stay up all night playing cards. They'd fall asleep at the table, wake up the next morning, and play through another day. Jamie could never get enough.

Kitchen table poker was one thing, but this place was for real, and without the deck in her hand the playing field would be level. This place attracted suckers after a quick fix, dads trying to stretch a paycheck, old-timers hoping to turn a pension check into another month of Early Times and Marlboros. Maybe she was just another chump, but she needed to turn things around and she needed to do it today. Besides, no one was forced to come here and put their money on the table. Luck was just that. It could hit her just as easily as it hit anyone else. She took the bill from Jack and said, "I'll need two of those."

Itchy Nose ordered a round for the table. He lifted his glass toward them and downed it.

"Fucker," Jack said. He took out another bill, and Jamie took the cash. She hesitated, but she had made this mess and he was trying to help. She took the money and the chair opposite the dealer.

"Yo, Hoodie sent his girlfriend," Itchy Nose said, and the men at the table laughed.

She saw their sideways glances, their subverted smiles, and sensed these guys had a history, that she was an outsider. Her throat constricted. The dealer counted out two hundred chips and slid them to Jamie. Her hands trembled as she collected her chips.

The dealer shuffled the cards and sent them around the table. She lifted the corners of her hole cards. A five/seven off suit. Not worth the cost of a big blind. She fumbled the cards when she slid them back to the dealer and was sure the other players noticed. They'd be watching for any sign of weakness. She jammed her fingers under her thighs and sat on them while the hand played out. The salami rumbled in her belly.

Up close she could see Itchy Nose's tattoo. It was a colorless black job, cheap, like he'd only paid for the outline. She counted backward from ten to try to slow her breathing. He caught her looking at him and smirked. "Name's Damon," he said. "Tough break for your boy."

Jamie nodded. She didn't care what his name was and there wasn't any reason to talk to him. She owed him nothing.

His nails were chewed, the calluses thick but clean, a few nicks on his knuckles. His hair was the color of sawdust and he was jumpy in the forearms. She guessed he worked some kind of labor that needed muscle but didn't involve grease. He raised the blinds, picked up a few dollars, and watched her watching him.

She ignored the hot nausea burning the back of her throat and waited for the next hand. Playing in a casino was a much bigger rush than playing online where no one could see her face or the movements of her hands or stare stupidly at her. An old guy at the end of the table stared openly at her chest, dropped his hands to his lap, and smiled. She clenched and unclenched her fist, testing her fingers. They were steadier now but she didn't trust them yet.

"Excuse me, miss?" Itchy Nose was talking to her. "You got a vein, right here," he said, pointing to his temple. "It's blue and for some reason it's throbbing."

Another player laughed and Jamie knew she was going to blush. In ten seconds her whole face would turn red and there wasn't anything she could do to stop it.

For her thirteenth birthday her uncle had taken her and Toby hunting. They'd sat in a deer blind for hours, Toby bored and carving his initials on the wall, waiting for the sun to rise. When it did, a buck stepped out into a meadow just fifty yards away. Loyal lined up the shot for her with a new rifle he'd bought from the Walmart and told her not to be a pussy. The buck stood solid and gray, morning dew setting around his flanks, and Jamie saw something she'd never seen before, something innocent, something majestic, something proud. "Now," Loyal had whisper-shouted and she'd pulled the trigger. The blast crushed her eardrums and ripped a hole in the buck's neck. He staggered sideways two steps and then his front legs folded. His back quarters hit the ground less gracefully, legs twitching like he was peddling a bike. She couldn't take her eyes off him, off what she'd done. That's when the trembling had first started. That's how she felt now.

The dealer tapped the table in front of her and said, "It's on you, miss."

She peeked at her hole cards and found a pair of queens. Another shot of adrenaline hit her bloodstream. She did the math. The right bet was forty. She reached for her chips and knocked the stack over, counted them out, and tossed them to the middle.

Itchy Nose said, "I'll see the flop," and he and another player called the bet. It was her hands. They were giving her away. Guys like these would call her all the way to the end, thinking she was trying to outplay them. Heat flushed up to her ears.

The dealer laid out the first three cards, and the ten of diamonds was the highest card on the flop. Itchy Nose bet a hundred and she knew he was trying to bully her. If she called him, she might as well bet her whole stack. Chances were her queens were still the best hand, and besides, if she didn't have the guts to play queens, she might as well fold and go home to face Loyal. Itchy Nose was staring hard at her and that jumpy muscle in his neck had smoothed out. His eyes went a little unfocused when she stared back. A classic bluff.

She pushed all her chips to the middle and felt the edges of the room tilt away when he and the other guy called the bet. Whether or not she won this hand, she'd never forget these bastards.

"Three all-ins," the dealer said. "Turn 'em over."

Itchy Nose flipped over a pair of twos; the other player turned over a jack/nine. They'd pegged her for weakness and come gunning. *Idiots.* Her fingers seemed like jumpy little animals but somehow she got the queens turned over.

The dealer placed the fourth community card on the table, an ace.

The jack/nine was drawing dead and Itchy Nose needed a two to hit a three-of-a-kind. The dealer turned over the last card, a seven.

"Fuck me," Itchy Nose said.

"Queens are good," the dealer said, and slid the pot toward Jamie. The relief was a lot like being high. Too high.

Winning was supposed to feel good, but something dark twisted in her gut. She grabbed her chips and stood up. Part of her wanted to laugh, part of her needed to run.

"Don't leave now," Itchy Nose said, the snake tattoo bunching at his throat. "You gotta give me a chance to win it back."

But she knew better. They'd each taken their chances and it could've come out different. She shoved the chips into Jack's hands and hurried down the hall to the bathroom.

A few minutes later Jack called to her from outside the bathroom door. "You need anything in there?"

Jamie was slumped on the floor. "Got any disinfectant on you?"

"Are you on the floor? That's gross. Get up."

Jamie flushed the toilet and pushed herself up. "I'll be out in a minute."

She braced herself on the sink and cupped some water to her mouth. The nausea was gone. She bought a disposable toothbrush and some aspirin from the vending machine, ignoring the impulse to stock up on high-priced condoms.

"Babe. Come out here. That was vicious."

Her legs were shaky but she managed to get out the door.

"You look better, less green." He pulled her to a quiet spot near the water fountain, his eyes wild like when he was hard. "You won six hundred dollars!" He grabbed her arms.

"I got lucky," she said, but she couldn't deny it. She'd felt the rush, too.

"It took guts to go up against that guy. It was more than luck; it was sick. You're on a heater," he said. "You need to strike while you're hot."

"Maybe." She leaned against the wall and locked her knees.

Jack said, "We need a plan."

"Okay," she said, nodding. The aspirin burned in her stomach, which meant that her headache would let up soon. "Here's a plan. Those guys I just beat? I made them look like fools in front of their friends. They'll come gunning for me now. I'll buy back in and wait for the right moment to raise the stakes. They won't back down. All I have to do is wait for the right cards to come along."

"What about Keating?"

"I'll call Toby. If he asks her, my mom will cover it. I mean, what's it pay? A hundred bucks? I need three grand."

She realized if she won enough, she wouldn't need the judge's recommendation for Toby. She could pay for the summer camp herself.

"I'm doing this." She held out her hand. "And I need it all."

"You're so hot right now. I love it when you get fired up." He hugged her then and she felt him getting hard.

She smirked and pushed him away. "Maybe we'll get that room after all."

When she got back to the table, Itchy Nose had bought in for another thousand. He joked with the new dealer and ignored her when she took a chair at the end of the table. She slid twenty-five hundred to the dealer, but the limit was two thousand. Already she looked like a rookie, not even knowing the table limits. She'd sworn to herself that she wouldn't play the first round, let herself relax and tamp down her nerves, hated it when she saw the ace/king of hearts staring out at her from her hole cards. She was out of position and the first to act and a little horrified when five players called her hundred-dollar bet.

The flop came. No ace, no king, all black clubs. She knew she should bail here, but checking would tell everyone she'd missed. She bet the pot, five hundred and change, and was proud of how still she was able to keep her hands. With nothing to back it up, though, her bet was too large.

"Here she comes again," Itchy Nose said. He tossed some chips into the middle and called the bet.

It was almost like he knew she was bluffing, and it made her think he'd picked up on some sort of tell. It was possible. She sat still, focused on the center of the table, but couldn't help cutting her eyes at him to see if he was watching her. He smiled. One other player stayed in the hand. She ran the calculations. There was fifteen hundred in the pot. There was fourteen hundred left in her stack.

The dealer turned the fourth card. A king. She had high pair now, but there were four clubs on the board. She felt calm as she thought it through. Neither of them had bet like they had a flush. This was the perfect spot to front the nuts and back it up with the pair. She'd made this move a hundred times online and it almost always paid off.

"All in," she said, keeping her hands in her lap.

"I want a count," Itchy Nose said.

She slid her stack toward the dealer for him to count. Her hands were steady allies now.

"Fourteen eighty," the dealer announced.

Itchy Nose watched her closely. She turned to face him directly to convey some confidence in her move and felt a little sick when he said, "Call."

He seemed unfazed. The top of her head went cold when he turned over the seven/eight of clubs. She'd played one hand. She'd lost it all.

Jack shook his head, walked away.

"Let me give you a tip, honey," Itchy Nose said, laughing and stacking his chips. "It's your hands. They shake when you got the nuts, but when you bluff, they're still as pond water."

She followed Jack through the casino, to the entrance, and out to the parking lot. There was nothing to say. An hour later he dropped her at the curb in front of Angel's house because there was no way she could show up at that game and face Keating and her uncle.

CHAPTER

6

PHOEBE LOVED THE sounds of the game, the shuffle of
the cards, the sifting of chips, the occasional snap of a
beer can popping open, the strike of a match, the sizzling
tobacco of a fresh cigar. She couldn't remember when
she'd been up this late in the company of men who weren't
wearing uniforms. It almost felt like old times.

She had arrived at Keating's house at five minutes to
eight. Keating's two-story Tudor and its sweeping roofline
sat at the end of a long drive with the usual rides parked
along the street: Cadillacs, Lincolns, and a sleek black
Lexus. While they poured drinks, she made her way to the
game room, took her place at the center of the table, and
waited. She felt sure it wasn't a parole violation to deal a
poker game at a judge's house, but she'd been in the system long enough to know that anything could land her in
lockup if she came up against a pissed-off cop with a hard-
on for trouble. Still, it was a chance she had to take. When

Toby had come to the diner with the message that Jamie was going to miss dealing a big game at Judge Keating's, Phoebe had seen it as an opportunity to do something to help her daughter, maybe build a little goodwill. Loyal would be angry at the change, but he might go easy on the girl if he had a decent night. She could throw him a few good cards for the sake of family peace. Besides, as much as she despised him, she owed him for taking in her kids when she'd gone away.

"I took a cut for the dealer," Keating said, handing Phoebe some folded twenties as the men took their seats at the table.

Introductions were quick. Most of the players, Phoebe guessed, were men immune to losing money at poker from years of excursions to Atlantic City or Las Vegas. Three were from out of town and wouldn't know her or her history, or that when she wanted to, she could pull an ace out of thin air.

Six players, six thousand dollars less the dealer pay. Unless someone busted out early and bought back in. She pegged the linebacker for that. Pocket money for Keating and Loyal. The rancher and the state rep probably had the good sense to see their attendance here as just another hazing ritual along their climb to power. An invitation to Keating's home game was an honor, and everyone expected a few laughs even if all they left with was a sick story about a bad beat. Hardly anyone was stupid enough to expect to win, but whichever way the night went, they'd all remember the moment when their luck ran cold.

The big guy seated directly across from her was TJ

Bangor, a retired NFL tight end who said he was in town to deliver a motivational speech to the men's breakfast club at the Methodist church. Phoebe had to smile. Beating a guy like that would mean lifetime bragging rights to any man in this room.

And, of course, there was a cop. There was always a cop. Carl Garcia sat in the chair to her right looking just like a detective—mousy hair, dull eyes, faded plaid shirt— but fit and muscular like a cop with ambition. She'd throw him some good cards to keep him happy. Chances were he was a decent player. Cops in Blind River sat on their butts a lot down at the precinct. Poker was their favorite pastime.

"We'll call the game at twelve o'clock. Winner takes all," Phoebe said, and cut the deck. "Keep your cards on the table where I can see them, please. Good luck, gentlemen."

A cloud of smoke already hovered beneath the paneled ceiling. Someone lit another Cuban. Phoebe breathed it in and watched as Loyal reached over and took one for himself from the humidor on the bar. She shuffled the deck twice, then dealt the hole cards.

She'd rummaged up a white button-down shirt and black vest and looked as legit as the pretty young dealers she'd seen in Atlantic City all those years ago. But she wasn't a girl anymore. A girl could get away with almost anything when it came to poker and grown men, but prison had left her run down. Bad food, bad health care. Her left eye drooped a little now—an injury from a fight over a bottle of ketchup. She sat up a little straighter realizing she still had good posture and was glad she'd had the foresight to buy some blush and lipstick from the drug-store last week.

Keating checked his cards and threw two chips in the pot. Loyal adjusted the extra weight that hung over his belt buckle and glanced over at her. She hadn't looked him in the eye yet, hated him despite how he'd stepped up for the kids. She dealt him a pair of jacks and watched as he calmly trimmed the ash from his cigar.

She held the deck in her hand and looked at the wall to her right while the action made its way clockwise around the table.

When it was Loyal's turn to bet, he stared stubbornly into space long enough that she had to say something. "The action's on you, sir."

Her eyes finally met his and she remembered the day, more than twenty years ago, when Jimmy had brought her home the day after they'd crossed the state line and eloped. Loyal had done nothing when his father sucker-punched Jimmy and screamed that he'd married trash. Things were never the same after that and even though Jimmy had never held a grudge against his little brother, Phoebe had. In all the years since then, she and Loyal had barely spoken to each other.

Keating knocked a knuckle on the felt and said, "Check or bet."

"Raise." Loyal threw two black chips into the middle, but no one wanted the action and he took the pot.

Phoebe pushed the chips toward him and said, "The raiser wins."

After an hour she'd worked Keating's deck to where she could read the cards like Braille, softened the corners on the aces, split the corners on the kings with her thumbnail. Queens got dented with a fingernail halfway down the side; jacks got the same indentation at the top. She barely had to glance at the cards when she turned them faceup on the table to know what had hit the flop, the turn, or the river.

The whiskey flowed. The rancher and the politician got tanked early and didn't put up much of a fight. They busted out in consecutive hands to Keating and neither seemed to care as they drifted out of the house.

The detective made her uneasy, but it was time to cast to the shallow end. She sent him a king/jack and watched him suppress a smile and swallow some whiskey when TJ, that big football player, bet a hundred dollars before the flop. She glanced over at TJ's cards, saw the warped corner of an ace, and gave him a little credit for trying to steal the hand with a single ace. The other men bailed but Garcia called the bet. Phoebe stuck another ace on the flop along with a jack and watched TJ's pupils dilate like he'd fallen in love. He bet two hundred on the aces but Garcia called with the two jacks. The turn was a three and TJ bet another two hundred. Garcia stayed with him. When Phoebe stuck a third jack on the river and Garcia won with a set, TJ threw his aces in the muck, poured himself more whiskey, and tried not to pout.

"Bad beat," Garcia said.

It was a typical nice-guy comment and Phoebe smiled because, deep down, she knew he had to be thrilled.

"That a Super Bowl ring?" Garcia asked.

"Yep." A bet like that was nothing to a man like TJ and he played it cool. He was easily the largest man at the table and could have bullied anyone here. She wondered how many concussions he'd had in his twenty-year career and if he'd keep his cool after getting fleeced by Keating and Loyal. There was no way he would know what was coming.

Keating said, "I saw a guy throw his wedding ring in the middle once. He was out of money and had a full house. Another guy had four kings, but he folded because he was worried that the guy's wife came with the pot."

Everyone laughed like they'd never heard the joke before. Phoebe shuffled the deck, but she was thinking about the next hand. She'd throw some good cards to TJ, put a smile back on his face. He'd bounce out soon enough on his own accord, but a guy like TJ would get his wallet out and get back in the game. He was still famous enough that his misery wouldn't be too pathetic. In fact, it would keep the night interesting. She remembered the play in his rookie year—hell, the whole country remembered that play. He was older now, his face gray and washed out. Probably spent a lot of time in card rooms. But it was stupid to come to this town and play this home game, a game that had been around for decades. What did he expect but to lose everything in his wallet?

Keating poured another tumbler of whiskey and passed the bottle around the table. With the whiskey flowing and the cards flying, the conversation turned, inevitably, to luck. She stifled a yawn. When it came to luck, poker players always had opinions.

"I've had my share of it," the tight end said, dropping his poker face, "but there is no luck without preparation, gentlemen. Every game I've ever won was the result of hard work."

Phoebe assumed he was borrowing material from the motivational speech he was known for on the church circuit. She stopped her eyes from rolling by staring at an old scar on the back of her hand. She'd stopped philosophizing about luck a long time ago when she'd learned the mechanics of dealing and started sending men into the night questioning their very existence. God? Luck? Fate? Men might not want to believe it, but none of that mattered in poker. Not when the deck was stacked. Not when she could place any card in any player's hand any time she wanted. The longer TJ talked, the harder she stared at that scar.

"Luck is a hard nut." Keating rapped the table with his knuckles and drained the whiskey from his glass. "I've seen the whole of someone's life hanging by a thread, and I've snipped that thread myself a time or two in my courtroom. But, TJ, my friend, you've always had Lady Luck by the tail. Let's get the country boy's view on luck, shall we?" Keating leaned back in his chair and rested his eyes on Loyal. "Surely, the old dog has given it some thought."

Loyal twisted his head until his neck popped. "I guess I don't know much about luck, but what TJ says makes sense. Work hard and say your prayers. You'll be okay."

"Ha!" Keating motioned toward Loyal. "Didn't take you for a praying man."

Phoebe caught the lift and fall of Keating's eyebrow, the smirk on his face. The two men stared at each other briefly. Loyal stretched and tensed his fingers, showing the true size of his fist. She'd seen this before. Good cop, bad cop, getting feisty with each other. No one would suspect they were in this together.

Garcia peeked at his cards and said, "As far as I can tell, luck is as reliable as a stripper on meth." He pushed his chips to the middle. "I'm all in and I'd feel better about it if someone would pass me that bottle."

"I call," TJ said, and flipped over eights.

Garcia had sevens.

The hand played out and the cop busted. He pushed back from the table. "Guess I should've saved my money for the big tournament this weekend."

"Buy back in. It's too early to leave," TJ said, a slur sliding through his words.

The cop poured himself a shot and said, "I'm a public servant. I don't have another thousand."

TJ stacked his chips. "I hate pushing someone out of the game so fast. Come on, Judge, let him back in. And someone tell me about this big tournament. Maybe I'll stay in town a few extra days."

Phoebe took her time gathering the cards while Keating decided.

"Normally, I don't do this." He tapped the ash off his cigar. "But I have a soft spot in my heart for public servants, especially ones that move here from out of town to serve in Blind River. I'll front you two hundred chips." He smiled when he slid twenty black chips to Garcia. "My treat. You came down from Albany, right? What brought you down our way?"

"Been here five years, sir. But it still feels brand new." He downed the whiskey.

"Seems I remember hearing some story about the feds stepping in and cleaning house, getting rid of deadweight. You part of that?"

"I was there about that time." Garcia poured another whiskey. "A new judge came to town. You know how that can go."

"I know you ended up here, divorced." Keating's face was deadpan and it seemed the air got still.

The men waited, shifting their eyes at each other, until Garcia cleared his throat and said, "I did indeed."

Phoebe figured he'd been invited to be educated on exactly who ran this town and knew Keating had made his point when he changed the subject. "Our annual poker tournament is a fund-raiser, Mr. Bangor. For our local veterans. It'd be a great honor for you to appear if you're still in town."

If Loyal asked her to deal at the tournament she'd come face to face with every boy she'd dated in high school and skip a shift at the diner. But she'd have to agree. She owed him that much.

Keating waved his hand toward Phoebe. "Shuffle up and deal, please. These boys are getting bored."

TJ started out with a hundred-dollar bet. A two/six/seven came on the flop and both men liked their hands enough to bet another hundred. The turn was a four. TJ was too drunk to see there was a straight on the board and pushed all in. Loyal called him and an eight hit the river.

"My nines good?" TJ asked, flipping his cards over.

"Not against my straight," Loyal said. "Sorry, buddy."

"Goddamnit," TJ said distractedly, and swayed a little in his chair.

Phoebe had seen it a thousand times before. When luck failed, God got cursed. She pushed the pot to Loyal.

"I'm down to two hundred," TJ said, and bought in for another thousand like she'd expected.

"Lots of bad beats tonight," Keating said, reaching for the whiskey. He poured his glass full and pushed the bottle toward TJ. "Take heart, buddy. Luck changes with the wind."

The whiskey was starting to show in their eyes and on their faces. They were all drunk enough to snap if they saw her fish a card off the bottom of the deck. She still had it, the ability to stick the cards when and where she wanted, but her hand was starting to cramp. She dropped it beneath the table, stretched and rubbed her fingers. The whiskey smelled good. A little sip would be okay, but she stifled that yearning and dealt the cards. Maybe she'd slip a beer in her coat pocket on the way out the door.

Empty beer cans and whiskey bottles sat on the bar. They'd gone through five bags of chips and pretzels. It was near midnight when Keating said, "Final hand, boys," and split the last of the whiskey between the four remaining players. Phoebe knew it was time to wind things up with a big hand when Keating smiled at her and said, "Cheers."

It was a genuine smile and she took it to mean she'd done an adequate job. Then his eyes rested briefly on her chest and she wondered if he'd meant something else.

Keating had twice the chips as TJ. Garcia had tripled the two hundred chips Keating had extended him on good-will. Loyal was down to fifteen black chips.

She was tired, but she had one more show to put on. It was time to bring the night to an end, so she chugged her bottle of water and sent the hole cards flying.

Garcia shoved all-in and so did Loyal. TJ called them both and Keating followed along.

She laid out the flop, an open-ended straight.

Garcia and Loyal groaned at the same time and mucked their cards.

TJ was dead serious as he shoved all his chips into the middle.

"I'm all in, too," Keating said. "And I've got you covered."

Phoebe glanced at their stacks and figured Keating had twice what TJ had. She started to turn the last card, but TJ held up his hand to stop her. He contemplated his cards and she could almost hear the booze washing through his frontal lobes. "Side bet," he said, and started to pull out his wallet.

Keating grabbed his wrist and said, "No, no. Your money's no good on this hand."

"What do you mean, no? I'm going to cover your bet with cash. There's nothing wrong with that."

"House rules," Loyal said. "You can't add cash to the pot after the hand's been dealt."

Keating let go of his wrist and tapped his forefinger on the table. "You want to cover that bet, you got to use what's already on the table."

"Everything I got is already in the pot."

"Not everything." Keating pointed with his chin. "You got that ring."

"This?" TJ laughed, his bloodshot eyes going wide. "My Super Bowl ring?"

Phoebe's grip tightened on the deck of cards. Her hand cramped. She'd been staring at that ring, had never seen one with so many stones. Only a drunk would use it to cover a bet, but she'd seen some crazy bets go down between inmates—like the time two upstate girls went after each other with blades over a bar of soap.

Keating, seemingly unfazed by all the booze he'd sucked down, said, "Yeah. You've been flashing it all night. In my house you only bet what's on the table."

"It's late," Loyal said. "What's it gonna be?"

TJ stared at the ring, wagged his head from side to side. He drained his glass and lifted his chin toward Keating. "Normally, I'd say no, but I got the best hand and I'm not letting you bluff me off it." He worked the ring off his finger and set it on top of chips.

The diamonds caught the overhead light. Lots of diamonds, lots of gold.

"Show me a winner," Keating said and motioned to Phoebe.

She turned the last card. Her hand ached with the motion, but she managed to pull the ace off the bottom of the deck. It snagged on the top card that was slightly out of place, but she recovered quickly and landed it on the table. She felt sure TJ had missed the fumble.

"Turn them over, gentlemen," she said, staring hard at the green felt.

Keating turned his cards over first. The ace gave him a full house.

TJ sank into his chair. His straight was beat.

Loyal and Garcia pushed back from the table like they didn't want any part of what happened next. Phoebe set the deck down but kept her hands in front of her just in case a fist came flying.

TJ slammed his hand on the table and the ring tumbled toward Keating. When Keating chuckled, Phoebe thought the whole thing might have been a joke, but he picked it up and slipped it over a knuckle, inspecting its facets in the overhead light.

"You know I can't let you keep that," TJ said, and reached his palm across the table.

"What did you say earlier about speaking at the Methodist church? Seems to me you're a man of your word, isn't that so?"

"I am a man of my word, sir. But I want that ring back."

"A man of his word only bets what he can afford to lose, and when he loses he takes responsibility for his actions."

TJ's jaw went slack as his face shifted, and he went pale for the second time that night.

Keating took the ring off and said, "I shouldn't gloat." He put the ring in his breast pocket. "Don't worry, son. I'll keep her safe."

TJ shook his head and pointed a finger at Phoebe. "That ace come off the top?"

Keating used his courtroom tone. "Don't blame her; she dealt those cards straight."

"You paid her though."

"She got paid out of the buy-ins."

"But you picked her."

"I hired her for the evening. Nobody made you place that bet. You lost fair and square."

"I want to hear her say it." He leaned over the table toward Phoebe, his breath foul with whiskey and cigars. "Lady, say you didn't cheat me. Say it in front of the cop." He motioned toward Garcia.

Keating raised his voice and stood up. "I'm telling you, there's no cheating in my house."

TJ pushed himself upright, but it took a moment for his feet to move. Phoebe watched him carefully. A man that big and drunk could take this place apart in seconds. He picked up his coat and turned toward the door. "Cheat," he said with as much scorn as the booze made possible, and walked out of the room.

It made her queasy to think she'd been part of that hand. The ring was worth thousands, enough to elevate a charge to grand larceny. She took her time collecting the chips and placing them back in their case, hoping to give TJ plenty of time to get to his car and drive into the night, hoping the cop hadn't been watching too closely when that last ace appeared.

Garcia stood. "I don't think he should be driving."

The front door slammed shut. Keating raised his voice. "Leave him alone. He's a grown man."

Garcia draped his coat over his shoulder, looked toward the hall, and asked Keating, "Are you really going to keep that thing?"

"I won it fair and square." He reached out and shook Garcia's hand. "Thanks for coming tonight, son. It's always nice to have someone from downtown in my home."

The implication was clear. Keating meant to use the cop's presence to prove the game had been legit. He'd invited the cop and expected loyalty in return. It chilled her, how effortlessly some men wielded power.

Garcia shook his head. "Thanks for inviting me, but what are you going to do with it?"

"Add it to my collection of priceless items handed to me over the years by drunk men," he said. "But first, I'll get it appraised."

A car engine started up outside, tires squealed.

"Let's go," Loyal said. He pointed at Phoebe. "You're square with her?"

Keating's eyes slid from her cleavage to her mouth. "Of course. I always treat the ladies right."

The look he gave her made Phoebe wonder if she should stay behind a minute, see what might come of things. It had been so long. His hair was gray, but it was full, and his belly wasn't as big as most men his age. As far as she knew he'd never married, never had kids. This house was too big for one person. Maybe he was lonely, too. But then he yawned and she reconsidered. It had been too many years anyway. Maybe if he gave her that same look another time, like in the diner when he dropped in each morning to fill his thermos with coffee. Maybe then, but not tonight. She buttoned her coat and followed Loyal and Garcia outside.

Low-slung oak trees lined the avenue. Streetlights glowed in the cold night air. Garcia offered them a ride.

She'd die before she ever rode in a car with a cop again. "No, thanks, I need the exercise." The three of them walked to the end of the drive.

"I'm just over there," Loyal said, pointing his key fob. A truck made an awful honk and its parking lights flashed obnoxiously.

"New Dodge?" Garcia asked.

"Yeah," Loyal said.

"Nice." The cop jiggled his car keys. It was obvious that he'd been upset by that last bet and wasn't ready to let it go.

"Man, you ever see anything like that?" Garcia asked.

"Like what?" Loyal asked. "A straight beat by a full house?"

"Not that," Garcia said, his voice incredulous. "He took that man's ring."

The two men stood under the street light. Garcia shook a cigarette from his pack, lit it, and offered one to Loyal.

"I think he took a lot more than his ring," Loyal said, tipping his chin and exhaling a cloud of smoke over the cop's head.

The cop scraped his shoe against the curb. "What do you mean?"

"The way I see it," Loyal said, climbing into his truck, "he took his soul."

Phoebe started walking. Their doors slammed shut, the engines started up. She jammed her hands deep into her pockets and picked up her pace for the dark walk home.

Tᴴᴱ ɴᴇxᴛ ᴍᴏʀɴɪɴɢ, Carl Garcia slipped inside the
sanctuary one minute before nine and took a seat
near the center aisle. The nave of the church was plain and
unadorned, with drab pine paneling, walls that hadn't
been painted in decades, and threadbare wall-to-wall car-
peting. Off to one side behind the pulpit, TJ Bangor sat
slack-eyed and pale in an ornately carved high-backed
chair, going over the notes for his speech, buttoning and
unbuttoning the tweed jacket that fit a little too snug across
his middle.

During the minister's introduction, Garcia learned that
TJ had been one of the few in his class to get drafted into
the NFL before his senior year at Ohio State, and that after
a long football career he'd gone back to finish his degree in
communications and launch a second career helping others
pursue their dreams through a relationship with God.

The minister droned on, and the more Garcia thought about that poker game, the more unsettled he got.

It wasn't the money—Garcia knew he wasn't a good player and hadn't expected to win. He also knew that losing had earned him more favor with the judge than if he'd won. But he wasn't sure he wanted the judge's favor anymore, not if it meant putting up with swipes at old wounds. Who brought up a man's divorce in front of a group like that? Keating was connected throughout New York, and everyone in law enforcement at the time knew Garcia's wife had left him for a circuit court judge. It had wiped out his credibility within the force and left him no alternative but to leave town. When he'd gotten a job in this little town, he'd told everyone his leaving had to do with the department's reorganization, but everyone knew the truth. He was just saving face. For five years now, he'd kept his head down and worked his way to detective. He figured the promotion had earned him the invitation.

The game wasn't illegal—the stakes set and agreed on by the players—but the dealing had seemed shady. He knew Phoebe Elders had done time and was pretty certain she'd been working that deck. She'd probably learned a lot of bad habits in prison.

He took off his jacket, loosened his tie, and was glad for the padded red cushions on the pew that vaguely matched the carpet. He'd been to every church in town over the years, funerals and such, and only the Methodists had the decency to provide seat cushions. This morning he was grateful for them and for the aspirin he'd taken before leaving home.

The minister stepped away from the pulpit, prompting applause as TJ heaved his big frame up from the chair. The tweed was a nice touch even if the gray tones matched the shadows below his eyes. In the dull light of this dim little church, the man's face was as colorless as egg white. Judging from the hollowed-out man standing at the pulpit, Garcia thought it could be true what Loyal Elders had said last night, that Keating had taken his soul. But to Garcia, the loss of the man's soul wasn't as worrisome as his health. He seemed a little caved in, like he'd been punched in the chest.

TJ was talking now, reading from some notes he'd pulled from his jacket pocket, but the microphone hadn't been adjusted to his height and Garcia heard only a few words. The air in the church was stale and warm. TJ seemed disoriented, pausing between sentences to swig water from a plastic bottle. Garcia had seen a man pass out from a hangover, but a man that size might take down the whole pulpit. TJ tugged at his collar trying to find his stride. Sweat soaked his forehead and dripped down his temples.

TJ adjusted the microphone higher and held up his fingers. His personal guide to success consisted of three bullet points. "Prepare hard, show up, and trust God." He dropped his hand to the pulpit and leaned toward the audience. "Success isn't rocket science. It's guts and determination."

The men of the Methodist breakfast club waited for more, and TJ finally got to the story they'd all come to hear. "We were on the fifty-yard line with eight seconds on the clock. Coach called for a Hail Mary. It was a long shot, but it was our only hope."

That play had made every highlight reel. Garcia had seen it at least a hundred times. TJ was the guy you wanted on your team, the guy who could jump higher than the defenders, the guy who could land on his head and still hold on to the ball. As he talked, spit flew from his mouth and his hair fell into his eyes.

Garcia recalled his own glorious moment on the high school team, the block he'd thrown that allowed the quarterback to connect with the receiver in the end zone. The tackle had cost him a groin injury but had won him the heart of the girl who, for better or worse, would become his wife. But TJ Bangor had won more than a game, more than a girl. He had lived every player's dream. He paused and wiped the sweat from his forehead, panting as though he had just finished that play once more. He'd been knocked unconscious, but when they'd carried him off the field on a stretcher, he'd still had a death grip on the ball. Now, he pointed at each man, making eye contact with as many of them as possible. "These life lessons can make you a champion, too."

TJ pushed out his chest and stood as tall as his frame would allow. Garcia had to give it to him. An hour ago he'd probably sucked down a handful of Tylenol and a quart of Gatorade. And he'd probably been thinking about losing that Super Bowl ring.

The men in the audience stood and applauded as TJ walked down the center aisle to introduce himself and shake hands. What a life, Garcia thought, to have grown men pay fifty dollars a pop for breakfast and a good story. Who wouldn't want that gig?

When TJ got to his aisle, Garcia said, "Quite a speech, TJ." He reached out to shake his hand, smiling hard to make sure the lines around his eyes crinkled. In his years as a cop he'd learned that if a smile didn't make it to your eyes, it meant nothing. He clasped TJ's shoulder, hoping that he'd remember him from last night.

TJ stood twelve inches over Garcia. His size alone was intimidating, teeth the size of marbles and a face as wide as a catcher's mitt.

"Garcia, right? From last night." TJ slid his arm around Garcia's shoulder and turned him away from the crowd. He bent over slightly and lowered his voice. "You got a minute?"

"Yeah, sure." They stepped away from the others.

"You're a cop, right?" TJ wiped his face with a handkerchief. "That judge, Keating, you know him?"

"Everyone in town knows him."

"I asked around. That game's got a reputation. I don't think it's on the up-and-up."

One of the ushers opened the double doors at the entrance and flooded the foyer with light.

Garcia squinted. He'd heard the rumors.

TJ leaned in. "The more I think about it, the more I think I got played."

Garcia nodded like it might be possible, though he was reluctant to admit he'd been thinking about that ring all night, too. "Huh. So, tell me, how did you get invited to the game?"

"I'm here to give a speech. Word gets around; I got a call," TJ said. "You saw what happened. All that whiskey. And betting the ring? That wasn't my idea."

"You called the bet, though. No one made you."

"I was on a roll. I mean, what are the chances he hits a boat same time I get a straight?"

"It happens. I've seen it before."

"I want that ring back. You have no idea how embarrassing it is to show up here without it. I called my daughter and told her to bring my second one, but she can't get here until tomorrow. I'm going to have to tell them I forgot to bring it with me. People pay to see that ring." He was whispering now and handed Garcia a business card. "Look, I'm not from around here and I'm not afraid of these boys. Those guys, Keating and his buddy, especially that woman—they paid her to cheat me. They were all in on it." He squeezed Garcia's shoulder like he was gripping a twenty-yard pass.

TJ's ruddy cheeks were blanching again and Garcia remembered how his face had crashed in on itself last night at the sight of Keating's full house. He could understand the anger, but it was easy for an outsider and a man of TJ's wealth to make an accusation like that.

"That's a hefty allegation," Garcia said. The more he thought about it, the more he suspected it was true, but he couldn't act on just a hunch. He'd need more proof than that.

"But you were there. What did you see?"

"We'd all had a lot to drink. I wasn't really sure what happened."

"Assuming you weren't in on it, right?" TJ gripped Garcia's shoulder. "Right?"

"Of course not. I'm just not sure what I can do."

"You're a cop, right? Throw your weight around a little. All I want is the ring, okay? If you can't get it for me, I'll get it myself, but no one wants this to get messy. Nobody needs to admit anything or apologize. Nothing like that."

The minister announced that breakfast was being served in the fellowship hall and TJ said, "I gotta go." He gave Garcia a card. "That's my cell. Call me anytime." He straightened and followed the crowd through the door.

Garcia put the card in his jacket pocket. He'd paid to stay for the breakfast, but he'd had his moment with Bangor and the man had asked him for help. He imagined Bangor on the other end of the phone, the surprised relief in his voice when he called—if he could manage to return the ring.

Help out a hero. Be a hero's hero. Face down a judge and maybe earn some chops on the force. Blind River was such a closed-up system, especially downtown. That had worked in his favor when he'd first moved here. He'd needed the isolation. But the more he thought about it, the more he felt that Keating and Loyal had taken things too far. Everyone knew they ran something on the side. That bogus annual veterans' fund-raiser was coming up, and what had they ever done with the proceeds but repaint the meeting hall and plant a few crape myrtles on Main? They should have at least planted oaks. *Huh*, he thought. *Follow the money. That might be my angle.*

Loyal, the good old boy with the new Dodge Ram.

Trucks like that ran, what? Fifty thousand? Where'd he gotten that kind of money? Unemployment in this county was at nine percent, and wages were busted flat as twenty years ago. They were taking good money from hardworking people. And Keating with that ivy-covered Tudor and creamy white Cadillac. Garcia would do some snooping around. Maybe get lucky fast.

He walked to his ten-year-old Toyota, wondering how many Super Bowl rings there were in the world—he guessed a few thousand total—and was struck by the effort required to win one.

He added TJ's cell number to his contact list. Then he started the engine. He lit a cigarette, inhaling deep enough to get a hot sting in his lungs, and put the car in drive.

CHAPTER

8

MONDAY AFTERNOON, JAMIE pulled her stocking cap over her ears and left Angel's house, where she had been holed up since Jack had dropped her off Saturday night. Overhead, the sky was fat and low with another front moving in from the west. She walked to the edge of the field next to the high school and stood at the chain-link fence with her backpack at her feet, her hands jammed in her pockets for warmth. The appointment with Jilkins and the principal had been set for three thirty, after the final bell.

She hoped that Toby was still inside the school, hoped he hadn't bolted and left her to handle them alone. She'd helped him out plenty of times and he owed her one. They had survived the last eight years by being human shields for each other, and she would need him there later when she told Loyal about having lost the money. That's how she planned to put it, make it sound like it had been misplaced on accident. He might buy that. Probably not. But the Monday night group were a bunch of laid-back shop owners, and if she told him right before they showed up things might go easy. He definitely wouldn't hit her in front of them and they would be there for hours. Maybe by the time they left he'd be passed out.

At three fifteen the school bell rang and kids poured through the doors into the parking lot like a flood of minnows rushing through the shallows, climbing over the fence into cars and buses, walking alongside the ditch that led away from the football field. All of them wound up from too many hours spent in a compressed space, most of them in need of a smoke and a couple of unstructured hours. It had been less than a year since Jamie had been stuck inside those walls waiting for life to begin. She remembered the impulse to flee at the end of the day. Now, a year later, she was nagged by the suspicion that those days might have been the best she'd ever know.

Toby was the tallest kid in his class and easy to spot in a crowd. She didn't see him leave the building. When the last school bus pulled away from the curb, Jamie went inside. She checked the detention hall behind the library, wondered if he was scamming the nurse again, and walked toward the main building to check the infirmary. She saw him through the tall glass windows, slumped on a bench outside the principal's office, pretending to catnap.

He looked up when she opened the door. "Jilkins is hell-bent on some stupid program." He rolled his eyes and dropped his chin back to his chest.

The school's guidance counselor spotted her through

the glass walls. She picked up a file off her desk and came out the office door. Ms. Jilkins followed her.

"We were expecting his uncle," Ms. Hollins said.

Jamie took off her stocking cap and twisted it in her hands. "He's sick today and sent me instead. Said to say he's sorry."

Ms. Hollins stretched her neck impatiently as if she'd expected something like this and said, "I guess you'll do, then."

Toby slumped forward, his elbows to his knees, hiding a smile.

"What's going on? I'm sure Toby will apologize. Right, Toby?"

"Apologies won't do this time," Ms. Hollins said. "We're seeing a pattern of behavior that needs to be addressed. We think Toby is a good candidate for a new program."

Toby groaned.

Jilkins took the file from Hollins, flipped through some pages, and found a form. She gave it to Jamie. "This is a program aimed at helping young men who show signs of . . . well, who struggle with social skills. Toby is inclined to push smaller students around, tell them what to do. We'd like to change that."

"He's just bigger than most kids his age. He's not a bully," Jamie said, not believing her own words. She looked at the form. It was an evening program run out of the school. Toby would see it as nothing more than detention, but all she had to do was take this home, sign Loyal's name, and this would be over.

"And we'd like to keep it that way. This program will help him learn to manage his temper."

Toby started popping his knuckles, and Jamie cut him a look. Everything they were saying was true; he was used to getting his way using those long arms and big fists. Most kids kept their distance.

Hollins tilted her head and adjusted her glasses. "With a little empathy training, though, Toby could work this out. He might even become a mentor, a student liaison for this program across the county."

Jamie asked, "That sound good to you, Toby?"

"It sounds gay," he mumbled.

Jamie held his gaze. They wouldn't get out of this until he went along. Finally he stood and said, "Yeah, I'd loved to improve my social skills."

"Good. Have your uncle look that form over and sign it. Toby, you should bring it to my office tomorrow," Hollins said.

"Consider it done," Jamie said, but Hollins wasn't finished. She pulled out a copy of Toby's numbers sheet. "And we found out about this today. Apparently, he's taking bets on the basketball team. This kind of gambling isn't legal and it certainly isn't allowed on school property."

Toby scratched the back of his head and looked toward the front door. "The thing is," he said, "I didn't know that."

Hollins cocked her head at Toby. "Yes, I think you did. You are to return all the money to the students you took it from. And you will get that done by the end of the day tomorrow. Do you understand?"

Toby splayed his big palms faceup like an innocent man and huffed. "Uh, okay."

Jamie wondered how much of it he'd already spent, how much more she'd have to come up with to cover it. "I'll make sure that happens."

Toby walked past the woman and leaned on the glass door at the entrance. "I have a lot of homework. Can we go now?"

Jamie followed him to the door, but Jilkins stopped her. "By the way, Jamie, how's college?"

"Fine," Jamie said straight-faced. "Good, fine, it's all good." She turned to catch up with Toby, who was holding the door for her.

"Oh, good. I always knew you were a bright kid," Jilkins called.

Right.

"Me too," Toby said when they were outside. He loved mocking Jilkins's high-pitched voice. "I've always known you were a bright kid."

"Shut up."

"Loyal won't sign that form. He'll say it's for fags."

"I'll take care of it," Jamie said.

They cut through the cemetery. Last week's storm had blown the plastic flowers everywhere. She hated plastic flowers and was glad to see the place torn up. She looked in the direction of their father's plot, somewhere near the back corner, and thought for the millionth time that she should take Toby there again, at least show him where to look for the headstone. They'd gone there once when Toby was ten. He'd covered the engraving on the headstone with his foot and rubbed his eyes till they turned red. He'd refused to speak to her for the rest of that day and, since then, they'd fallen into an unspoken ritual of silence when they walked by the cemetery on their way home.

Each time a car came up the road, Toby ducked his head and stepped off the curb.

"What're you so twitchy about?"

"Billy Pivens. He says I owe him."

A snow tractor had shoveled Main Street, leaving clumps of mud and snow along the curb. Cold, flat air slapped the blacktop dry. She wondered again if she could leave this town if her brother never did.

"Do you?"

"I sold the same square twice by accident and it hit. I paid him half but he wants it all."

She stopped midstride and swung around to face him. "Jeez, Toby. How'd that happen?"

"I said it was an accident."

"Christ."

"It didn't go like I thought."

"You got to be tight if you're going to run a sheet."

"The fuck you got to tell me that for? I think I know that now, don't I?"

She rubbed the back of her neck, sensed a headache traveling up from beneath her left shoulder blade, and switched her backpack to the other side. "Listen, you aren't the only one in trouble."

"Yeah, Loyal was pissed when you didn't show up at Keating's or all day yesterday."

"It isn't just that." She realized her eyes were dampening. She stopped and, after a couple of steps, so did Toby.

"What?"

"I didn't get the deposit to Jack."

Toby stepped closer and lowered his voice. "What the fuck did you do? Spend it?"

"I just needed a loan, for a day or two. Loyal wasn't supposed to find out."

He squared up to face her. "How much was it? Can you get it back?"

"No, we went to Mimawa. Lost it all."

Toby wrapped his arms around his chest and rocked forward. "Jesus. He'll kill us both."

"He won't take it out on you," she said.

"Right," Toby said. "Because we both know he never takes it out on me."

It was true. Toby was the boy and he got smacked harder, longer, and more often.

"He's been good to us, Toby. I mean overall."

"Yeah," he said. "Sort of. He'll go crazy when he finds out about this. He called you all day yesterday."

"I know. I turned my phone off and stayed at Angel's house, trying to come up with a plan."

"Hiding out is more like it."

Jamie wondered if she should lay low for a few more days or face her uncle now, wondered which option would be less painful. She could show him the laptop, explain how she thought she had the money to cover it, how she had planned to pay him back. It wasn't her fault the government had shut down the sites.

They turned at the corner of Main and First and slowed to look in the storefronts. The same set of golf clubs had been sitting in the front window of the pawn shop for over a decade. A new gun shop sat between Blind River Funeral Home and the men's shoe store. Farther down was a wholesale casket store that was perpetually empty.

Mack Dyson, the pawn shop's owner, came out of the Main Street diner cleaning his large teeth with a tooth-pick. He was a tidy man with thick-soled shoes and vacant eyes. Everything about him seemed bland until he smiled, and then he resembled the Doberman he kept chained at the back door of his store. The dog lived out there during the day and inside the store at night.

They stopped at the diner and Toby shaded his eyes, looking through the plate-glass window.

Dyson walked the twenty feet from the diner to his store. As he went inside, he called back to them, "She's out sick today."

Jamie hated that everyone in town knew they were Phoebe's kids.

"Damn. I wanted a burger."

"We'll get something from the 7-Eleven. Myers still has my last paycheck."

He pulled a box out of his jacket pocket and opened it to show Jamie. "Her birthday's tomorrow."

It was a silver chain with a tiny cross on it. "You bought her a necklace?"

"Well, I didn't steal it." He snapped the box shut and stuck it back in his pocket. "It'll make her happy."

"Try not getting your ass expelled from school before you graduate," she said, and started walking. "That might make her happier."

"Like you should talk. Try not getting your ass sent up for grand theft."

He turned up the street taking long angry strides. He'd grown a couple of inches this year, his cheeks losing some of their roundness. The peach fuzz was gone from his chin and she figured he'd shaved that morning, maybe for the first time ever. She followed behind, letting him cool off.

When they got to the 7-Eleven, Myers was behind the cash register. "I saw you out back the other day, you know. You got balls coming in here after that."

"Wasn't me. I've been out of town," she said.

Toby went straight to the back and grabbed two hot-dogs off the grill.

"Uh-huh," Myers said. He reached, blank-faced, under the counter where she knew he kept a pistol. Jamie froze. For an instant she thought he might pull the gun on them. He could say he thought they were robbing him and no one would be able to prove different. All the cops that came in here every morning to buy coffee and cigarettes, they were all his friends. So, who would take their side if he shot either of them right now?

He pulled his hand out from beneath the counter and held up an envelope. "Your last paycheck."

Jamie stared at the envelope feeling ridiculous, letting the air reenter her lungs.

Toby filled a Big Gulp cup, drank half of it, and refilled.

"Hey," Myers snapped. "It's not a goddamn water fountain."

She looked at the amount of the check. He'd docked her for a uniform she'd spilled grease on and twice because she forgot to mop the floor. She slid it back across the counter. "Just cash it."

"Take it to the bank." He rang up their drinks.

"Come on." She pushed the check toward him on the counter. "It's fifty-two dollars."

Myers folded his arms over his chest. "No."

"You want to get paid for this stuff? 'Cause we're broke."

He shook his head hopelessly and searched his pocket for a pen. "Sign it then." He took the cash, less the sodas and hotdogs, from the till and slapped them on the counter. "Got a new guy for the morning shift. A good worker, does everything I ask."

"That right?" Jamie said, stuffing the money into her pocket. Toby walked to the door and pushed it open.

"That's right," Myers said. "Goes to show you really can still find decent help these days."

She smirked. She had definitely not been decent help. Her heart wasn't in it. Never had been. She didn't want to be good at a minimum-wage job that would keep her stuck in this town. She wanted to be good at something that would get her the hell out of here.

Toby held the door for her and she briefly glimpsed the man he might become. He muttered, "I bet he bends over for him, too," and she laughed.

He spit on the sidewalk, stepped on the splat, and ground it with his boot. "Let's cut through the woods."

"As long as you don't fuck around on the tracks."

Sleet was beginning to fall. Jamie put her stocking cap on, and even though she hated walking beside the tracks when the afternoon train was due, she followed him. They took the south end of the trail through the woods and in a few minutes were walking alongside the tracks.

"Who'd you go to Mimawa with?"

"Jack."

"What the fuck, Jamie? That's your way out, right there."

"Blame Jack? No. It wouldn't be right."

"Oh, yeah. We're back to doing the right thing, are we? He was there, right? It would take the heat off you. You, meaning us."

Jamie sipped her soda, debating the idea quietly.

"Mom went there once," Toby said.

"Where? Mimawa? Huh-uh. That was Atlantic City. Remember, she brought you that T-shirt with the dice on it?"

"Yeah," he said. "The dice."

"Why'd she go there anyway?" he asked.

"Mom?"

"Yeah, why'd she go to Atlantic City?"

"I don't know. Probably met a guy," Jamie said, but she wasn't really sure.

"Which one?"

"Elvin, you know, the one with the Camaro."

"Oh, man, that was a nice car."

"You remember that? You were so little then."

His eyes darted back and forth as he searched his mind for the memory. "It was red with yellow flames on the side. Man, I loved that car."

Jamie nodded, though the car had been green. She remembered that guy and all the others Phoebe had brought home. Toby had fallen for every one of them. But that was before Phoebe went to prison and they ended up sharing that room in the back of Loyal's trailer.

A mile out, the train sounded like distant thunder. In another minute it would come barreling around the bend, just fifty yards away.

Jamie said, "Come on," and walked down into the gully.

Toby stayed on the tracks, turned around and faced the direction of the train, spread his arms Christlike, and raised his face to the sky. She hated when he fucked around like this, hated him for needing such a rush.

"Get off!"

The train came into view, hurtling toward him.

She screamed.

He opened his eyes and smiled. The conductor leaned out the window and tugged on the horn. A screeching wind boomed down the gully as Toby jumped off the tracks. He hit the ground, rolled into her, and took her out at the knees. The train whipped past them, pinning their hair to their heads while the conductor shook his fist at them, mouthing something like *fucking kids*.

"You're a goddamn ass," she screamed, but he was curled in a ball at the bottom of the gully laughing too hard to breathe.

CHAPTER

9

JAMIE AND TOBY were drenched with melted sleet by the time they got home. The sun had set and it was freezing inside the trailer. Out of habit she started cleaning: bagging garbage, emptying bottles and food wrappers that Toby could never seem to throw out on his own. He wrapped a blanket around his shoulders and parked in front of a space heater that glowed so red-hot at its center they sometimes used it to toast marshmallows. Toby turned on the TV and flipped through the channels until he found bare-knuckle cage fighting, his favorite. She set the garbage outside the back door and rounded up his clothes and the other crap he'd left around the living room and hauled it to his cot in the back room.

Loyal's room was shut. She twisted the doorknob thinking that blackmail wasn't completely out of the question or that maybe she'd come across some old family heirloom she could hawk at the pawn shop, but she'd scoured his room a hundred times and it was the same pigsty as always. The place stank of unwashed bedclothes and moldy carpet. His shotgun leaned in one corner, several cartons of shells stacked beside it on the floor. She'd priced that shotgun on eBay before and knew that even with the cartons of bullets it wasn't worth enough to cover the cost of shipping. She checked the box he kept under his bed and found his collection of nudie postcards from his buddy begging him to ditch Blind River and get on down to Key West, the small black lockbox she'd never been able to pick, a snapshot of him and her father when they were boys, one of the grandparents she'd never met, and a new bank statement she was tempted to open but didn't because the seal hadn't been broken yet. Sometimes there was cash, but not today. She heard the rumbling of engines outside, and Toby yelled, "You better get out of there before he comes inside."

By the time the engines cut off, she was in the kitchen wiping out dirty ashtrays.

Toby, glued to a blood fight on TV, said, "I hope he's got pizza."

Outside, Loyal yelled for him to open the door.

"I got it," Jamie said, and opened the door, stepping behind it to let him through. He had a case of beer under each arm.

Two more cars pulled in. The Monday night crowd was made up of Dan Remsen, who owned a gun shop on the north side of town; Charlie Creel from the liquor store; and two other men she'd seen but hardly ever spoken to. These were men Loyal had grown up with and in whose stores he kept some of his gaming machines. And then there was creepy Mike Tuckahoe who came in carrying six boxes of pizza. She hated the guy. They stomped their boots, grunted halfhearted threats at each other, and filled the trailer with the cold, musky smell of seldom washed winter coats. Just as she'd hoped, they'd arrived at the same time as Loyal.

When her uncle noticed her standing behind the door, he dropped the beer on the counter. "Where you been?" He made that scowl that used to scare her when she was little.

She hated when he made faces and opened the freezer, pretending to look for ice. "Oh, sorry about the other night. I got hung up."

"Keating hired you for the night and you're telling me you got hung up?"

"But Mom showed, so no problem, right?"

He slammed the freezer door shut, barely missing her nose. "Who were you with?"

"Jack." *Shit.* She'd meant to play this differently.

"What the fuck you doing with him?" His eyes narrowed and she saw the possibilities snapping together in his brain. Across the room, Toby was shaking his head at her.

"We went to Mimawa." Every time she opened her mouth, things got worse.

"You went to the casino instead of doing what I told you?" He took a step toward her. "With my money? Goddamn." He balled up his fist and pressed it against her jaw.

"Traffic was worse than I expected. I couldn't get back in time."

"Now you're lying."

He'd never done more than slap her before now, but she'd never lied right to his face. She backed against the freezer.

"You blew it, didn't you?"

"I fucked up. I'm sorry. I lost it." If she pushed his fist away, it would only make him angrier.

"Lost it. That's what you call it?" His spittle splashed on her cheek. She could barely meet his eyes, but then she spotted Dan moving in slowly on her right.

"Hey, now." He stepped between them and put his hand on Loyal's chest. "Take it easy, man. She's just a girl."

Mike Tuckahoe opened a pizza box and stuffed half a slice in his mouth. He stared at Jamie's chest. "Yeah, she's just a girl."

Loyal dropped his hand. "We'll finish this later."

The worst was not over, but if he let her play it might give her a chance to prove she could make back the money. "Maybe I could sit in on the game," she said.

"No room," Loyal said.

"Willie's not coming," Dan said. "She can have his seat."

Loyal shot him a look but said nothing, so Jamie took a chair.

"Me too?" Toby got off the couch.

"Not happening. Count out the chips if you want to play, Jamie. It's another five if you want pizza."

Jamie got the last of her cash from her pocket. Loyal nabbed her money off the table. "The pot's four hundred, winner take all."

Toby went back to the couch with his pizza and surfed the channels.

"Turn that down, Toby," Loyal said. He pushed the cards to Jamie. "You deal."

The game moved slowly until the food was gone. She folded her hand for the first round so she could get the feel of the group. They played old style, like she expected, limping in for cheap, hoping to hit the flop, folding every time the pot got raised.

"That VA tournament's coming up, isn't it?" Dan asked. He'd been a part of the group for five years even though he'd never won and Loyal often called him a donkey to his face. He was usually the first player to bounce out.

"Saturday," Loyal said.

"What's the buy-in this year?"

"A thousand." She knew Dan would never play for that much money.

"Goes up every year," Dan said.

"It's been a thousand for three years," Loyal said. "Takes a lot of work to put that thing on." He crushed a beer can in his hand.

Jamie knew better, though. He'd run the tournament so long it wasn't work anymore. Make a few phone calls, rent some tables, and hire a few dealers to come in from Mimawa. No advertising necessary because the locals couldn't wait for this event. She'd been watching the show for years and knew he took a big rake. But nobody seemed to care. Not even the vets. Everyone got lunch, free beer, and a chance at one big prize. It generated goodwill among the local boys who had actually served their country.

"Got a surprise this year." Loyal twisted the top off a new bottle of Jack. "Got a big celebrity coming. Good player, too."

Charlie said, "I heard TJ Bangor speak at the Methodist church. That the guy?"

"That's the guy," Loyal said. He swigged the whiskey from the bottle and set it on the table.

"Oh, man. He's huge, big as a door and still in awesome shape. Everyone wanted to see his ring, though, and he didn't have it on. Said he'd left it home on accident. I might scrape up enough to try my hand against him. Rich guy like that, though, probably plays high stakes all the time."

Sleet turned to ice and struck the roof hypnotically. "Sounds bad out there," Dan said.

The chatter quieted while the men cocked their ears to the ceiling and murmured their agreements.

An hour into the game, the beer was gone and Toby was snoring on the couch. Loyal hadn't said a word to her but Jamie felt his eyes on her each time she shuffled. She made a point of keeping her hands on the table where everyone could see them. She kept an eye on him, too, hoping to see it when he marked an ace because she'd never known him not to find a way to cheat. A few good pots came her way, and she made enough bluffs to build a decent stack.

By nine o'clock the ice had stopped falling and the room was warm. Jamie cracked a window to let in some fresh air. In another ten minutes three players had run out of luck and gone home. It was down to her, Loyal, and Dan.

She had the lead but she knew better than to bully Loyal in front of Dan. She folded three hands in a row, trying to pit them against each other. The next hand Dan busted Loyal's trips by hitting a straight on the river. Loyal glared at the cards, pushed his chair back, and joined Toby on the couch to catch the local news.

"Go easy on me," Dan said, and gathered up the cards to shuffle.

She needed this win and shuffled the deck until she felt the corner of one of the aces that Loyal had bent and dealt it to Dan. Any ace and she knew he'd go all in.

It was fifty-fifty luck, the kind of luck she knew to bet on, and she paired a ten on the river.

"Sorry, man."

Dan shook his head. He pushed away from the table and grabbed his jacket. "It's okay. The wife won't like me out in this weather anyway."

At the door he covered his head with his jacket and ran to his truck. She went to the porch, watched the mud fly at his feet, braced when she heard Loyal's footsteps come up behind her. He stepped outside and lit a cigarette. There was nowhere to go. The halogen lights of Dan's truck backing out of the driveway hit Loyal's face, lighting the gray scruff on his cheek, the jowls that sagged beneath his jaw. Dan's lights turned up the road. She knew the worst was coming, hoped it would pass quick.

When the truck was out of sight, Loyal grabbed her wrist and held it at an angle. Pain shot up her arm. One time he'd twisted Toby's arm hard enough to crack it in half. She waited for the snap.

"You know I'm going to have to cover this, don't you? If Keating realizes you ever even thought about stealing from him, you'll be in his cross hairs for the rest of your life."

Jamie winced and grabbed his fingers, but he was too strong. "I thought I could cover it."

"It didn't belong to you."

"I'd won some online. I needed a new computer. The money never came because the feds shut down the site." She tried to keep the pleading tone out of her voice. Pleading never set well with Loyal.

"You played poker online and were fool enough to think you wouldn't get cheated?"

"I won four hundred here tonight," she said, keeping her eyes level with his. "It's a start. I'll pay it back. Every dime of it. I will."

He squeezed her fingers into a fist and white pain filled her brain so fast she couldn't breathe.

"What does Jack have to do with this?"

"You're going to break my fingers." She tried to twist her hand free, but he gripped her fist tighter. She couldn't look him in the eye. "We tried to win it back."

Pain crept up her arm, beyond her shoulder, into her throat.

He landed an open hand on the side of her face and shoved her into the door frame. The back of her head smacked the wall. Pain like lightning seized her arm. She thought of Toby because if he saw this now, he'd jump in between them. She slumped to the porch floor and pulled her hand to her chest, trying to unfold her fingers and listening to see if the noise had woken him up. Loyal had never been this rough with her but it was all her fault.

"Then you both owe me. Was Phoebe in on it, too?"

"No," Jamie said, drawing the word out and holding her wrist. She couldn't straighten her fingers.

"So you clowns run off to Mimawa and I'm in to Keating for six grand."

"I can get it back in a few months." She'd done the math and knew it would take closer to a year.

He stood over her, his big knuckles in her face. "It'll take a year, maybe two, for you to win that much. And that's if it goes your way every time. Which it won't."

She knew that.

"I'll tell you what you're going to do. You, Jack, Phoebe. The three of you are going to work that tournament, exactly the way I tell you to, and you're going to make that money back."

"Okay." She tested her fingers again, flexed them until it seemed nothing was broken.

"I didn't ask you. I told you. And from now on you do exactly what I say." He stepped back inside the trailer. "Born a thief."

It was an ancient accusation but she hated when he threw it in her face. He had no idea what her choices were, what it was like being an Elders girl.

"I'm not like her."

"The hell you aren't," he said, and slammed the door.

An engine started beneath the streetlight across the street. She sat in the corner beside the door and peered through the dark. Her first thought was of Jilkins, but it wasn't her style to sit outside their home, and besides, no one from Family Services would be out in this weather. All Jamie could make out was the shape of a man's shoulders and a dingy brown sedan. Inside the trailer Loyal banged around the kitchen. In another minute the door to his room slammed shut and she knew he'd gone to bed. But it was safer out here, so she waited a little longer before slipping inside to her cot.

10

EARLY MONDAY MORNING, Garcia had gone to the Dodge dealership in Bracksville, just south of Blind River, and shown his badge to the owner. It took some convincing, but thirty minutes later he was looking at a fifty-two-thousand-dollar cash sales receipt for Loyal Elders's brand-new Dodge. The upgraded edition. Who had that kind of cash? Garcia had never seen that much money in one place outside of a stint on the narcs unit ten years ago. He got the address from the DMV and was a little surprised when he ended up in the trailer park on the south side of Blind River. Abandoned cars were everywhere—in the street, in the side yards, up on blocks. There was no way to know which one went with which trailer. The sun had already set by the time he parked his Civic beneath a broken streetlight. He got lucky quick when a half-dozen cars and trucks converged on the address.

He ran the plates on each car, but nothing hit. Still,

he touched his revolver in its holster—an old habit—locked the car doors, and pulled his lapels up around his ears. The temperature had dropped fifteen degrees since sunset and now it was sleeting. An hour later a thirty-something white male came out of the trailer and stumbled to a banged-up El Dorado that Garcia had ignored because it was parked three houses down. He got the license number as the truck drove by and ran the plate.

Mike Tuckahoe, registered sex offender. *Fuck.* This was not the direction he'd expected.

By nine, the cars were clearing out. He could have arrested three of these guys for DUIs, but that wasn't what he was there for. He wiped the fog off the windshield. It was coming down hard again, and his feet had turned to ice but he didn't want to announce his presence by idling his engine and running exhaust out the tailpipe. He sank lower in the front seat.

Another man came outside, followed by a young woman who stayed on the porch while the man got in a truck parked in the driveway. Loyal Elders came outside, the bulk of his frame filling the doorway. The truck backed out, briefly lighting the two people on the front porch before it turned up the road. The woman was slight, more like a girl. Garcia looked back at the porch and saw Loyal grab and twist the girl's arm, smack her once in the face. Garcia reached for the door handle, but then the girl got away from Loyal and crawled into the corner. Loyal went back inside and the porch light went out. She seemed okay.

A girl, though. It didn't sit right.

Garcia pulled up the address for Tuckahoe and started the engine. In a few minutes he was halfway across town and the warm air from the car's heater was thawing his toes.

From the street it could've been a crack house. The boxwood hedge looked like it had been trimmed with a hatchet, what with the mess of limbs jutting out beneath scant greenery. The glass on the front door was cracked and repaired with glue and tape. The front porch listed toward the street, its floorboards gaping and warped. He parked, got out, and banged on the door, hoping the glass window wouldn't fall out on his shoes. On the other side of the door he heard bare feet approaching, slapping like wet mops. The porch light came on and Mike Tuckahoe, pulling a T-shirt over his head, peered out through the fringe of curtains. "What do you want?"

Garcia held his badge up. "You hanging out with kids again, Mikey?"

"Huh? No. I was just playing poker with a couple of guys. They can vouch for me."

Garcia motioned at the door. "Open up."

Tuckahoe arranged the T-shirt over his belly and opened the door. The smell of whiskey and backed-up sewage hit Garcia in the face. He put his hand over his nose and stepped to the edge of the porch. From the back of the house a woman's voice called out, "Who's there?"

"Go back to bed, Ma." Tuckahoe stood flat-footed in a pair of dingy boxers, scratching his crotch.

"Who's the girl?" Garcia asked.

"What girl?"

"The girl at the Elders's place tonight. You've got one chance to give me a straight answer."

"Hold on there." Tuckahoe rubbed a thumb over his left eye. "That girl lives there, or used to. No, wait. She stays somewhere else now."

"The court told you to stay away from kids, all kids, by a hundred yards."

"Those are my buddies. Besides, she's just some scrawny girl. I can't help it she lives there."

"Yeah, and I can't help that I saw you breaking the conditions of your parole. You could get sent back for that."

"Man, don't do that. I'll be out by lunchtime tomorrow and for what? I didn't touch that girl."

"But you looked, didn't you?"

"Nobody told me I couldn't do that." He scratched his crotch again and looked over his shoulder.

"What the fuck, dude! Why do you keep touching yourself in front of me? Punk. Sitting on your butt in a warm house while my balls freeze in this crappy weather."

"Take it easy. I got bedbugs is all." Tuckahoe put his hands up. "It won't happen again."

"Who else was there?"

"Same guys every week, just local boys. Dude, it's just poker."

"What are the stakes?"

"A hundred dollars, winner takes all. Nothing illegal about that."

"You ever been to Judge Keating's game?"

"Fuck no. He's the one sent me off."

Garcia tapped a cigarette from his pack. "What's Loyal Elders doing at the judge's house, then?"

"How would I know?"

He blew smoke in Tuckahoe's face.

"You gonna stand on my porch smoking, least you could do's offer me one."

A pain started in Garcia's shoulder, a sharp pinch beneath his clavicle. He'd met too many guys like this. They knew no limits and were easy to buy. He shook another cigarette out.

"How's a guy like that come up with the money to buy a brand-new truck?"

Tuckahoe took the lighter, lit his cigarette, and leaned against the doorframe. "He works at the fertilizer plant, don't he? That's a good job."

"He hasn't worked there in years. Not since the explosion. What's that been? Three years."

"I don't know his business, man."

Garcia flicked the cigarette into the damp yard. "Maybe we should go downtown, get a cup of coffee, and continue this conversation someplace warm."

A light came on in the back of the house and the woman hollered, "What kind of trouble is it at this hour?"

"Leave it, Ma." Tuckahoe closed the door behind him and blew smoke out the side of his mouth. "I'm just trying to live my life. What do you want?"

"We were talking about your buddy, Loyal."

"Okay. He knows lots of folks, enough to run some numbers now and then. That girl? Maybe she helps him."

"Is that right?"

"Might be, but you didn't hear it from me."

"That girl, she's a sweet one, eh?"

"Heh." Tuckahoe reached for his crotch but instead hooked his thumb in the waistband of his underpants. "I don't know. Girl like that, though? Tight little ass. *Sweet* don't even touch it."

Garcia fought the urge to hit this perp. "There you go again, you stupid shit. You don't know how to act." He slammed his hand against the doorjamb and Tuckahoe jumped.

The lights in the house came on. A dog started barking across the street. Mrs. Tuckahoe, wrapped in a pink housecoat, came to the front door. Her mouth opened, then snapped shut, and she pulled the housecoat tight to her neck.

Garcia rubbed the back of his neck. This wasn't what he was after. He stepped off the porch. "Don't let me see you near a kid again."

CHAPTER

11

Phoebe watched Keating put on the robe and tie it at his waist before getting out of bed. They were older now, but he showed less wear. Living on the outside did that for a body. Doctors, dentists, supplements. He was pudgier than he'd been in high school, but he wore his hair in the same style as he had back then. Longer, though, than suited her taste in a man, and gray at the temples, but still as wavy as in their youth.

High school. The prom. Going with Keating had been an inside joke among her friends. It still made her smile, how she'd agreed to go with him and then left him holding her shoes and standing beneath the basketball net on the opposite side of the gymnasium while she danced with every other boy there. Oh, how she had loved torturing him.

One week later she'd gone and eloped with Jim Elders. Eventually Keating had left for college anyway. She knew his type. Screw a local, marry a highbrow. But he had never married.

He returned from the bathroom and crawled under the covers still wearing his robe. The modesty surprised her. He touched her lips and cupped her chin a little rougher than she liked.

"I always liked your smile. Sly and cocky. The crooked little mouth of a liar."

She didn't know how to take that. He hadn't been gentle with her when she arrived, hadn't even offered dinner. Earlier at the diner, he'd slipped her a note that read, *8:00 tonight, my place.* She'd been adequately late, but he'd seen through her fake ambivalence and taken her straight upstairs to the master bedroom. The room was dowdy, though she could get used to it. She'd never felt sheets so soft, carpet as thick as pudding.

"A sly smile hints at a quick mind," he continued. "I always thought you were smart. Maybe too smart for your own good."

She wondered if he meant then or now and just how much resentment he still held against her. Well, two could play that game. "Is that what you thought when I eloped?"

His face turned hard. "I thought you got what you deserved."

She sat up. "And now? Do you think I got what I deserved?"

He was quiet for a moment. "No. I didn't mean it that way."

Whiskey and sex had made her drowsy and she wanted to lie back down and close her eyes. But she wasn't comfortable here anymore. She'd finally given him what he'd wanted all those years ago and now she felt foolish. Now he'd turned mean.

"I only meant you deserved Jim. I mean—That's not what I mean."

"Well, what do you mean? Just say it, for Christ's sake."

"Look, that jail sentence wasn't my fault. I don't know why you agreed to it. That was all the prosecutor presented me with. All I did was sign off on it."

Her only weapon was silence and she decided to let him stew in it. She lay down, closed her eyes, hoping for a few hours of sleep and to leave before he woke. It was dicey, being here in his house, much less in his bed. But it was riskier for him. A judge with an ex-con. He had more on the line than she did and she wondered if she'd stumbled across a secret weapon. If anything, he could improve her image around town. At least get her a better job. As she contemplated the possibilities, her mind began to drift to white. Then a dull thump from downstairs startled her.

"What was that?"

He dismissed it as noise from the foundation settling but sat up at the sound of a small crash. She sat up, too, suddenly alert, and moved quickly to pull on her blouse. He found his slippers.

"Don't you have a security system?"

"I left it off in case you left in the middle of the night," he whispered. He opened a drawer, got a handgun from the nightstand, and walked across the carpet to the door. "There's another pistol in the drawer if you need it, but you stay put."

"You're not leaving me here," she said, and found the second pistol. Briefly she thought to hide, but there was no way out of the house from the second floor.

They went down the carpeted stairs, and when he stepped into the kitchen, she was right behind him. The deadbolt on the back door had been jimmied loose and the door was ajar. She thought about running out the door, but it occurred to her that a second person might be outside. There was safety to numbers, so she stayed behind Keating. The door to the basement and game room was half open, and inside it a flashlight flickered across the walls. Keating released the safety on his handgun and went down the stairwell first. He pushed the door open. A man was stooped low over the bottom drawer of the bar. When Keating flipped on the light, TJ Bangor stood to his full height and smiled slowly. The crystal decanter in his hand was half empty. He took another swig.

Recognizing his face made her feel better—until she remembered what they'd taken from him.

Keating lowered the barrel of the gun to the floor. "What are you doing in my house?"

"I came for what's mine."

"You're not welcome here. Get out."

TJ pulled out the drawer he'd been looking through and carelessly dumped its contents on the floor. He threw the drawer down and it broke in half. "I'm not leaving here without my ring."

"You set the alarm off and the police are on their way. You leave now and I'll tell them it was a misunderstanding."

TJ laughed at the lie. He was so big, he made Keating's gun seem like a toy, like he could just walk over and take it if he wanted. Keating had taken this too far and she wished he would give the man his ring and end this now.

"Good. Maybe they can help me find my damn ring." TJ waved the decanter at Keating and took another drink. "Nice stuff you got here. A lot better than the swill you served the other night." He threw the decanter against a bookcase and it shattered, leaving amber splotches on the wall and carpet.

"What the fuck! That belonged to my mother!"

TJ wasn't threatened by the gun or Keating's advantage, which, if he ever had one at all, was fading every second they stood there talking.

Phoebe thought about running for the back door, but a man that big could overtake her in two seconds.

"Give me my ring," TJ said.

"We both have a lot at stake here, son."

TJ slurred, "Don't call me son!" He swayed like a pine in a windstorm. "I'm not leaving here without it."

"Okay, calm down. It's right there on the bar in the humidor."

TJ lifted the lid. The Super Bowl ring was on the center cigar.

It seemed like it was settled. He could take the ring and leave. Phoebe started to back away from the door, but TJ caught the motion and wheeled toward her. His face shifted to comprehension. "You're that bitch."

Her heart pumped in her ears.

"Take it easy. It's not what you think," Keating said,

but TJ lunged—or maybe he tripped. It would never be clear in Phoebe's memory. Shots blasted the air and bullets lodged in the man's midsection. He looked surprised as his legs gave way and he hit the floor. TJ let out a gasp of air as blood bubbled in his mouth, oozed down his cheek. He convulsed once, then again, and finally stopped moving altogether.

CHAPTER

12

JAMIE WOKE TO the sound of Loyal's cell phone ringing in the kitchen and his footsteps thudding down the hallway to answer it. She refused to open her eyes, flopped onto her back, and pulled the blanket over her head, but she heard Loyal say, "Goddamn it, I'll be right there."

In another moment he came back up the hallway, opened the door, and pointed a flashlight at her.

The light hit her eyes through the threadbare blanket. "I'm sleeping. Can't it wait till morning?"

"Get up."

"It's still dark."

"Get up." He yanked the blanket off her.

Across the room, Toby sat up. "What's going on?"

"Go back to sleep," Loyal said.

"You two going somewhere, I'm coming, too." Toby threw his blanket off and groped to find his sweatshirt.

"Stay put," Loyal said. He pointed at Jamie. "You, grab some jeans and come out here."

She recognized the tone in his voice and knew from the frown on Toby's face that he did, too. "It's probably nothing," she said, hoping to appease him. "Go back to sleep."

In the kitchen, Loyal poured a cup of day-old cold coffee into a glass and guzzled it. "Goddamn, it's early."

The oven clock read three AM. "Can't Toby do whatever this is? I mean, it's rare when he actually wants to help."

Loyal sloshed some water on his face and spit in the sink. He rubbed his head hard, the gray hairs standing up on end. "Toby's strong, but he's got no guts," he said in a low voice, then pointed at her. "And you goddamn owe me."

She couldn't argue with that. "I'll put some coffee on."

"No time for that. Keating needs help. Needs it right now." Loyal started pulling on his boots. "If you want a chance to get out from under your debt, you got it tonight."

"Doing what?"

"Everything I tell you till sunup. But you play by my rules."

Right there she knew that whatever he needed help with couldn't be good.

He stepped closer and towered over her.

Her jaw clenched, knowing she had no choice, but it was a chance to get back on her plan to leave this fucked-up town.

"And you don't ask questions. You keep your mouth shut and don't speak unless you're spoken to. Understand?"

She glanced down the hallway.

He lowered his voice. "And Toby can't know." He grabbed his keys. "Get your jacket and come on."

"Okay," she said, and pulled her boots on. "Where are we going?"

"Keating's place and that's the last question you ask," he said. "You see any cars come up on us, you get down on that floorboard, you hear? The fewer people knowing our business, the better."

*　　*　　*

They looped north on the county road to avoid Main Street. It was after hours but there were a few cars at Crowley's Pub, likely Eddie and some of the servers kicking back with a nightcap or two.

On the other side of town, the houses on Keating's street were dark and silent. Loyal turned into the driveway beneath a row of sagging elms and pulled around to the back of the house. A porch light spread yellow over the backyard. The door to the freestanding garage was propped open with a metal bucket, a thin light on inside. Keating came out from the garage carrying a folded blue tarp, the yellow porch light like a stain across his hands. He dropped it in front of the truck when Loyal cut the engine.

"The hell you bring her for?"

"What? You going to help me? You skinny bag of bones."

"It's a one-man job."

"The hell it is. That man's huge."

Keating climbed the few steps to the back door. "It's not her damn business."

Jamie got out of the truck. A light in the upstairs window backlit a familiar silhouette.

Loyal picked up the tarp and carried it inside. He pushed Jamie's shoulder as if to wake her from a dream. "Stop staring. Back the truck up to the porch and drop the tailgate." He followed Keating inside.

She looked back up at the window. The curtains shifted slightly and the light went out.

Fifteen minutes later, the men reappeared at the back door dragging the tarp, bundled and wrapped with twine, their breathing labored and fogging the cold night air. The tailgate of the truck sat a good six inches above the level of the porch and transferring it into the truck bed took everything they had. Loyal climbed out of the flatbed and straightened his back stiffly. He rubbed his left shoulder and slammed the tailgate shut. Keating waved toward Jamie. "What about her?"

"You got big enough problems. Leave the girl to me."

Keating grumbled something and spit on the ground, but he went inside and closed the door behind him.

"Get in," Loyal said, but Jamie just stood next to the truck, staring at the tarp.

"I'm not getting in there." She turned for the woods. She'd rather hike alone at night than help dig a grave.

Loyal caught her near the garage and grabbed the wrist he'd twisted the night before. White light shot behind her eyes and her knees nearly buckled.

"You are getting in this truck."

"That's a dead man and this is a felony."

"Just being here puts you in over your head. You best come along."

"Seeing is not the same as participating."

"Damn it, girl. I had a choice and I chose you. I could've had Toby help me with this, but I gave you a chance to get square. Besides, you think he'll get into the Army if this thing comes to light and he helped? You really want to drag your little brother into this? You made your bed when you took what didn't belong to you."

He took her by the back of her neck and steered her to the passenger door. "That man is dead and there's nothing going to fix that, but if you play this thing smart you might improve your situation."

The way he put it, she had no choice. It was horrible and gross, but she'd never dump this on Toby. And if Loyal was willing to cut her a deal, she might be able to pay him back in one night. She opened the door and got inside.

He climbed in behind the wheel and handed her the flask. "Take some whiskey if it helps, but get down on that floor."

13

JAMIE SAT ON the passenger side floorboard staring up at her uncle and the truck's dashboard lights reflected in the window beside his head. It was stupid, having to hide like this. She could jump up, yank the door handle down, and roll out backward, but she kept quiet and thought about her brother. Everyone thought he was such a bully, but she knew better. That first year after Phoebe left, he'd barely slept through the night without waking up crying. Something like this would scar him forever and he'd already been scarred too much. If she bailed now, Loyal would drag him out of bed and into this nightmare.

She pushed her back against the door and bent her knees to her chin. Loyal cracked his window and lit a cigarette, driving slowly and making so many turns that she lost her sense of direction. Each time he opened his flask, the smell of whiskey cut the night air. He passed it to her and she took it. The whiskey bit at the back of her throat but warmed her chest. They hit a pothole and the load in the flatbed bounced and thudded with a sickening sound. She took another sip and passed it back to Loyal.

The truck veered left and her body leaned into the curve of what she guessed was the highway. They were quiet now, driving straight and fast. She wondered what her uncle was thinking, if he'd done this kind of thing before, moved bodies wrapped in tarps in the middle of the night. Whoever it was inside that tarp was so big they'd had to bend his legs and angle his body to fit him between the toolbox bolted to the truck's cab and the tailgate.

Loyal threw the cigarette out the window and lit another one. "I saw her in the window. It's bad she was there," he said. "Complicates everything."

Jamie felt an unexpected need to defend her mother and took another drink. He stared straight out the windshield as if racing toward a house fire.

"She won't talk, you know." The whiskey slowed her tongue and slurred her words. "She won't say anything that might get her in trouble." Talking helped, helped keep the image of the tarp, and the body wrapped inside it, from taking complete possession of her brain. "What's it matter?" she asked, just to keep the conversation going.

"The more people know about a problem like this, the more likely something gets out."

"Huh," she said, considering the numbers. That the problem had a mathematical equation reassured her, though anyone could see that four people were three too many.

He took another sip. "You see her much?"

"No. Some. Now and then. Toby's crazy for her."

"Uh-huh," he said. They passed a lighted billboard and the inside of the cab flashed bright green. He held the cigarette and the wheel with one hand, capped the flask with the other. "Boys love their mothers, no matter what."

Flashes of light swiped the interior of the cab as they passed another billboard and then a third and she realized they were headed toward Mimawa. She expected to feel the truck lift as it climbed the ramp to the freeway but was surprised by the echo of a roar: the engine inside a tunnel. He'd taken the underpass.

"What are we going to do with him?"

"A ditch or a gully. Can't dig until after the first thaw."

She tried to guess where, but there were abandoned farms and hunting reserves all over the county. The underpass told her they were moving north, but she hadn't been out this way in years, not since they'd gone hunting that one time. Maybe she was safer not knowing.

He let the truck slow to a crawl, then turned left onto an unpaved road that dropped off sharply, weeds slapping at the fenders. He stopped once and backed the truck up at an angle and stopped again, looked out each window, switched off the engine, told her to get out.

When he cut the lights, the woods fell black all around them, trees looming on every side high enough to block the sky. A gully dropped off at her feet. Beyond that, the sharp line of a tin roof caught a fraction of moonlight. Some old barn.

They slid the tarp out of the truck bed and it landed

hard on the frozen ground. Something cracked within the bundle and the sound was nauseating. Jamie thought about another sip of whiskey but leaned against the truck instead while Loyal grabbed the edge of the tarp in his big fists and pulled.

"We'll leave him down there," he said, nodding toward the ravine.

But the ground was dirt and rock and they could barely budge him. Jamie grabbed one corner of the tarp and together they moved him about an inch before she landed on her ass, the tarp damp with the night air and slipping out of her hands.

"Let's roll him," Loyal said, his breath jagged with exertion.

Jamie got on her knees for leverage, and together they rolled the tarp to the edge of the embankment where the ground sloped away and gravity kicked in. The bundle slid at first, then tumbled and gained momentum with a series of nauseating thuds. The corner of the tarp snagged on a branch of a fallen tree limb and tore loose, unwinding, but the body kept falling, gaining speed, and rolling freely to the bottom of the ditch, a shoe flying off, a hand waving absurdly, then stopping where the ground leveled out. It came to an awkward rest, face up, the legs twisted, one arm bent all wrong, the mouth open and slack-jawed, and the face unbelievably pale with blank eyes staring at the star-filled night. Jamie had seen that dead-man stare once before and the memory of her father's corpse filled her brain before she could stop it.

Loyal switched on his flashlight and scanned the

beam down the ravine. "Jesus," he said, "he still has his watch on."

She sat at the top of the ditch staring at the man's vaguely familiar face, his blood-soaked shirt, the grotesque and distorted posture. "Who is that?" She'd never seen a man so big and from that alone knew he wasn't from Blind River.

Loyal skidded halfway down the graveled embankment, grabbed the tarp, and slid the rest of the way to the body. "No one you know."

He searched the man's jacket and trousers, fished out a wallet and a set of keys. "Damn Keating. Didn't even go through his pockets."

Jamie sat on the ridge, unable to look away. "That stare. Do they all look like that?"

"What?" Loyal looked up at Jamie. He threw the tarp over the man's face and started tucking it underneath his body. "No. Get down here and start bringing me rocks."

She was relieved that he'd covered the man's face, but the tarp was still in the shape of a corpse. Or a mummy. She tried not to dwell on it, grateful that her uncle seemed to know what to do next and for the simple chore of finding stones and small boulders and carrying them to him so that he could begin to build a fortress, a wall of sorts, something that would stand between them and this unholy thing they were doing. She thought about the dams beavers built and how this was similar but not really because there was no purpose in this dam, no water in this ditch, just an embankment left over from what she guessed used to be a working farm, and how ridiculous her thoughts were considering there was a dead man lying at her feet. Loyal placed the stones around the tarp, then on top of the tarp, building a pile, and she worried briefly that the rocks would settle and drop and crush the body, guts and all.

She gathered rocks for what seemed an hour, ignoring the dirt gathering beneath her fingernails, the split nail that tore deeper as she dug another rock from its place in the frozen ground, the sting from another and then another until all her fingers bled. She accepted the pain, the split fingernails, and the cold cracked cuticles because this little bit of blood made the thing they were doing seem almost sacred.

They dragged brush from the woods and threw it over the pile and eventually it began to look less like a burial mound and more like a landslide. She imagined setting it on fire—it only seemed fitting—but overhead the black night began lifting to purple, and her uncle, tossing the last of the brush on the pile, rubbed his hands against his trousers and told her to go start the engine. A fire would attract attention and lead authorities to the body, identifiable in so many ways. Jamie climbed up out of the ditch, sick at what she'd taken part in but relieved to be done and to be finally going home.

In the truck, she shivered and sipped some whiskey, certain that one day she'd need to find her way back here. It seemed they weren't that far out of town but she never came out this way.

They bounced over the uneven ground back toward

the road. The whiskey sloshed in her belly and threatened to come back up. She gripped the armrest and swallowed hard.

At the road he told her to get back down on the floorboard.

She folded her body in half and hunkered there, rubbing her hands, impatient for the engine to warm. Her tailbone smacked against the floorboard each time they hit a pothole. She sucked at her fingernails, the sting worsening as they warmed, and wished for the cold again. Even though she knew Loyal wouldn't say, she asked, "You gonna tell me where we were just now?"

He lit a cigarette. "Private property, and that's the last time you ask. Some things you're better-off not knowing."

She saw the logic there, but made note of the lights she'd seen on the drive, the sudden drop of the pavement, the moonlight on the tin roof in the distance. There'd come a time, she felt sure, she'd need to remember all this and more.

He offered her the flask again, but the heater was blasting in her face and she waved it away.

The truck slowed and then climbed a small rise. Now they were back on the highway and the road smoothed out. In the sallow light of the cab, the stubble on Loyal's face seemed wolfish, his eyes eerie with the backlight from the dashboard. They passed the casino billboards again, the green neon blinking on the windshield. The wheels whined against the highway, the heater blasted. South. She could tell that much. She rested her head on the seat cushion and almost passed out but wouldn't give herself the relief, not yet.

"We square now?" she asked, lifting her head.

"No. Not square." He set the flask between his knees and wiped his mouth with the back of his hand. "But, if you want, I'll give you a route and double your pay."

She closed her eyes and tried to count backward from a hundred to empty her mind.

"You listening?"

"I'm listening," she said. But the words left her mouth like oblong echoes.

"Tomorrow, you make the rounds. Collect the money from the cashboxes and take it to Jack's. Same as always."

Jack. She hadn't thought of him all night.

"I'll leave you a list and a set of keys for the machines and you can keep using this truck. I'll buy the gas. Make sure it gets cleaned, though, first thing in the morning. You got that?" His voice was hollow and distant.

"Okay." She closed her eyes and had the sensation of standing on the edge of a cliff, of something vast and dark spreading like a shadow beneath her feet.

"You help me, I help you. But make no mistake; one word gets out about tonight and all deals are off."

Sweat dripped down her back. The whiskey had turned her brain to lead. Darkness crept up the back of her skull and she saw that man's face again. She opened her eyes and shook it off.

"There's one more thing you should know. Things change, maybe I disappear, you got something on Keating. Keep that in your back pocket."

"But I don't know where we were."

"If need be, I'll tell you what you need to know."

The truck turned abruptly, its wheels crunching over gravel, and they stopped in front of the trailer. Loyal turned off the engine and opened his door, told her to go get some sleep.

The cold air was a relief. She stumbled out of the truck, stared dully at the gray haze of dawn rising in the field behind the house, and went inside.

On his cot, Toby opened his eyes at her for a moment then turned toward the wall. A draft lifted the curtains at the window as she burrowed beneath her blankets, fighting the image of that dead man's face, forcing herself to think instead of the many stones she'd carried.

14

THE NEXT MORNING Toby stood next to Jamie's cot and watched her sleep. He said good morning three times in an increasingly louder voice and poked her in the cheek when she didn't respond. After an eternity of winter gloom, the sun had finally come out, busting through the window and slanting across her eyes, but that didn't wake her either. When she groaned and rolled toward the wall, he pulled on his boots and jacket, stuck the box with the necklace in it deep in the front pocket of his jeans, and left for town. He was already late for first period but it was just study hall and who cared anyway? It was his mom's first birthday since she'd come home and he had a present for her.

If he walked fast he could get to the diner in twenty minutes. She worked the breakfast shift every morning, and unless she'd taken it off for her birthday, she'd pour him a cup of coffee like he was one of her regulars and he'd drink it while she shuffled plates of scrambled eggs and toast to her customers. He'd wait for things to get quiet, even if that meant missing his morning classes, and surprise her with the necklace. The scene played out in his head, her surprise, the happy tears in her eyes. He passed on his usual breakfast of two Snickers and a Monster from the 7-Eleven and cut straight through the woods to Main Street.

Most of the storefronts on Main—the hardware store, the Army recruitment center, the pawnshop, the insurance broker, the bank—were still closed, but Mr. Lu's dry-cleaning and the diner were open.

The bells on the diner's front door jangled when he stepped inside. Phoebe looked up from pouring Mack's coffee and, seeing her face, Toby felt a pang of regret as he realized he'd forgotten to buy a birthday card. A sergeant from the recruiting center came in right behind him and it was him that Phoebe attended to first by motioning to an open table by the window and handing him a menu.

Customers always came first. He knew that. Besides, his favorite stool at the end of the counter by the kitchen door was vacant. Even before he sat down, she turned over a cup and filled it for him, said, "Morning," then went to take the sergeant's order.

Her eyes and nose were red and puffy, and he wondered if she'd been sad to wake up alone, her first birthday after eight behind bars, and was glad he'd planned it this way. Women were healed in mysterious ways by presents of jewelry from the men in their lives. Despite having never done it himself, he'd seen this fact proven a thousand times on television. He'd never had the chance to create that kind of smile on a woman's face before today.

But she was here now, and he was here, and he'd planned the whole thing himself.

He set the black box on the counter, leaned forward on his elbows, and kept it hidden under his hand. At the right moment he'd reveal the box and watch the surprise spread across her face. While she took a to-go order over the phone, he tore open three packages of sugar and filled his coffee with cream. She stuck the order through the cook's window and the cook, a guy named Tommy, snagged it, and then Toby's mom came back to him.

"I got here late and I can't talk much this morning," she said, leaning over the counter, her words rushed and low. She set a pamphlet next to his coffee. "This is for you. The recruitment officer comes in here every day. He said you can apply before your eighteenth birthday if you have a parent sign."

She wasn't her usual self, but that's what he'd come here to fix. He pushed the box toward her—she hadn't noticed it—and said, "Happy birthday, Mom."

She stared flatly at the box and Toby realized she didn't understand. She'd gone without for too many years.

"It's for your birthday. Open it."

He flinched when she seemed to recoil, to step away from the box and straighten her back. "What is that?" She wiped her hands on her apron and glanced sideways down the counter.

He slid the box toward her. She didn't take it, so he opened it for her. "Happy birthday," he said again, more as an explanation than anything.

She frowned.

"How did you afford that?" Phoebe was still talking in

that low rush, but people were noticing now. Mack peered down the counter. The necklace was too simple. He should've known she'd want something nicer, bigger, better. A tiny silver cross on a thin chain. How could he be so stupid? Mack turned back to his newspaper.

"Let me put it on you," Toby said, but Phoebe snagged the box and shoved it in her apron pocket.

"I'll put it on later. Let me get you something to eat."

His face reflected hers now and his mood went tumbling toward that empty feeling he couldn't name but hated anyway. He saw a string hanging around her neck. A string, when she could have worn this necklace. "I'm not really hungry," he said, knowing that empty feeling would be with him the rest of the day.

Tommy slammed the cook's bell and called, "Order up." Phoebe went to the pass-through and grabbed the steaming plates.

Toby's eyes felt hot as he sat there at the counter, trying to recover. The pamphlet showed a picture of a soldier driving a tank across the desert. He knew what happened to those guys. They came home as heroes, smiling in their uniforms and prosthetics like they were still whole men, but what did the uniform matter when they'd been blown up by cowards who dressed like women and hid behind children? And how could she want him to leave, especially after she'd just come back?

She returned to refill his coffee cup, but it was still full. "Don't you need to get to school?"

"You don't like it."

"I like it, honey." She reached over and touched the

back of his hand. "I just don't want to get it dirty while I work. I'll put it on later, okay? After I get home."

She unfolded the pamphlet and spread it on the counter. "John, over by the window, gave me this. He said for you to come talk to him at the recruitment center."

Inside there were more pictures of soldiers, men and women, a guy walking through a crowd of dancing kids.

"Have you thought about what you'll do after graduation?" she asked.

"I'm working with Loyal."

"Loyal? That's not a career. You should join the Army and learn a real trade."

"And get blown up."

"Shhh, Toby." She glanced toward the window. "You could have a life, get out of Blind River for a few years, come back, and build your own family."

"I don't want a family." How could she say this to him? She wanted him to leave? All those years spent waiting for her to come home. All those years wondering what she could possibly have done that they'd taken her from him, her child, and locked her away. He'd cried so hard that first year, believing that she'd be home soon, not understanding, not accepting, just waiting and waiting for her to come back before finally getting it, getting that she wasn't ever coming home. And when he grew tired of crying he'd started hitting things, then people. Hitting Jamie, hitting kids at school, hitting anything he wanted whether it meant a broken knuckle or not. Hitting was better than crying. He knew that much. But he wouldn't hit his mother even though right now it seemed like she deserved it. Instead, he picked up the brochure, ripped it in half, and walked out the door.

He walked down Main cussing and rubbing the corners of his eyes, his nose that had started to drip. Snow crunched beneath his boots. He cut across the soccer field with its frozen brown grass, bent and dead from the winter. She'd been gone most of his life and he'd been fine without her. Bitch. Most mothers took care of their kids; most mothers didn't steal shit and go to prison. He pushed open the school door and instantly wondered why he'd come. But he knew why. Inside these walls were people and what he needed right now was someone to hit. He stopped and turned to leave, but the second-period bell sounded and the halls filled with kids, so he put his head down and pulled his collar up around his chin and tried to cruise past the front office. Ms. Hollins and Coach Palmer stepped out of their weekly staff meeting just as he, fists clenched in his pockets, rounded the corner.

"Hold up there, Elders," Palmer said, and put his hand on Toby's shoulder. "School started an hour ago."

Toby flinched and pushed the man's hand away. "Keep your hands off, faggot."

"Whoa. In my office now, Toby," Ms. Hollins said, pointing in Toby's face. "You need to cool down."

"No!" Toby yelled. He didn't want to be here. Not for one minute. He hated this place, hated these people. He turned to back toward the doors, but Coach grabbed his arm. Toby wheeled on him, came around swinging his fist at no one, at anyone, at everyone, at nothing and everything, at the first thing stupid enough to stand still and let him connect.

CHAPTER

15

WHEN SHE FINALLY opened her eyes, Jamie could tell it was way past noon. Slatted light cut through the plastic blinds, casting broken shadows on the wall. She sat up, groggy from the boozy sleep, and opened the blinds. Out back, sunlight glinted off the snow all the way to the ridge. Above that, the sky was a blinding bluish-white.

Her fingernails were cracked and split and caked with dirt and she remembered everything that had happened the night before. That man, his big head and lifeless eyes. The big bloody hole in his stomach.

God. She'd helped dispose of a dead man. That made her a felon. Except she was just an accomplice and she'd sort of been forced into it. But she wasn't a minor anymore.

Even with her eyes open she saw the image of his slack face, the distorted angle of his neck. She'd stared too long before Loyal scrambled down the embankment and thrown the tarp over him. She hated horror films and zombie faces.

That shit was fucked. The only people who could laugh at it were people who'd never seen a corpse. She started counting backward from ten before that image had a chance to set in and went to the bathroom to look for peroxide and ointment.

A man that age. He probably had kids, a wife. She chewed a thumbnail off and spit it out. How many rocks had she dug up and carried to cover him? Maybe a thousand.

This is how it starts. A life of crime. Except that it had started months ago. Making cash runs for Loyal. Small-time stuff, things that a public defender could get dismissed as a first offense. She weighed her age against her uncle's and the judge's and figured a court would take that into consideration. But that was stupid. Keating was a judge. Nothing weighed against that.

The trailer was quiet and she knew Toby and Loyal were gone. She turned the TV on and ran the faucet in the kitchen hoping for hot water. The keys to the old truck and a ledger were on the table along with a note saying that Loyal had hosed off the flatbed. *Good.* She studied the list: addresses and four-digit codes that would give her access to the machines in eight locations on the west side of town, ten up north, and thirteen on the east side. Almost the whole operation, but she had days to get to it all. She could do this. If it moved her closer to getting out of here, she could get it done. She thought through a few calculations, figured that between the extra work and the tournament she'd break even by summer. Steam billowed over the sink; Loyal had finally fixed the hot-water heater.

On the television, the weather man pointed at a map and predicted another cold front of freezing temperatures and snow.

She stepped into the hot shower, let the water beat down on her. She scrubbed her nails, peeled off a couple of broken ones, scrubbed them again, thought about that man, tried to remember what the Bible said about the sins of the fathers being visited on the children. She couldn't recall it exactly, but the notion was like this mess with Loyal and Keating. Their rivalries and alliances went back decades, without any logic that she could decipher. Small-town bullshit. She'd been born into it and knew exactly how her life would play out if she stayed. Two or three kids, a divorce or two. A dead-end job that would keep her half-starved if she didn't eat junk food and get fat, get diabetes and lose her feet, or die of a heart attack. She saw it all around her, doughnuts and caffeine for the early-morning despair, booze after work just to take the edge off a twelve-hour grind. She thought about her mother standing behind the curtain in the window at Keating's house. The woman had never had a chance in this town. No Elders did, not really.

If there was a window to escape, it was closing fast. Right here at the underside of twenty, there was an opening, maybe a month, and it might be the only time she'd be able to leave, find her way to some city where there were real jobs, where winters weren't so fucking cold, where no one would ask her to help move a dead body in the middle of the night. Somewhere she'd have half a shot, before she got in too deep and this town pulled her under. Like it was doing right now.

The shower turned lukewarm and she turned it off and wrapped herself in a towel.

Outside, a car's wheels crunched over the gravel in the driveway, its engine idling. Someone was probably looking for her uncle and she hoped whoever it was would see the Dodge wasn't here and move on, but the engine went quiet and seconds later someone was banging on the front door. She grabbed her robe and peeked around the corner through the small window on the door and came face-to-face with Keating, peering through the glass.

"Loyal home?" he yelled through the door. His gray hair was smooth and slicked back. "Saw his truck." Keating thumbed over his shoulder at the Ford sitting on the street.

"He doesn't drive that anymore. Bought a new one." Jamie thought for a minute that was all the information the man would need to leave, but the knob turned and the door opened and she cussed Toby because he could never be trusted to lock a door. Keating pushed through and she stepped sideways, knocking into the table by the couch.

"We need to talk," he said.

"Like I said, he's not here." She knotted the sash around her waist and tugged the towel tighter around her neck.

"He should've left me a package. Do you have it?" He cut his eyes around the room, at the broom leaning against the kitchen table, the dishes stacked in the sink, the muddied floor, and openly cringed. Then he asked, "Where'd you take him?"

"Take who?" She ignored the question about the package, knowing he'd let it drop rather than bring up Loyal's business.

He stared at her flatly. "Don't play stupid with me. That man. Where'd you take him?"

She shook her head. "I don't know. Loyal made me ride on the floorboard." Besides, she was supposed to play dumb about last night.

Keating picked up a piece of mail off the kitchen table, read the address, and tossed it back. "So you really don't know?"

She thought he said this with some relief, so she added, "I only helped pull him off the truck. I don't even know who it was." It came out so calmly that it sounded absurd. Her feet—she hadn't had time to towel them off—were freezing.

"Do you understand how important it is to keep quiet?"

"Seems obvious."

"Don't get smart." Keating pulled a kitchen chair away from the table and wiped the seat with the palm of his hand. Up close and in the bland light he seemed older than her uncle. His hair was whiter and there was something stiff and wary about the way he moved his body, as though he thought the trailer might collapse on him.

She didn't sit, hoping he wouldn't either. But he did.

"That woman," he said, leaning forward on his elbows.

"Your mother, I mean, was invited into my home. My home. A judge's home."

Jamie tried to follow, but last night's whiskey was making it hard to keep up.

He snapped his fingers. "Are you listening, young lady?"

She moved her eyes to meet his, felt her shoulders hunch up around her neck. It was starting to sink in. They would be linked forever by this, she and this man.

"I knew her history. I knew she was an ex-con. But I looked beyond that and extended hospitality. What happened was an accident, but if word gets out, the authorities won't be kind. Her parole will be revoked and that's just the beginning. I'm willing to go along with this for her sake, for the sake of her children. But if anything comes to light . . ." He lifted his palms. "A woman like that? Well, a lot of assumptions will be made. It could be bad for everyone involved. For her family, her kids."

She slapped at the water dripping down the backs of her legs because it made her think of spiders and, right now, she needed to concentrate.

"There's no weapon. I assure you that's been taken care of. It was the least I could do."

Weapon? She hadn't thought of a weapon. But what did she think? That someone could rip a hole in a man with their bare hands?

"Could be seen as a crime of passion, I suppose, but who knows, really, why some people turn out the way they do." He looked her up and down. She hated that. He was big enough to take her if he wanted. She backed closer to the hall and pulled the towel tighter around her neck. He'd been with Phoebe in a way that made Jamie ill to think about, but she doubted that screwing a lover's daughter would matter to a man like him.

"I don't know what happened before I got there," she said, to remind him what he'd come here for. "I just did what my uncle told me to."

He stopped staring at her legs and bobbed his head almost imperceptibly. "But she had the gall to steal something from me. I want what's mine. Get it back. And tell her to keep quiet. If she's quiet long enough, this thing will blow over."

"What did she take?"

He sighed impatiently. "Do I have to explain everything? No. No, I don't. This is all her fault. She'll know exactly what I'm talking about. Get it from her and bring it to me."

"But, I don't—I mean, I never see her."

He slammed his fist on the table and Jamie jumped. "Go, damn it. Go see her!"

He took out a silver money clip from his pocket and peeled off some twenties. "This is for you. Girls like you always need a little extra money."

She just stared at the money he set on the table. What good would a hundred bucks do her if she had to deal with this lunatic?

He stood up. "There's more if you keep your mouth shut. And believe me, darling, you want to keep your mouth shut. You don't want anyone knowing you were an accomplice to—to anything."

He started to say more but just shook his head and

waved his hand in her face. He walked out the front door and Jamie locked it behind him. Water dripped from her hair as the wheels crunched on the driveway and the noise of the Cadillac's engine faded down the street.

Accomplice.

There it was, hanging over her head.

Darling.

Like he had the right to call her that.

16

O NE WORD SWIRLED through Jamie's brain. *Accomplice.* As she drove to the first stop on the route, the word kept repeating itself, like a living, breathing thing spinning inside her head. *Accomplice.* She turned up the country station, wishing for the first time in her life that she smoked. Surely smoking helped stop obsessive brain chatter.

Crowley's Pub was Loyal's most lucrative spot. She parked the truck out front, let the pub door close behind her, and waited for her eyes to adjust to the dark.

The air inside was dank. The floor and baseboards were caked with grime as thick as chewing gum. Garbage cans overflowed with plastic plates and cups. The place smelled of humanity, stale smoke, vats of cold grease, old beer, and beneath that, cheap perfume, aftershave, and backed-up toilets. The dance floor was mirrored and jammed tight with human-size speakers and a low-hanging disco ball.

Crowley's Pub was just as much a part of the bedrock of
Blind River as the Methodist church, but far more profit-
able and always more crowded.

The back door had been propped open, so she stepped
around a few high-top tables and walked toward it. Out
back, a guy in a torn black T-shirt with a cigarette clamped
between his lips was hosing down kitchen mats. He glanced
up when she said hey and apparently found her uninter-
esting or at least unthreatening.

"Not open till five," he said.

"Here to check the machines," she said, dangling the
keys where he could see them.

"You work for Loyal?" He looked more closely at her
face. "Oh, yeah. I seen you before. You got keys for them,
fine." He went back to dousing the mats.

Jamie and Toby had waited in this bar's parking lot
twice a week for the last eight years while Loyal went inside
and collected money from the machines. Two legal pinball games sat near the entrance, but the coin pusher and
the slot machine were tucked in a corner in the back where
gamblers would sniff them out.

She wrestled the coin pusher away from the wall and
squeezed in behind it, wishing she'd brought a flashlight.
The lock was at chest level and impossible to see in the
dark. She felt her way along and it felt like magic when
the key fitted in the hole and clicked open. She bagged
what she guessed was twenty pounds of quarters and put
them in her backpack. The teaser bills had moved too
close to the front, so she repositioned those at the back of
the machine and wondered just how many drunks had

contributed to the proceeds. She locked up the unit and shoved it back against the wall, swearing because the thing weighed twice as much as she did. The glass and chrome were filthy from spilled drinks and fingerprints, so she wiped them until they shined. Shiny things attracted more money and, come five o'clock tonight, the machine would begin filling up again.

Five years ago, Loyal had had the bright idea to slap nonprofit labels on the units, some with children in wheelchairs, some with underfed kittens in cages, or busted-up veterans holding American flags. People believing they were contributing to a worthy cause usually saw nothing wrong with the possibility of scoring a little cash in the process. Cops saw the images and decided to look away at what might not be legal but would definitely involve a load of paperwork.

The slot machine was in a corner between a cigarette machine and the wall and impossible to move. She squatted down to reach the knee-high lockbox mounted underneath and cringed when she had to touch the floor with her hands. From now on she'd carry sanitary wipes in her backpack. The lock cooperated on the first try. She slid the tray out and set it on the floor.

The front door opened and Jamie looked around the legs of a pinball machine to see a narrow figure standing in a rectangle of light like a Hollywood alien exiting a spaceship. Her first instinct was to hide the cash but the silhouette was as slight as a girl, so Jamie relaxed.

"Anyone here?" It was definitely a girl's voice.

Jamie started to say something but didn't want to

explain why she was sitting on the floor under a slot machine, so she stayed put and hoped the guy out back would handle it. He did, slipping inside the back door and explaining they didn't open till five.

"Um, okay, but I'm from out of town and I'm meeting my dad here. TJ Bangor? Have you seen him?"

"The tight end? That's your dad?"

The name sounded familiar. Jamie remembered it from Toby and Loyal's mutual NFL obsession. Watching football together was about the only thing the two did without fighting.

"He's retired, but yeah, he's my dad."

"No. I'd remember if I'd seen him."

"Can I wait in here? He's not answering his cell." She waved her cell phone as if to prove her point.

He glanced at his watch and said, "The boss doesn't let anyone hang out till we open. There's a diner on Main."

From the dark corner Jamie saw the girl shaking her head.

"Jeez. Is it okay if I wait in the parking lot?"

"If you want."

The girl left and the guy closed the front door. Jamie heard the deadbolt slide into place, heard the guy's rubber boots coming toward her, squishing on the grimy floor. He slapped the slot machine as he walked past her. "Leave out the back door, will ya? I've got to keep it locked up front."

Jamie bagged the cash from the machine, a wad of bills as thick as her wrist. She'd have to be more careful with people walking in. One meth-head wandering in could cost her plenty. She zipped up her backpack, got up, and wiped her hands on her jeans.

When she got outside to the truck, Jamie heaved her backpack into the passenger seat. The girl sat in a little black Mercedes two spots away, talking on her phone. Flashy sunglasses covered half her face, but Jamie could tell from the highlights in her short-cropped hair and her plump lips that she was pretty. She backed the truck out and rolled slowly forward, wondering what it felt like to grow up with a guy like that as a dad. NFL money, rich little girl. Big money. A big man gone missing. A big man in that tarp. People starting to look around and ask questions. Things were adding up in a way that made her want to run. She rolled passed that little black Mercedes and gunned it onto the highway.

*   *   *

By six o'clock Jamie had collected the cash out of seven of the eight gaming units on the north route. There'd been a slot machine snugged in beside an ice machine in the back of a liquor store and another one next to a money changer in a convenience store. Most of them were pretty well hidden, but Grizzly's Beer Hub out on the highway had a draw poker unit sitting right on top of the bar that had taken in over three thousand in twenties alone. Driving back to town, she estimated there was enough cash in her backpack for a decent start on the professional poker circuit and wondered what the going rate was for helping to dispose of a body and if she couldn't leverage that somehow. It was fun to think about that for all of two seconds, but her cheek was still tender from the back of Loyal's hand. At least he hadn't broken her nose.

Her last stop was Mr. Lu's dry-cleaning. Loyal paid a ten percent rake to Mr. Lu, so he often disappeared to the back when a customer came in for their clothes. Eventually the customer would get bored and wander over to the coin pusher, eye its piles of coins and the perpetual twenty-dollar bill jutting out toward the front, and play however many quarters were in their pocket. Mr. Lu would listen from the back of the store and wait for the silence that indicated the customer had run out of coins, then appear with their order.

Jamie unlocked the back of the collection box as Mr. Lu came to the front.

"Hello" she said. "I'm Loyal's niece." She turned toward him and raised her hands so he could see them.

"I know who you are," he said.

Of course he did. She was the Elders girl. The whole town knew her, had known her for years. When they'd been little she and Toby would wait in the truck drinking Cherry Cokes while Loyal went inside and took care of business. When they got older they would sometimes carry the toolbox he kept for repairs and beg snacks from the proprietors. Sometimes Loyal would try to show Toby how to change out a fuse or a lightbulb, but it was Jamie who paid attention.

"Oh, okay," she said, feeling stupid. "I work for him."

"If you got a key, it's okay."

"I got them." She unlocked the box in the back and poured the quarters into a plastic grocery bag.

She repositioned the twenty behind the pile of quarters and locked up the machine.

"See you next time," she said, but Mr. Lu had already gone to the back.

She parked on Main, locked the truck, and walked half a block to the diner. Sunlight bent at the horizon and threw such light against the brick and clapboard buildings that Jamie had to stop for a moment and stare at her hometown. Moments like that made her wonder if she'd miss the place if she ever got out. But she figured sunsets were pretty everywhere and waited for the moment to pass. The smell of supper was in the air and the street in front of the diner was lined with cars and pickups. Including a small brown sedan parked right up front that she was sure she'd seen before.

Inside, Phoebe was behind the counter serving plates of meatloaf and country-fried steak to the regular dinner crowd. Jamie started toward the counter but halted when her mother looked up and widened her eyes. Jamie scanned the room and saw him right off. Brown suit, polished shoes, loose tie. Everything about him said cop. And now that she thought about it, she connected that car to the cop. When he turned to see what Phoebe was looking at, Jamie suspected this was the man she'd seen outside the trailer the other night. He sat at the counter and the only open stool was the one to his right.

She backed up toward the door but the cop called over. "Hey," he said motioning to the stool beside him. "There's a seat right here."

Jamie set her backpack on the floor beside the stool

and sat down, knowing that any other move would have made her stand out.

Phoebe brought Jamie a Coke. "I got a spare BLT with your name on it."

The guy said, "I was just reminiscing with your mom about the other night. She tell you about it?"

"Do I know you?" Jamie asked.

"You're Loyal's kid, right?"

"He's my uncle."

Phoebe said, "She's my kid," and got busy ringing up checks at the cash register.

"Right," he said. "I knew that. I'm Garcia. Detective Garcia."

Jamie unwrapped a straw, noted the fake friendliness. All the locals knew the Elders had a history with the law.

"She tell you about the game the other night?"

It was just like a cop to poke around with questions and she didn't like it, didn't like that she'd been the one to cause her mother to end up at Keating's. Jamie worried what the game might have to do with that man's body. A weird paralysis chilled her spine between her shoulder blades as Garcia rattled on.

"The game at Keating's. You know TJ Bangor was there? You know who he is, right?" He didn't wait for an answer. "Biggest hand of the night, Bangor uses his Super Bowl ring to cover a bet. Loses to Keating big-time. A full house over an ace-high straight. You should have seen it."

"Huh," Jamie said. "Who's TJ Banker?" She'd tried all afternoon to put this thing out of her mind. She sipped the Coke, watched her mother. Phoebe was at the other end of the counter but obviously listening to everything Garcia said.

"Who is he? One of the greatest tight ends in NFL history."

Phoebe worked her way down the counter refilling coffee cups. When she got near them, Garcia said loudly, "Thing is, he wants it back. Asked me to help him."

"Sounds like you need to talk with Judge Keating about that," Jamie snapped. She felt a little odd speaking up for her mother and knew her tone was no way to shut down a cop.

Garcia gave her a glance that could have been a warning. "As a matter of fact, I saw the judge downtown this morning and did just that. Told me he never saw the thing after that night. Said it was a joke gone bad and he meant to give it back but when he looked for it he couldn't find it. He thinks the housecleaner might've thrown it out the next morning. Seems awful something so expensive would just disappear. Don't you think?"

The French fries smelled like old fish sticks and the Coke was flat. Jamie chewed a piece of bacon from her sandwich and felt her stomach tighten. There was no way to know if Garcia had really talked to Keating, but she couldn't see why he would've mentioned it to her when he showed up at the trailer. She wanted to check her mother's reaction but Garcia was watching them both too closely. She dipped a French fry in ketchup and fought the feeling that the entire dinner crowd was listening in.

"Rings are small. They go missing all the time." She forced herself to chew and swallow and watch as a red splotch appeared on her mother's neck.

"Not a ring like that. Big as a golf ball."

Her mouth had gone dry. "Did he check his garbage can?"

"Trucks ran this morning."

"Huh. There's your trouble." She sucked at her soda.

"Anyway," he said, pulling a twenty out of his wallet, "there's a reward for it if it turns up."

He watched Phoebe's face as he said it, but she just stared back and cocked her head toward the kitchen.

"Hey, Tommy, any big diamond rings in the lost-and-found box?"

The cook stuck his head through the pass-through. "Yeah. A whole box full. In fact, I'm heading to Miami on a private jet when I get done frying this chicken."

Garcia laughed, but it was fake. Phoebe wiped her hands on her apron and rang up his bill. Jamie watched her mother as she made change from the register, cool hands and calm fingers, the growing splotch on her neck the only sign of distress.

Phoebe set his change on the counter. "Maybe he shouldn't have bet it in the first place."

"No, he shouldn't have. But there's a big difference between losing and getting set up." Garcia took his time putting his money in his wallet, holding Phoebe's gaze the whole time.

After a moment, she said, "Drunks bet stupid and lose big."

"Yep. But he's a hero in these parts—or you been up the river so long you don't know that?"

It was a low blow, and Jamie cringed.

Phoebe didn't even blink, but she looked fragile, the bones of her knuckles going white as her fingers curled into fists. The flush on her neck crept up to her face. There was no way Garcia could miss it.

A hush went through the diner. It was her imagination, Jamie told herself, it was just her imagination, but it was the same horrible silence she'd experienced the first day of every school year when the other kids pointed at her and whispered to each other, "That's the girl whose mom's in prison."

There was a slow widening in her brain; she had let herself believe those moments were behind her, but now she saw that those days would never be completely gone. Not when a cop, one of the good guys, was throwing it in their faces again. It made her ill. She had to get out of there. The talk with her mother would have to wait. She picked up her backpack and wound her way through the tables and the staring faces, most of them too polite to make eye contact.

Outside, the cold air cut her lungs, but Jamie refused to let the nausea turn into the spins. She walked in the wrong direction, then remembered the truck. The sky was dark, the street dimly lit with yellow streetlights. She got into the truck as the diner's door slammed behind her. The bastard had followed her. He came to the window and made a little rolling motion with his hand. She lowered the window halfway.

"Lose your appetite?" Garcia shook out a cigarette.

"Seemed greasy."

He leaned his elbow on the door, looked around the cab, and asked, "You in school these days?" He flipped a lighter open and blew the smoke to the side.

"I'm taking a break."

"Must be bored, all that time on your hands. You spend a lot of time at Jack DelMar's store?"

Fuck you. She started the engine.

"I'm just saying. You're a little young to have to worry about your mother, your brother. Jeez, you're just a kid. Now you're running around for your uncle."

Phoebe appeared at the diner window and looked out at the street.

"I'm late," she said. The truck bounced when she put it in reverse, but Garcia reached inside the cab and blocked the steering wheel.

"Cop asks a question, you give him an answer. You working for Loyal?"

"Some," she said. "There's an event coming up."

He laughed. "Yeah, that so-called fund-raiser."

She said nothing.

He took his elbow off the door and took another drag from the cigarette. "You got that whole Elders thing going on, don't you? Fuck the law, live by your own rules. You might want to give that a second thought, consider a plan that doesn't include prison time."

The back of her head felt cold. For a moment it seemed he knew everything she'd done in the last twenty-four hours. He was so close that if she backed the truck up fast she could run over his foot. She gripped the wheel and pressed hard on the brake to stop herself from doing it.

"I think I made my point," he said, and tossed his cigarette on the ground. The smoke drifted and curled.

Jamie backed the truck up slowly and slipped it in drive. When she passed the diner window, she glanced up but her mother was gone.

CHAPTER

17

BEYOND THE TINY, wire mesh–covered window, the small square of sky was the color of steel. Toby balled up the thin mattress from the built-in concrete shelf and stood on it. Who the fuck puts a window seven feet off the ground? Daylight was fading, but if he pulled himself high enough he could almost make out the roof of a building he judged to be about a football field away. The mattress slid out from under him and when he landed, he smacked his elbow against the metal toilet. He held his arm and rocked back and forth, trying to breathe. Being locked up wasn't as scary as he'd thought it would be, but all the same, he fucking hated it here. All this steel and concrete. It wasn't natural. Tiny mesh windows bolted closed, big guards pushing him around, everything locked up tight, no Xbox. Somewhere down the long corridor he could hear a TV blasting a *Judge Judy* marathon, her voice a parrot screech in his brain.

There was nothing to hit but the walls, nothing to

kick or break. His legs ached to run, and now his elbow throbbed.

The biggest guard on the cell block walked past his door and glanced in. He carried the standard gear on his belt: a can of mace, a nightstick, and plastic restraints.

"Sir? Sir?" Toby had been in the center twenty-four hours and no one had spoken to him since they'd processed his fingerprints and locked him in this room.

The guard stopped and faced the cell door. "What?"

The sound of a human voice nearly brought him to tears. He stepped closer to the door and read the man's badge. "Brewster, huh? It's lonely in here, you know? You're the first one to talk to me."

"Must be the first time you said sir."

"What?"

"You want to address someone in here, you call them sir. Understand?"

"Yeah."

"Yes, sir," Brewster said and turned away.

"Wait!" Toby called. He refused to cry, but that only made his nose run. He swiped at it, hating the pleading tone in his voice and how it made him feel like a girl. "Sir!" Toby yelled. "You got any Red Man?" But the man kept walking.

Toby took a piece of toilet paper and folded it until it was a small tight square, stuck it between his cheek and teeth like he'd done when he was little and starving. He sucked at it, slumped on the mattress, and tried to think why his uncle hadn't shown up yet. Or Jamie. She was nineteen now. Didn't that mean she could bail him out?

An hour later the man returned.

"Sir," Toby said.

Brewster stopped and faced the boy's door again. "What?"

"Why am I here? I threw one punch. What's the big deal?"

"You punched the high school coach."

"He got a bloody nose is all," Toby said, moving closer to the door.

Brewster stepped in front of the opening, his height blocking the light. "You broke his nose."

Toby feigned a right hook. "I can't help he's a pansy, can't take a hit."

The man's face was flat, his hands big as paddles, an eagle in military green tattooed on his forearm.

Toby smelled the stink of a rotten tooth and backed away. "Hey, nice tattoo, man. Army?"

"Marine Corps. Retired."

Despite the bad breath he liked Brewster and wanted to keep him talking. "I'm joining soon as I graduate."

"Huh. Don't know they take punks."

"They'll take me. One of 'em will. Army, Navy. Hey, man, I came in with some Red Man. Can I get it?"

"Don't know if you noticed, but this is a jail. Ain't no room service in here."

"I want my stuff!" The cell was too small, the light too low. Someone turned up the volume on the *Judge Judy* marathon.

"Your *stuff* is at the front door. You get it on your way out."

Toby gripped the bars and shook them. Nothing moved, nothing even rattled.

Brewster didn't flinch. "Settle down. You're not going anywhere soon."

"Where's my uncle? I'm a juvenile!" He pushed away from the door. "You can't keep me here! I got rights! Where's my sister?" He was trembling with rage.

"See now, that's where you're wrong. You got nothing, boy. Assault with intent to harm? At your age, that don't get you sent to juvie. This here's downtown jail."

Toby picked up the mattress and threw it, kicked it, kicked it again, fell on it and tried to rip it in half.

"You best calm down, boy," Brewster said.

"Don't tell me to calm down!" Toby screamed. From somewhere deep in his belly a howl made its way through to his lungs and out his mouth. He beat his head with his fists.

The door clanged on its hinges and three officers rushed in. Brewster caught Toby's arm and bent it behind his back. Another man guarded the door. The third man picked up the mattress, folded it like a sheet, and walked out the door.

"You're going to have to earn that back," Brewster said.

Toby jerked to get loose but Brewster pulled his arm tighter. Pain shot through his shoulder, and Toby dropped to the floor. Brewster let go of his arm and pushed him to the far wall.

"Let me know if you can't get that back in its joint," he said, and slammed the steel door shut.

J AMIE PULLED THE truck to the curb outside Jack's store. He was inside, stooped over a computer, and scratching the scruff on his cheek. When they'd first hooked up she'd expected an older guy to be different from her high school boyfriends. She was wrong about that. Except for the slightly receding hairline and the crinkly lines around his eyes, he was like any other guy. It was almost cute how he was stuck in a time warp when it came to music, playing boxed collections of The Beatles and Pink Floyd. In the beginning, she'd believed his devotion to Bob Dylan meant a thoughtful, reflective mind. He was cool enough, though, the kind of guy who turned off the porn video when she walked into the room. And he always kept it wrapped, not like the jerks in high school that always had money for booze but not for condoms. She was grateful for that because right now a baby would ruin her plans quicker than an STD.

The store was empty and that was good. She felt the weight of her backpack and thought it through one last time. There was at least fifteen grand in there. She could take off right now, catch a train to Florida. There had to be at least five casinos down there that she was old enough to play in. She might hit it big. Or she could crash and burn like at Mimawa. And then what? She'd never be able to come back to Blind River and she'd always be looking over her shoulder because Loyal would certainly hunt her down.

And then there was that man's body. She was already too easy to frame and if she left now it would be easy to pin the whole thing on her. The timing couldn't be worse. Her cracked fingertips were beginning to throb from the cold. She was hungry and all she really wanted was to curl up under a blanket, but she stood on the sidewalk wondering if she'd ever have another chance like this one.

Then the door opened and Jack stepped outside. "There you are," he said. "You okay? You look funny." He pulled her inside the store and locked the door behind them.

She started to unload her backpack. "It's been a long day."

"Hang on. Let's do this in the back."

His office was small and cluttered with a metal desk left over from the fifties, four tall filing cabinets from the scratch-and-dent store, a low ceiling, a fluorescent light overhead, and that dumpy futon in the corner.

He spread the envelopes over the desk. "This it?"

"Just the eight stops on the west side."

"Okay." He emptied an envelope and started sorting the denominations.

"I marked where each envelope came from, but I didn't have time to count it all. That big one's from Crowley's Pub," she said, pointing.

Jack totaled the money in that envelope, thirty-five hundred and change, and tagged it with a Post-it note and rubber band. Seeing the cash piled up like that, Jamie judged the total to be way more than fifteen thousand. Closer to twenty.

"I saw my mom."

"Huh?" He put a rubber band around a stack of bills. "Why?"

The impulse to tell him everything was nearly overwhelming, but she couldn't answer truthfully. "I stopped in for a bite."

"Yeah, how was that?" She could tell he wasn't listening. He got a ledger from the back of a locked drawer and entered the totals.

"It was fine. That cop, Garcia, was there giving her a hard time about some bullshit at Keating's the other night." She didn't mention the girl she'd seen looking for her father or her suspicions that everything was connected in ways she couldn't see yet.

"The game you missed?" He opened another drawer and swore. "Fuck. Where's my damn calculator?"

"Yeah. Pissed me off."

He stopped for a moment and looked up. "Why would you get pissed about that? You say it all the time, you don't even know her."

"I don't know. I was supposed to deal that game. Now it sounds like things got a little crazy."

"Your mom can take care of herself, Jamie. You know, prison toughens a person."

"Or breaks them."

She'd been caught off guard by that cop sitting there quizzing them and then hassling her at the truck. And Phoebe had looked awful, the circles under her eyes dark and puffy, struggling to conceal her nerves. "You wouldn't understand."

"Well, no. I guess I wouldn't, would I?"

She couldn't tell if it was a put-down.

"Relax. Talk about something else." He locked the cash in a safe and walked out from around the desk and stood face-to-face with her. "Why does counting money make me horny?" He kissed her forehead, then her mouth.

" 'Cause you're cheap like that," she said.

It was a line from a porn video she'd caught him watching. The line was funny, the video pathetic, and she'd felt bad for the woman in it. She'd never make a sex tape, even though Jack nagged her about it all the time.

He wrapped his arms around her waist and she bent backward under his weight, his lips on her neck, the smell of his skin. It was enough to fill her mind with this, with him. They got to the futon in two awkward steps. He pulled her on top of him, yanking at the zipper on her jeans.

She pulled his shirt over his head. He ripped open a condom. This was the dance they'd perfected over the last month. In a minute they were naked and he was pushing in deep. A few more minutes and he was done.

Jamie wished it had gone longer but it rarely did. One time he'd stayed with her for nearly ten minutes and she'd seen lights exploding behind her eyes. She wanted that again, but he was catching his breath now and soon he'd get up. She kept him inside her for as long as she could, breathed in his scent, knowing that in a minute he'd be on the phone ordering pizza and the ordinary world would return.

"That was nice." His breath was slowing.

She knew he was thinking about food. "Yummy." He liked to hear that he was good.

"Pepperoni?"

"Sure." She found her sweater, wondered why she didn't feel any different than before, wondered if he felt anything at all.

He grabbed a blanket off the back of the futon, threw it over his body, and texted an order to the pizza joint down the street. "Ten minutes," he said, and pulled her back on top of him. "Time for another round."

"Stop bragging," she said, but relaxed on top of him and buried her nose under his chin. "I've been thinking about stuff."

"Not surprising." He ran his finger along her spine. "Bright girl like you. Probably always thinking and scheming."

"Loyal wants me to play in the fund-raiser."

"The vets' game?"

"Yeah."

"That's weird. They don't usually invite the ladies. You know those old guys, they don't like getting shown up by a babe."

"I thought Margaret Freeland played last year."

"Yeah, but she's a vet. Nurse in 'Nam, I think. Loyal still put a bounty on her. Everyone knew it but her. She was out in twenty minutes."

"Are you kidding? How do you know that?" Jamie sat up and double knotted her hair in a band.

"I'm the one who took her out. He gave me two hundred bucks right after she walked out the door."

She looked for her boots and found one under the futon.

"It's different this year. He wants us to make up for the cash we lost. Wants you to play, too. And that jerk, Tuckahoe. Phoebe's going to be one of the dealers."

"Us?"

"You know, Mimawa."

"You told him about that?"

"What else could I do? Lucky he didn't kill me," she said, remembering the way Loyal had handled that man's body. For a moment she thought about telling Jack, but she'd taken money from Keating to keep quiet and talking about it now would only make it more complicated.

"Is he pissed?"

"Not at you. He's pissed that I blew Keating's take. Now I got to work for him till I pay him back."

"Huh. So what does he want us to do at the tournament? Basic shit like rat-holing, chip dumping? We take it down and Keating is paid off?"

"Yep. Exactly."

He waved his head back and forth like he was

weighing his options. "That's cool, if it settles the score. And Keating gets to win in front of his constituents, which amounts to free publicity for his reelection. God- damn. Those two work every angle."

"Yeah, but I don't care," she said. "I need this to work. And I need to find a way to get ahead."

"Ahead? What are you going to do then, pretty girl? Leave Toby, leave Blind River?"

She noticed he didn't put himself on that list. "I want to try the circuit, make some serious money. After Toby turns eighteen and joins the Army."

Jack smirked. "You still think your little brother is Army material?"

"Yeah." She turned her sweater right side out. "I think he could be."

"You haven't heard, have you?"

"Heard what?" She pulled the sweater over her head.

"Toby's been in jail since this morning. He punched out the wrong guy."

19

T OBY YANKED HIS boot off and bashed the heel against the window latch. The latch broke off but the window frame was frozen with rust and it wouldn't budge. His lip throbbed, his head banged, his vision was blurred. Beating the shit out of him and locking him in the back room of the trailer only proved how fucked up his uncle was. No way Toby would stay here and wait for the bastard to come back for round two. He'd take this trailer apart before he'd stay locked up in here one more minute. He broke the window and knocked out the glass fragments until it was wide enough to climb through, then went around the outside of the trailer to the front door which, go figure, Loyal had left unlocked. Inside the bathroom he checked his lip in the mirror, soaked a towel, and wiped the dried blood, which only opened the cut and set it bleeding again. He jumped at the sound of a car's engine, relaxed when he realized it was just a neighbor passing by.

At first he'd been relieved when Loyal had shown up at the jail to post bail, couldn't wait to get away from that guard. But as soon as they got in the truck, he realized he'd been safer in that cell. Bail was a thousand bucks and Loyal had ranted on the ride home about how much money Toby had been costing him lately. Toby had promised to make it up if Loyal would give him a job, but Loyal had shouted no and started in on his flask. As soon as they got inside the trailer Loyal had taken off his belt. He was pretty sure the welt over his eye had come from the buckle, hated how he'd cried out when metal connected with bone. When Loyal got tired he'd stopped, grabbed his coat, and locked him up in the back room.

No doubt he was at Crowley's Pub right now getting tanked on whiskey and beer chasers and when he got home there'd be nothing holding him back. Toby splashed water on his face, the lump below his eye still swelling.

The beating wouldn't have been so bad if Jamie had been home. Loyal always pulled his punches in front of her. Goddamn her. She was probably with that pervert, Jack. Goddamn all of them. He held a towel to his lip and went to Loyal's room to rummage through the box under his bed where he kept his stash of nudie postcards from his buddy in Key West. There was almost always money in that box, and today he found a wallet with a few dollars and credit cards belonging to some schmuck named Theodore James Bangor. He stuffed the wallet in his pocket and grabbed his jacket and a box of Pop-Tarts, paused at the door and looked around for something more, but there wasn't anything more and he walked out the door.

He took the long walk that wound through the back valley and headed toward town. It had once been a cornfield, but land speculators, predicting a boom, had bought up all this acreage years ago. The boom fizzled the year after the fertilizer plant exploded and left a cloud of toxic smoke hanging over the town for a month. Now it was an empty field of brown weed not even fit for grazing. Standing water sloshed under his boots. He looked at the land his grandfather, Nate Elders, used to own. Twenty acres. Some of it turned into a trailer park, some of it set aside as a dump. If the old man hadn't sold out they'd still be farmers. Maybe they'd still have cows, maybe a tractor. Maybe a good life. Toby went up the rise on the other side of the valley and took the road to town.

He needed to find Jamie. She'd know what to do, maybe help him find somewhere to hide for a few days until Loyal cooled off. Maybe they'd go away together on the bus like they'd always wanted. They were older now and no one would care if they bolted. Kids did that all the time. No one would even look for them.

When he got to town, he took the alley that ran parallel to Main. He thought about stopping by the diner, but his mother was so weird now. He'd paid a hundred dollars for that stupid necklace and she'd hated it. Fucking waste of time. He saw the Ford sitting in front of Jack's store and knew Jamie was in there. She'd been different lately because of that guy. Like they were keeping a secret that wasn't really secret. It was gross. Technically, Jack could have been her father, he was that old.

The sign said they opened at ten and it was already

past noon. He tried the handle but it was locked. Toby peered around the ten thousand stupid posters taped over the windows. The office door in the back was cracked open and he banged on the door.

Finally Jack stuck his head out of the office and yelled for Toby to knock it off, then called something to the back and came to let him in.

Jamie came out front, tying her hair up in a ponytail. She stopped short when she saw him. "What the hell happened to your face?"

"What the hell are you doing here? With him?"

Jamie made her what-the-fuck face that always pissed him off. "I don't answer to you, Toby. Why did you hit the coach?"

He jammed his fists into his pockets, wanted to hit something now, but his knuckles were sore and his lip throbbed. The whole side of his head ached.

Jack said, "I'll get some ice," and went back inside the office.

When he was gone, Toby said, "Jesus, Jamie, why are you hanging out with a perv?"

"Take it easy. I like him."

"Does Loyal know?"

"What does it matter what Loyal knows? I don't need his permission. Did he do this to you?"

"Yeah, he hit me. Locked me in the back room and left me there. He's pissed that I got arrested, pissed that bail was a thousand bucks. Says I owe him." He slammed his back against the wall and crashed to the floor, yanked at his hair. He was so enraged, but there was nothing to do about it. Everything hurt, so he cried.

Jamie crouched in front of him. "What happened?"

"I don't know. I was at school. He touched me, the faggot, so I punched him. As hard as I could. He went down; I think he cracked his head when he hit the floor. They said I broke his nose."

"What do you mean he touched you? Where did he touch you?"

"Not like that, stupid. He grabbed my shoulder, told me to calm down. You know I hate that shit."

Jack returned with ice folded up in a rag and handed it to Toby. "The coach is in the hospital with a fractured nose and cheekbone."

Toby took the rag and touched it to his forehead. "How do you know that?"

"I got takeout from the diner this morning. Some kids from the team were looking for you. They're pissed because the principal canceled tonight's game. You better stay low a few days. Let this thing blow over."

"What kids?"

"That tall kid who plays guard and the short one with the big head."

"Fuck." Toby stared at his hands. "They're worse than Loyal."

Jamie sat next to him. "You got to fix this, all right? Apologize to the coach. Go to that mentoring program. You got to graduate."

Toby saw Jamie's keys sitting near the cash register

and thought about the highway. He'd rather drive head-on into a pylon or off a bridge than endure another minute of this bullshit town.

Jack bent down behind the counter looking for something. "Right. How can he fix it? He assaulted a man who ended up in the hospital. Apologies don't make that right."

Toby jumped to his feet. "Shut up! You don't get a say in this. You're just some creep messing with my sister!"

Jack held his hands up. "Take it easy, man. I'm just saying what's true."

Toby knocked Jamie on her ass and grabbed her keys.

She hit the linoleum floor but scrambled after him. "Toby, stop. Give those back."

"So what if I don't graduate?" He pushed her back down before she could get her balance. "I hate this fucking place."

He ran to the truck and pulled out before Jamie could stop him. As he drove off, she stood in the middle of the road screaming his name until he turned off Main and she disappeared from his rearview mirror.

CHAPTER

20

B Y THE TIME Jamie got to her feet, there was nothing she could do except watch the taillights of the truck disappear as it rounded the corner. Jack had just stood there behind the counter, hadn't even followed them outside. When she went back in the store he was closing his cell phone.

"Shit, Jack. Who did you call?"

"Loyal."

"You shouldn't have done that. Why didn't you ask me first?"

"Thought he should know. It's his truck." He pocketed the phone. "Doesn't matter; he didn't answer anyway."

"You leave him a message?"

"Told him to call me. Don't worry. Toby just needs to cool off. How far can he go anyway?"

"I don't know. The tank's a quarter full."

Jack was right though. There wasn't really anywhere

for him to go. No aunts, uncles, no cousins. The farthest from Blind River she'd ever been was the casino, but Toby had never been farther than that one failed bus ride. He loved water, though, and had always wanted to see the beach. "He might go east, toward the ocean."

"We'll have to wait then. See if he calls," Jack said.

"He doesn't have a cell phone."

"Well, what then?" He lifted his hands. "You want me to call the cops?"

"No. They'd just throw him back in jail for auto theft, and Loyal is so pissed off right now he might press charges." There wasn't much she could do except let him cool off and decide to come back on his own.

"Exactly. Look, that boy's a mess. He's always been a mess. And the rest of us have work to do." He put his glasses on and opened a ledger.

He could be such a tool. She was back to footing it around town and there were only five stops left to complete the collections on the route, but they were scattered around the edge of the county. Jack's Toyota sat out behind the back door. "If you're going to work for a few hours, can I use your car?"

He looked up, confused.

"Your car?" she said. "The one out back just sitting there?"

"I guess," he said. "But be quick about it. I've got to be home in time for dinner."

She couldn't ignore the edge in his voice and the snarky reminder of his wife. "Never mind," she said, and grabbed her backpack.

It was drizzling outside. For the first time she wondered what she was doing with Jack, if she wasn't making just another stupid mistake. The secrecy had made it thrilling at first but it wasn't a secret anymore, and it was way past thrilling.

A car rolled up behind her, and she glanced over her shoulder. Jack rolled down the window and put his head out. "Get in, Jamie."

She kept walking.

"Come on, Jamie. Stop acting like a kid and get in."

He was a dick but she needed wheels. She got in the car. They drove silently back to the store. He left the car running and got out. "Go drive the route. I have to be here till five anyway."

She waited until he closed the door before climbing to the driver's side.

She drove along the river with the windows cracked, the heater warming her feet. The air smelled clean outside of town, and she caught glimpses of the narrow river beyond stands of old pines lining the road. She loved the cold air, the sharp scent of pine, but more than anything she loved the sound of the wheels on the pavement and the odd and unexpected comfort of solitude.

Her first stop was a convenience store with a small arcade in the back near the coolers. A bony-faced boy in red overalls played a pinball machine in the corner, too absorbed to look up. She collected the money from a coin pusher and another pinball machine. She had to wait for him to stop playing before she could get to the last cashbox.

She stared at him for a solid minute before he let the ball drop and looked up. "I'm a pinball wizard. Who are you?" he asked.

"Jamie. My uncle owns that machine and I need to get inside it."

"Huh," he said, and went to the register at the front of the store.

She opened the unit, collected the quarters, and locked it up. The boy stared out the large window overlooking the parking lot. She paused at the front door, and when he didn't look up she asked if he worked there.

"I watch things for my mom. She's in the back doing inventory," he said, unwrapping a candy bar.

When she got back to the car, she wrote the store's street number on the envelope and stashed it under the front seat where she found an old copy of *Poker Max* magazine that she guessed Jack had borrowed. She paged through it briefly. Out there in the big wide world there were dozens of tournaments, people winning buckets of money, trophies, even cars. She stuffed the magazine into her backpack and drove on.

When she got to her last stop, the clerk was watching TV and two security camera screens. He absent-mindedly chewed a thumbnail.

"I'm checking the equipment in the back," she said, and dangled the keys where he could see them.

"Huh-uh. No." He pried his eyes off the screen. "You can't do that."

She dangled the key ring in the air, surprised that someone finally questioned her. "No, it's okay. I got the keys."

He shook his head. "Doesn't matter. That money goes missing and they'll take it out of my check."

"Call your boss, tell him Loyal's niece is here to service the machines."

The hot bar smelled of overcooked burritos. While she waited, she took one from the rack and browsed the magazine racks. She spit out the burrito. "You can't sell this shit. It's three days old."

He picked up the wall phone, held the receiver to his chest, and dialed. "Hey," he said. "You eat it, you pay for it."

Through the front windows she saw another car pull in the parking lot and realized she'd already seen it twice this morning. *Goddamnit.* The front door opened and he walked in, his collar turned up and hat pulled down over his brow. She threw the burrito in the garbage and circled around to the back of the store, then up the cold aisle back to the front. She threw a ten on the counter on her way out the door. "I'll come back later."

The clerk hung up the phone. "The owner said you're okay."

She was halfway out the door when she heard Garcia say, "Don't you want your change?" He stood near the cash register and pointed to the TV. "You seen the news this morning?"

A girl's face filled the screen. The pretty lips, the hair, and the highlights were unmistakable: the girl from Crowley's Pub. The volume was off but the closed caption said she was in town looking for her father, TJ Bangor. The screen changed to a photograph of a man with a big square head, marble-size teeth, and a grin that seemed a lot like the dead man's grimace. Garcia stared at Jamie as her stomach turned liquid. Her hands started to shake.

That little bit of burrito she'd swallowed threatened to come up fast. "I don't watch the news," she said, and pushed through the door.

21

GARCIA FOLLOWED THE girl to the parking lot, watched as she pretended to ignore him and get into her car. Jamie Elders. Nineteen and going nowhere fast. There was nothing for a kid like her in Blind River and he guessed she probably knew it. A semi bore down the highway, its draft bending the grass in the field across the highway where a small black mare grazed behind a barbed-wire fence. Her tail and flanks twitched at the blast of air as the semi passed.

Jamie started the engine as he approached. He tapped on the window. "Let's talk."

She opened the window an inch and turned the radio down. "What's left for us to talk about?"

"Plenty. Step out of the car."

"Why?" She raised her chin in that typical insolent teenager way he hated.

"First thing you need to understand, when a cop asks you to get out of your vehicle, you do it."

She turned off the engine and got out.

Another semi blasted up the highway and the mare pawed at the ground with her front legs. It was clear she wanted to run, but a lead tethered her to a fence post. It was distracting and bothered him. Who tethered a horse so close to the highway?

"Look," he said, taking a notebook out of his jacket pocket, "I've known about your uncle for years. He's got an operation, right?" He put his hand up and said, "Wait. Don't answer that. Everybody downtown knows about it." It was a guess but he would have put money on it. "He's connected. Tight with the judge. Everybody looks the other way." He opened the notebook, pretended to check his notes, wrote down the date for lack of anything better. He was sure she'd heard something from her mother or uncle that would help him find Bangor. He rubbed the spot between his eyebrows like he was frustrated and said, "Thing like that can change any minute. And changes? Well, you know how it is. Sometimes changes bring trouble."

Her eyes danced sideways. He couldn't tell if she followed his meaning. A girl like her could be thinking about anything—a boy, her next meal—and was unlikely to give up much on purpose.

"So, I'm wondering," he continued, "maybe you could help me out."

The wind pushed her hair across her forehead, and she pulled it behind her ear. "I'm just running errands. Doubt I can help much."

Her tone revealed nothing, but she hunched up her

shoulders and it dawned on him that she might be scared of her uncle. Maybe that was the crack he needed. A gentle tone might convince her to follow his lead.

"I know what you're doing. I've been watching you all morning. I know these aren't your gambling units and you're not the one running things. Hell, by the looks of things, you're probably not even getting paid."

Her silence made him think he was on to something, but then she stepped away to wipe a smudge off the car window and the gesture caught him off guard. His ex-wife had hated smudges, was always wiping his fingerprints off windows, the fridge, the toaster oven. He took a deep breath and focused, made a mental note to run the plates on the car she was driving. He'd seen it around town.

"Look, that guy on the news?" He pointed back at the store. "He seems to be missing and that's not good news for anybody in Blind River."

"Big guy like that can probably take care of himself. Maybe he's just having some fun on the down-low."

"On the down-low?" He tried to laugh but knew it sounded fake. Sometimes he was shocked by what kids knew these days, so he kept talking. "What do you know about all that?"

She shrugged. "Gay Awareness Day in high school, sir."

"Uh-huh. Sounds like you got an answer for everything." Now she was being a smartass and that meant she'd seen through the good-guy shtick. He'd never been good at getting through to girls her age. It was time to switch it up. He looked up at the sky and snapped his notebook shut. "The thing is, his family says he's never disappeared before. It's not like him and they're worried. We found his car but no one has heard from him."

"Like I said, I wasn't there that night. I never even met the guy."

"But you know a few of the people who were there. You might've heard something that seems unimportant to you but might be a lead for me."

"That's not exactly my crowd, you know? So nope, no one said a thing to me."

A police cruiser came over the top of the hill and the little mare danced until her butt was aimed at the highway. "You probably know more than you think."

She just stared at him.

"All right. Play it your way, but just so you know, I am going to have to start paying more attention to details." He handed her a business card. "You think of anything, call me."

The cop inside the cruiser squeaked his siren as a greeting. The mare jumped and threw her head back so that her lead rope was pulled too tight over her shoulder and she couldn't move her head.

Jamie turned to face the wind, her hair flipping in her eyes. She pointed at the mare. "What's wrong with that horse? Why doesn't it just back up?"

The sudden curiosity made her seem so naïve. "Horses can't naturally walk backward. They don't know how until they're taught."

"So she'll stay stuck?"

"Yep. Lots of that going around these days." He turned toward his car. "Horses are pretty but they're a pain in the ass. I almost bought one once and I'm glad I didn't."

"Why didn't you?" she asked.

The truth was he had arranged to buy a horse as an anniversary present for his wife, but that wasn't this kid's business. He'd hoped a gift like that would prove something to his wife, but she'd left him that same day and he'd never even told her about the horse. All those days and weekends she'd claimed to be working at her friend's barn, teaching riding lessons, had been spent falling in love with another man.

"Why didn't you buy the horse?" the girl asked again.

She was such a kid, suddenly nosy, convinced she was immune to the world's trouble. He shook his head. She was just a girl looking at a horse, a kid who deserved better than what she was getting but living in a world that offered her few choices. He was losing his edge again. This girl and that little mare were bringing up things he'd worked hard to forget.

Then she looked him in the eye with such intensity that he couldn't read her and he realized she was reading him. She'd sensed an old wound and wanted to poke at it.

"Huh." He laughed at himself and walked to his car. "I guess I wised up in the nick of time."

CHAPTER

22

PHOEBE WIPED HER hands on her apron and opened the door to the pawnshop. Mack was near the back of the store polishing a large glass display case. The big Doberman got up from her rug by the cash register to sniff Phoebe's pockets for the strips of bacon she had come to expect in the middle of each afternoon.

The lunch shift had been a killer. An unexpected church group had taken up three tables and driven her crazy with coffee refills. The cop had sat at the counter pestering her with personal questions, stressing her out even more than the church ladies. He was starting to piss her off, acting like he knew something when there was no way he could know anything. Feeding Mack's dog and browsing the familiar aisles had become a soothing part of the afternoon lull, but the dog was putting on weight and growing lazy and she worried Mack would blame her for that. She let the dog eat from her hands, feeling the softness of its muzzle, then watched as it flopped back onto the rug.

Mack scowled at a scratch on the glass case. He seemed prissy to her. The way he fussed over things, straightening a tray of watches, polishing a silver service, sweeping the front sidewalk every morning. Keeping everything in its place. It wasn't manly to love all these household items, blenders and mixers, even if they were antiques. She could understand it if he were a woman. She could've made a life of these things, too: the neatly arranged shelves, the store's musty odor. It was calming just to be in here. At night, when she couldn't sleep, she would visualize the merchandise, name each brand, and try to remember exactly where it sat on the shelves. It helped some. But Mack knew what he'd paid for every single item and what its retail value was. She didn't have a mind like that.

"Some watchdog," Mack said as the Doberman rolled onto her side.

Phoebe began her usual loop around the store. The shelves were packed with stuff most people would consider junk, random china plates, teacups, jewelry, bits of collections he'd gathered over the last forty years. It seemed outrageous that one person could own so much. Eight years in prison, one year on the outside, and what did she have? A hot plate, a mini-fridge, a fold-out couch. A three-hundred-square-foot garage apartment, paid for by the Methodist Women's Outreach Committee. She couldn't afford new sneakers or a haircut; even her hair dryer was used. She stopped at the display case in the back where Mack kept the expensive items locked.

"See anything you want?"

He was teasing, but the first time he'd asked she'd taken it as an insult and realized that everyone in town knew her story. But then she'd seen his face go red and decided he meant nothing by it and it had become a joke between them. Between his morning breakfasts at the diner and her afternoon visits to his store, an unexpected ease had built up between the two of them.

At the beginning of her parole it had taken such an effort not to be pissed off at the ordinary comments people made—people said stupid things to her all the time—but he made an effort to put her at ease. She felt welcome visiting his store even though it was understood that she could never afford to buy a single thing.

And yet, it seemed any question she asked resulted in a lecture, like he meant to train her to work as a salesclerk in a store where nobody ever shopped. Two weeks ago she had looked twice at a toaster only to get caught in a ten-minute discussion on housewares. Once, she'd helped him polish a tea set and learned that it had been sitting in the store for nearly a decade. They never sell, he'd said, and always tarnish. One time he'd tried to give her a few pieces but she refused, embarrassed as hell—he clearly had no idea how she lived—and she hadn't come back to the store for a week.

She bent to look inside a display case and felt the ring shift beneath her blouse. She tucked the string under her lapel, but he had seen. "You looking to upgrade that string?"

"Huh? No, it's just a key." She hoped he hadn't seen the ring hanging there.

"That makes you a latchkey kid, then," he said, and laughed a little.

She pointed to a tray of rings. "How do you figure out how much these things are worth?"

He set the dustrag down and found the keys to the case. "There are lots of ways to appraise a piece of jewelry," he began, and she knew she'd have to put up with another lecture. The man could never give a simple answer. He picked up a wedding band. "See this? This isn't worth much in weight, but they sell pretty well. A man on his way to the courthouse will pay a hundred bucks for it."

"What about the one next to it?"

It was a big rock, set in twenty-four-carat gold. He glanced at the front door before he took it out of the case, like he always did with expensive pieces. "This one is special. Beautiful, isn't it? Lots of color." He held it up to the light and the facets caught fire.

"It's pretty, but how do you price it?"

"It's tricky sometimes, but I had this one appraised by a jeweler last fall when I was in Atlantic City."

He could sound so pretentious.

"Priced it at twenty thousand, though it's only worth that if someone is willing to pay it."

She stared at it. She'd never owned a diamond and guessed she never would. In another life she might've had a living husband, be celebrating a twentieth anniversary. She might've had all sorts of jewelry by now, but these days, when she bothered to look in the mirror, all she saw was a worn-out woman whose clothes didn't even fit. There was never anything her size at the thrift store, the only place in town she could afford anything at all. That might change soon.

"Try it on," he said, handing it to her. "It is a universal truth that any woman hanging out at the jewelry counter loves to try on rings."

"Well, this one doesn't." She set it on the glass, suddenly aware of her reddened hands, her fingernails that hadn't seen polish in ten years.

He smiled. "You know, looking's free."

"What about that one?" She pointed to a gaudy piece with dozens of diamond chips mounted in white metal.

"Not much," he said, getting it out. "Maybe two hundred." He held it up for her to study.

"It's as pretty."

"Not to the trained eye. I can show you the difference in these catalogs." There were dozens of old copies stacked on the counter. "These prices are outdated, but it'll give you an idea of how diamonds are rated."

He opened to a page and started explaining the difference between styles and cuts, but she tuned him out and flipped through the photos, checking prices.

"If you tell me what you're looking for, maybe I can help. You want to sell something. Maybe a family heirloom?"

She shut the catalog and stooped to pet the Doberman one last time. "No, I was just killing time."

"Hey. I didn't mean anything."

"No offense taken," she said, and managed to give him a smile. "I just need to get back. Tommy will need help peeling the potatoes."

At the front of the store, he made her take an old copy.

She hated being the constant recipient of charity, but sometimes it was better to take what was offered than to insult someone out of pride. Phoebe folded the catalog into her apron pocket.

CHAPTER

23

Jamie watched her mother come out of the pawn-shop and slip between the buildings to the alley that ran behind the storefronts. Phoebe turned over a plastic bucket and sat on it, lit a cigarette, and started flipping through a magazine. The back door of the diner was propped open and the air was filled with smoke and the smell of frying grease. It was a full minute before Phoebe looked up from the magazine and saw Jamie. When she threw her cigarette down, its smoke drifted sideways along the wet ground. She lit another one and offered the pack to Jamie.

"I don't smoke."

Phoebe blew a cloud out the side of her mouth along with the words, "Don't start."

Jamie leaned against the back porch steps and wondered why it was so hard to talk to the woman. Never mind that their lives hadn't been normal for years, mothers and daughters should be able to talk. A decade ago there'd been an ease between them. At least that's how Jamie remembered things.

"What is it?" Phoebe asked.

"What do you think?" She closed the back door of the diner and checked over her shoulder. "That cop has been following me."

"Asking questions?"

"Uh-huh."

"He's been coming in the diner, too. Tommy says he's not from around here, came down from Albany a few years back. Moved here after a divorce or something. He gives me the creeps. Nosy effer. I think he might've seen me catch a hanger sticking an ace on that last hand. But they were all too drunk to be sure."

"You caught a hanger? That's it? All this happened because of a hanger?"

"It wasn't just that. It was a big bet."

"Bets are always big at the end of a game."

"A really big bet. Keating wanted fireworks. You know how it is. He doesn't care about the money. He just wants to crush people, leave 'em reeling, stand back and smirk."

"Maim and neuter."

"Yep. But he pays, so he gets what he wants."

"What about the next night? Why were you there?"

Phoebe sucked on her cigarette and studied the dirt beneath her nails.

"Jeez." Jamie shook off the image of that bloated man

and her mother, alone in the dark. Jack came to mind but she pushed that thought away, too.

Phoebe exhaled a long stream of smoke. "I was lonely. It was just one night."

"You think TJ came back to get even?"

"He came to get what he'd lost."

"In the middle of the night? He broke into a judge's house to get his money back, or did he really come to get that ring?"

Phoebe looked around the alley and got to her feet. She felt under the neck of her lapel and pulled a string from under her blouse. "Look at it."

The ring was enormous. Bright and shiny. Impossible to mistake for anything other than a Super Bowl ring.

"How the hell did you get ahold of that?" But she knew the answer as soon as she asked. Her mother in the window that night at Keating's. His rage that Phoebe had stolen something from his house.

"You had that all along, didn't you?" She looked up and down the alley. "That complicates things."

Phoebe tucked the ring back under her blouse. She opened the catalog and pointed to a dog-eared page. "Look at these prices. With these diamonds? This is worth a fortune. Enough to get us out of Blind River forever. Enough to start over."

All her life, Jamie had heard random bits and pieces of stories about her family. Jilkins often hinted at the criminal tendencies of the Elders clan. Loyal never talked about his brother or his death, but she knew they had been in business together. Every story she'd ever heard had the same thread running through it: theft.

She couldn't look her mother in the eye. She looked at the buttons on her blouse instead and, referring to the thing hidden there, said, "You're going to fence a dead man's ring?"

Phoebe stood and held the catalog at her side. Jamie waited for the slap, wanted it, and the permission to walk away it would bring. One single blow would make it easy to leave. But her mother turned and threw the catalog into the dumpster. Her hair was uneven in the back where she'd tried to trim it in the mirror. The waist of her skirt puckered at the belt loops. And Jamie understood—it was stupid to think Phoebe Elders could resist a payout this big.

"They're going to be looking for it, you know? If they find the body. That thing will tie you to that."

"We could get a long way from here before then," Phoebe said, flipping the ashes off her cigarette.

"We?"

"You and me." She cocked her head sideways. "You could come with me."

Jamie considered the idea. "What? You want to be a team now? Go all Thelma and Louise or something?"

"Don't be stupid, Jamie. You need to get out of here. There will be trouble if you stay. Why do you think Loyal had you help him that night?"

She raised her shoulders. "I owe him, so sometimes I help him."

"Is that what happened to your face? You helping

him?" Phoebe reached out and touched Jamie's cheek, but Jamie pushed her hand away.

"You're a scrawny kid who eats like a bird. He needed *you* to help him move a two-hundred-and-fifty-pound man?" She pushed her bangs off her forehead. "Watch yourself, Jamie. He put you at that scene for a reason. DNA, fingerprints. He's leaving a trail in case he needs to cover his tracks. He and Keating need to put this on someone, and it's not going to be me. I am not going back to prison. Not in this lifetime."

"What happened that night?"

The back door bounced open and Tommy stuck his head out. "Pheebs!" he yelled. "They're backing up at the counter." He tapped a spatula against his leg and locked eyes with Jamie. "Everything okay out here?"

"Go back inside, Tommy. I'm coming."

Tommy went back inside and Phoebe took a long drag off her cigarette.

"He recognized my face, Jamie. From the Saturday night game." Smoke clouded the air in front of her face and she waved it away. "He charged. What do you think happened? He surprised us."

"So you what? You just killed him?"

"What?" Phoebe stepped backward, her face turning to a sneer. "God. I never know what to expect from you."

"To expect from me? What you expect is for me to clean up after you." Liquid rage weakened her legs, but she couldn't back down now.

"What mess did I ever leave for you to clean up?"

"Toby! You left me to take care of him."

"Lower your voice," Phoebe said. "I couldn't help that and you know it."

Jamie braced herself against the back porch, the muscles in her legs turning hot.

"Fuck this." Phoebe threw her cigarette on the ground and went inside.

"Right, just walk away!" Jamie yelled, but Phoebe had already slammed the door behind her.

The woman was weak. Weak and selfish and she obviously didn't care about anything but money. Jamie picked up the bucket and slung it against the dumpster. Picked it up and threw it again. The handle flew off and hit her leg. The pain calmed her down. As she rubbed her shin she watched the smoke from her mother's cigarette snag on a breeze, twist, and disappear into the air.

CHAPTER

24

As Phoebe walked from the bus station back to the diner, she contemplated the cash she had left, adding it up to the dollar. Three hundred and twenty dollars wasn't much for a start in a new city. All that could change, though, if she played this right. The two one-way tickets to the shore had cost her plenty and the second ticket was probably a waste of time, but it was redeemable for cash if things didn't work out the way she hoped. She'd hated watching Jamie throw that fit, but she hoped if she gave it some time, the girl would cool off and maybe come with her.

When she got to the alley behind the diner, it was quiet. She had five minutes left on her break, so she turned over the mop bucket and sat down. It struck her, not for the first time, how comfortable she was out here, away from the eyes of the good people of Blind River. It seemed there was no end to their curiosity about her, the woman who'd spent time in prison. Sometimes she felt like the town's only novelty.

Sometimes she just needed to be alone on the outside of fences and walls and feel the freedom to walk down a dank alley at any time of the day or night. People complained about their bosses or the price of milk—they had no idea how lucky they were to simply open a door and walk through it. When she got out eight months ago, the world had seemed too large, the sky too high, the colors of sunset gaudy and bright. Getting to work on time, opening a checking account, buying aspirin at the drugstore—it was all she could do to get through a day. The choices overwhelmed her. How could there be so many brands for a single product, and why would anyone buy expensive shampoo when the knock-off brand was half the cost?

She'd been determined to put the past behind her, to never look back or think about prison. But with what she'd done at Keating's, those gray walls loomed behind everything. Behind the dumpster, a gray wall. Behind the metal barrel where Tommy burned trash, a gray wall. Even the wall behind the metal staircase that led to her apartment was gray. The color was closing in on her. And it was her own fault. She'd put herself in this position. She'd had help, that's for sure, and maybe she had some leverage, but this had come about because she had gotten comfortable with freedom and the few things she owned. And she had wanted more.

She finished her cigarette, went inside, tied on her apron. When she pushed through the kitchen's swinging doors, Loyal was sitting on a stool at the middle of the counter, waiting. The way he stared meant he had something to say, so she was glad the diner was empty.

"What do you want?"

"Coffee."

The pot from the lunch service had gone cold, so she started another one. "That isn't what I meant. What else?"

"Pie."

It was awful being alone with him. She owed him so much, hated him even more. "I got apple and sweet potato but they're still frozen."

"Give me the sweet potato."

She got it out of the freezer, popped it out of its tin, and whacked a piece off with a knife big enough to field-dress a buck. The coffeepot beeped and she tossed the pie in the microwave, punched a few buttons. From five feet away she smelled the whiskey on his breath, his unwashed hair. His silence pissed her off, like he had all the time in the world. She grabbed the coffeepot and filled his cup. It would be easy enough to accidentally trip and send that scalding liquid flying across the counter at him.

"What do you want from me?"

He pulled his old flask from his jacket pocket. It stunned her to see that thing again and it brought back a memory she hadn't thought of in years.

The whole gang had gone out drinking. She and Jimmy had hired a sitter for the first time ever and left the kids home to go to Bobby Smiley's birthday party at Crowley's Pub.

Bobby Smiley. Everyone called him BS for short and it was an apt nickname. He was Loyal's best friend on the high school football team and the only person Loyal ever spent any time with, a fact people noticed. Some folks talked. Joked about Loyal being Bobby's *center* and

snickered about just how *tight* Bobby's end really was.
Bobby moved to Key West a few years after graduation and
gave Loyal that flask as a parting gift. No one saw Loyal for
months after Bobby left, but the rumors about the two of
them remained as some of the best gossip in Blind River.

Loyal poured some whiskey in his coffee, stopped
when he saw her staring.

"You ever hear from him?" she asked, motioning to
the flask.

"Who?" ·

"You know who."

"Sends me a postcard sometimes. Want some?"

She took the flask and read the inscription though it
was nearly rubbed off: *Friends Forever*. It was silver-plated
and dented in the middle. A piece of junk like that wouldn't
bring five dollars in the pawnshop.

"Looks like it got run over by a truck."

"I didn't give it to you to inspect. Give it back if you
don't want some."

She handed it back. "No, I don't want any of it."

Loyal poured cream in his coffee and drank half the
cup. She thought about refilling it but wanted him to ask
for it or, better yet, just leave.

"Tommy's in the back doing dishes, so we're alone.
Why don't you just say what you came in here to say?"

"I don't know. It seems redundant."

Sometimes he threw out a big word like that, like he
thought he was so smart. She laughed and it came out
mean.

"I saw that cop's car parked outside of here yesterday.
You know he is not your friend, right?" he said.

"You came here to tell me who my friends are?"

"There's no way he will help you, okay? The only thing for you to do is sit tight and let me take care of things." He forked the pie and stuffed half of it in his mouth.

"Last time I let you take care of things I ended up with a dead husband."

He clenched his fists and she stepped back. A noise came from the kitchen and she said, "That's Tommy. You better say what you want and get going."

Loyal finished his pie and pushed his plate away. "Look. If I'd known you were at Keating's house that night I wouldn't have helped at all. I promise you that. I don't want no more to do with you than you do with me. But I'm stuck with this and so are you."

She picked up his plate and tossed it in the gray bin with the other dishes. "You can't control the wind by telling it what direction to blow."

"Just don't talk to anyone about anything. Including Jamie." He slapped a ten on the counter and said, "Anything happens, I'm your first and only call. You understand?"

One thing she knew for sure was that a good bluff starts—and ends—with a blank face.

He leaned toward her and waited.

"You're my first and only call," she said.

She could see he didn't believe her but she'd said what he wanted to hear. Doubt clouded his eyes as he walked out the door, but he'd tipped his hand without even knowing it. He hadn't mentioned the ring and that meant Keating hadn't told him she'd taken it. And that meant she still had a chance.

CHAPTER

25

Toby got a hundred miles from Blind River before he ran out of gas and had to flag down a passing truck. The window lowered as it pulled to the shoulder, and a skinny old man with a neck too stiff to turn leaned his head out.

"Out of gas," Toby said.

The old man said, "It happens. One of them cans in the back might have something in it." He pointed a crooked finger up the road. "There's a station, ten miles up this road. Should be enough to get you there."

The back of the old man's truck was full of garbage: bags of aluminum cans, a broken weed eater, unrecognizable spare parts thick with grease, three gas cans. Toby found a small one that was half full. After he grabbed it, the truck pulled back onto the road.

"Wait!" he yelled, but the old man just waved out the back window, his back wheels spinning gravel at Toby's feet.

The gas station was closer to twenty miles away. Toby coasted in on fumes and radio static.

The cashier was a wiry girl with sunken cheeks and a blue tattoo crawling down her arm that read *Reveal Your Soul*. He smiled at her to test the possibilities. She glared back, and he wondered what kind of girl would have a tattoo like that and not smile at a guy.

"Turn the pump on?"

"Sign says prepay."

He had twenty-eight dollars in cash. "Give me twenty," he said, and got three Snickers bars and a six-pack of Cherry Cokes with the rest. She flipped a switch for the pump and turned back to a small TV—that dyke talk show host with the sneakers and the boy's haircut who he hated.

"What's it mean?"

"What?"

"Your tattoo. What's it mean?"

"It's English. You know English?"

"Yeah."

"Then figure it out." She rolled her eyes and turned up the volume with the remote.

He lost interest because girls like that were never fun. He headed to the truck and started the pump, then found the bathroom on the side of the building. The toilet was brown and furry so he pissed in the corner, threw water on his face, and dried off with five yards of paper towels. All his life he'd loved pulling paper towels out of those machines and the righteous feeling that came from wasting the stuff.

As he stepped outside a guy rounded the corner from the back of the station. He was narrow at the waist with a forward lean that made him look slinky and dark eyes that he kept aimed at the ground except for a single glance when Toby let him pass on the concrete walkway. His long black hair trailed behind him smelling like fresh water. Before he could block the thought, Toby realized the boy was the prettiest thing he'd ever seen up close and a crazy longing opened up inside his belly. He started to speak but tripped off the walkway and landed on his stomach in the dirt. The boy just smiled and went inside the bathroom. He left the door cracked and Toby sat in the dirt not knowing what to do. His dick pulsed against his leg, a reaction so whack he wanted to strangle the thing. The crazy thing in his belly made him want to run hard and fast, but the boy's smile—he wanted to see that again.

He stood up and slapped the dirt off his pants. As he was wondering what to do, a semi pulled off the highway and stopped at the farthest edge of the parking lot. A big bearded man in a camo ball cap tugged low over his brow left the truck's engine running and hurried to the bathroom. He shut the door solidly behind him without even noticing Toby standing there, his dick going soft. That boy's thin hips, that man's burly torso. His mind tumbled through a dozen scenarios. He wanted to go in there but his feet wouldn't budge. The crazy in his groin settled into a not-unpleasant sensation that he could live with and he turned away.

By the time Toby made it back to the pump, it had clicked off. Seventy-eight dollars and fifty-seven cents. The cashier was watching him out the window. He raised his hands as if to say thanks but she pushed the window open and shouted, "You got to pay for that."

"It was supposed to shut off at twenty!"

"No, you were supposed to shut it off at twenty. The cops will explain how it all works if you want." She came to the door with the phone in her hand.

He had hoped to get to the shore before he used the credit cards.

She slid behind the register when he followed her inside. Toby tossed her a card and said, "It should've cut off."

"Not my problem you don't know how to use a pump, Mr. Bangor. That your daddy's AmEx?"

"That's my card."

"You're too young to have an AmEx. That's your daddy's or it's stolen."

Heat pulsed in his cheeks and scalp. "Well, it's not stolen."

"Uh-huh. You got an AmEx and you're driving a rusted-out pickup?"

The part about blushing he hated the most was when it brought tears to his eyes, some kind of bad wiring in his head he hadn't yet outgrown. Outside the big plate window the pretty boy was walking toward the highway and Toby watched to see which direction he would turn. The semi started rolling out of the parking lot. Those two hadn't been inside that bathroom for more than five minutes.

"Hey," she said, almost kindly. "Makes no difference to me. Sign here."

The boy got to the highway and Toby was thinking through the possibilities when a car slowed to a stop and the boy got in.

It was a relief in a lot of ways.

* * *

Fifteen miles east on I-15, Toby had eaten one of the Snickers and finished two Cherry Cokes, but he couldn't get that boy's smile or that girl's stupid tattoo off his mind. What the hell did it mean? An eighteen-wheeler passed and blew the Ford slightly toward the shoulder.

He tried the radio, but this far out in the country, there was nothing but static. For the first time in his life he was on his own. He loved the rolling hills, the horizon always out of reach. Another half-dozen semis passed him going west and he watched them flanking each other in his rearview mirror. Big trucks like that could take a body clear across the country a hundred times a year. He finally found a station playing Joplin, popped another Cherry Coke, and made up his own lyrics. "Freedom's just an open road and nothing left to do." He slapped the steering wheel, wondering where he could get his hands on a semi.

Toby thought about the boy again and the hair on his arms stood up. He'd never known a boy could be pretty. He imagined the two of them riding down the highway, sharing a joint with the windows rolled down, their hair blowing free.

* * *

Toby was taking a piss in a field behind a small bale of hay when a cruiser pulled up and stopped behind the truck. The officer stayed in the car with his warning lights cutting at the bright sky. Toby tucked his head. Behind him was a barbed-wire fence and beyond that a bare field extending to the top of a hill. The cover of nightfall was hours away. Another cruiser pulled in front of the truck and backed up until the truck was trapped between them. He'd feel better if they just turned off the damn lights. The second cop, a big round guy, got out.

He couldn't believe Jamie had called the cops. He had just as much right to the truck as she did, or almost, anyway. The big round guy drew his gun and crept up to the window.

Toby buttoned his pants and stuck the stolen wallet deep into the hay where it wouldn't be found for months, and by then, hopefully some damn cow would have chewed it up and turned it to shit.

They were checking the inside of the cab now. Maybe this was just routine. Cops find an empty truck, they check it out. Standard. No big deal. They'd probably let him go if he came out and explained he was just taking a piss. He'd apologize for the confusion; cops loved apologies. He practiced saying it in his head. *Sorry, Officer; sorry for the confusion.*

But if they did let him go, he'd need that AmEx. He considered circling back for it later, but he couldn't chance finding the same hay bale. There really were cows out here and one of them really could find this bale of hay and eat the wallet. Besides, a single card was easy enough to ditch in a hurry. He got the card, slipped it into the waistband of his underpants, and stuck the wallet back into the hay.

He stepped out from behind the bale. The cops were studying the hinge on the tailgate, picking at something stuck there. One of them got a camera out of his pocket.

Toby yelled, "Hello."

The cop with the camera jumped behind the truck, but the fat one dropped into a crouch and aimed his gun at Toby. "Get down, motherfucker! Get down on the ground."

The barrel of that gun seemed as big as a canon. Toby raised his hand but his knees caved on their own accord.

The first cop fumbled with the safety latch on his holster. In a heartbeat, another 9mm was pointed at Toby's head. Another cruiser pulled up and another gun was drawn.

"I'm . . . I'm sorry for the confusion, officer," Toby mumbled as he hit the ground.

"Facedown, arms out straight out from your sides." The fat one lowered his gun.

Toby fell forward, partly out of compliance and partly because of gravity, but mostly because the sky had begun to cartwheel.

CHAPTER

26

JAMIE WATCHED JACK sleep and thought it was crazy that he looked so innocent, his mouth slightly open, lips pale but full against his black three-day-old beard. She wanted to touch the scruff on his chin, especially the hollow dark spot of the dimple there. Her crotch was sore and she remembered a fraction from the night before, him on top of her, but the rest was a blank. When she'd arrived at his store after that fight with her mother, she'd been wound up. He'd been so cool about it, staying with her even though he should have gone home. Finally, he'd given her one of his pills, and she'd slept. It was the best sleep she'd had in a week.

She pulled the quilt over his shoulders and left a note saying she'd be back before five on his laptop.

Outside the sharp air snapped at her cheeks. She tugged her cap down over her ears and sloshed through the top layer of snow and the crunchy layer of ice that had frozen overnight. Her lungs clenched from the cold air, but halfway there she warmed up and loosened the top button of her jacket. The air felt good and clean on her face.

As she turned the corner at Sikes Avenue, she saw that Billy's truck was already gone from the driveway. Good. Maybe she could take a hot shower, catch up with Angel, pretend for a few hours that things were normal.

There weren't many cars in the neighborhood, most workers having left for the day, so the sound of ice beneath wheels made her look up and straight into the sunglasses of that damn detective. *Shit, shit, shit.* There was no one else in sight and there was no way to pretend she hadn't seen him.

He stopped at the curb and turned off the engine. That meant only one thing: this would be a longer conversation than she wanted with questions she didn't want to answer.

"Been looking for you," he said, getting out of the car.

She tried for a nonchalant smile. "You seem to find me easy enough." It wasn't exactly what she meant to say. She knew he'd seen she was rattled because he took off his sunglasses and stepped closer.

One time in high school she had smelled sex on the coach's breath when she ran into him in the parking lot behind the gym, so now, even though she'd brushed her teeth at Jack's, she stepped away from Garcia. When she pulled at the collar of her jacket, she caught a whiff of Jack on her hand and jammed it back in her pocket.

"No wheels today?"

"Got a flat."

"A flat, huh?"

"Yep." It was a gamble, but she was counting on Toby joyriding outside the county last night, maybe sleeping in the truck on a back road.

"You got anything for me yet?"

"I told you, I can't help you." She tried to sigh like she was bored, but her heart was starting to pound. If she took her hands out of her pockets now, they'd be shaking, so she clenched them and pushed them in deeper.

"You never know. You might have the key that unlocks this whole thing. You seen your brother lately?"

It bothered her that he kept bringing up family—first Phoebe, now Toby. What if he started putting it together? Cops got paid to fill in missing pieces.

"Let me tell you something, Jamie. I'm the guy you want for a friend."

"I don't know anything about it, man. I told you that. How am I supposed to help you?"

"I got the addresses of four coin pushers. I know there are more. And those posters claiming to raise money for pediatric charities? That's bullshit. Coin pushers are illegal, and no one believes that money is getting donated. Your uncle's making money off them just like he makes money off that bogus veterans' poker tournament. That's fine. Maybe one day Loyal will buy a bench for the town square, put up a plaque for the boys in this town who actually served their country."

The fucker had been writing down addresses while he'd been following her. But four was nothing in the scheme of Loyal's operation. "What's that got to do with me?"

"I don't know exactly, but your choices are narrowing, and you're going to have to figure out something soon."

"What's that mean? You want me to choose the law over my family?" The anger in her voice startled her.

"It isn't a choice between the law and your family."

"Sounds like it. Sounds just like that to me."

"It's a choice between right and wrong."

"You're the one who's wrong. Wrong to think I'd put anything over my family."

"That's good to know," he said turning toward his car. "You don't want to work with me, fine. I'll spend more time with your mother. But you need to understand, this is an ugly situation for a parolee."

"What situation?" He was wrong—she didn't want him as a friend. But then she didn't want him as an enemy either.

The cell phone in his pocket buzzed and he reached for it.

"You know," he said, walking back to his car. "Parole violations. She's crossing some dangerous lines."

"You just run around town making threats all day long? That what you're paid to do?"

He glanced at his phone. "I'm going to ignore that for now. Think about what side you want to land on, Jamie. And don't go far."

"Where am I going, huh? No wheels."

"Right. No wheels."

Fumes bellowed from his tailpipe as he drove away. She

was trembling as she climbed the porch steps to Angel's house. The curtain in the front window rustled and a shadowed figure stepped back. Angel threw the door open and yanked Jamie inside. "Babe, what was he doing here?"

"Fucker's been dogging me for days."

"You're freezing." Angel threw a blanket around Jamie's shoulders.

"I just need to warm up." It wasn't true, though. It was fear and anger getting to her. At least it was warm inside.

There were piles of laundry on the floor and the baby was sleeping facedown on one of them. The place was the kind of lived-in mess that made her want to stay. Dirty dishes on the coffee table, the smell of baby formula coming from the kitchen, a low hum coming from a local news channel on the TV.

"Sit," Angel said, and took Jamie to the couch. "You know he's a cop, right? What does he want?"

"Some shit. I don't know."

Angel lowered her voice and looked around the room as though someone might overhear. "I can't have the law coming around here right now. Billy brought home a half pound last night. It's going to take days to sell all that weed."

"He's not looking at you. He doesn't care about some skanky weed."

"Yeah, you're probably right. But keep your voice down; don't wake Tucker." Angel lit the remnants of a joint and handed it to Jamie, started folding a pile of baby clothes. "I don't think you should come around here for a few days, you know? Just until we unload this stuff."

Jamie took a drag, held her breath, stared at the television. The local news came on, *Nine on the Nines*, and a headshot of TJ Bangor filled the right half of the screen. The reporter mouthed the words *Foul play suspected.*

That was the guy. It had to be. Big square head, wide-set eyes. *Fuck. Am I going down for this?* She coughed. "Turn that up," she said, waving at the smoke.

"Why? Some old football player goes missing. Who cares? Probably got his ass shot up in a bar."

There was video of three people stapling posters on telephone poles. Jamie grabbed the remote and caught the last few sentences.

"Mr. Bangor's agent says he hasn't heard from the former NFL star in two days. And now there's been an arrest."

In the background, Loyal's old Ford was being rolled up onto a flatbed tow truck.

Shit. The connection was right there. She'd seen Loyal take the man's wallet out of his back pocket that night and knew he would have stashed it under his bed in the box she and Toby always rummaged through for cash.

The reporter continued. *"A young man from Blind River using Mr. Bangor's credit cards is being returned to local authorities. Stay tuned for more details as the police continue their investigation."*

Fuck. She needed to get to Toby before he said anything stupid.

27

Jamie showered and borrowed a clean sweater from Angel. By the time she got to Main Street her buzz had worn off and she needed caffeine and some wheels. Jack's car sat in front of his store and she was wondering about borrowing it again when Loyal's big red Dodge turned the corner and stopped at the curb beside her. The passenger window lowered and he said, "Get in."

"I got to be somewhere," she said, wishing she had her own place, a place with a door she could shut and lock.

"No you don't." He reached across the cab and pushed open the door. "Get in. We need to talk."

Jamie stood on the curb, sunlight glinting off the storefronts. She didn't want to go anywhere with him.

"Get in, dammit. I ain't asking a third time."

She climbed up.

"Careful with your boots."

She knocked the sludge off the soles. "It's just snow."

A persistent dinging started when she sat down and closed the door. The interior was spotless and she hesitated, not wanting to touch anything. "Damn, this is nice."

"Try not to mess it up."

The dinging was relentless until she buckled the seatbelt.

"Where you so bent on going?" he asked.

"Where do you think? My brother's in jail."

"Huh. You got the bail money this time?"

She didn't, but she thought of the cash she'd collected yesterday—and left with Jack last night. "I thought maybe you—"

"Maybe I'd what? I got him out once already. Cost me a thousand. You know what happens to that money now? Gone. Forfeited. And he wasn't even out eight hours."

She'd figured as much. "Maybe Phoebe will help."

"You think she can? Doesn't have a dime to help with you kids. Never did."

"There might be another way. Maybe she could call her parole officer."

He laughed. "You think she can pull some strings? That's not exactly how parole works." He turned north at the stoplight.

They drove another minute, then Loyal turned onto a brick-lined street. Houses on either side of the road were set back behind deep lawns of sycamores and their snow-covered limbs. She recognized Keating's car when they turned into the driveway. *Shit.* She looked back at the street, suddenly worried that Garcia might have seen her get into Loyal's truck. "You think Keating might help?"

"He'll be home for lunch. We'll talk it through." He pulled to the back and parked behind the Cadillac.

When she got out, she looked up at the window where she'd seen her mother that night. The curtains were drawn tight. Four bottles of bleach were strewn on the ground outside the garage.

"Come inside," Loyal said.

She smelled the bleach as they approached the back door.

Keating sat at his kitchen table inside his bright yellow kitchen eating a massive tuna sandwich. He scowled when he saw Jamie. "Why'd you bring her here?"

Loyal pulled Jamie inside and slammed the door shut. He spread his big palms out, level with the ground. "We got to get everyone on the same page."

Keating sank into his chair. "You better have a plan to fix this mess. That boy of yours is causing too much trouble." He picked up the rest of the sandwich and stuffed it into his mouth.

Loyal pulled a chair out and sat down. "Or not. He might offer a solution to everything. Seems to me we could play this thing to suit our needs."

"What are you getting at?" Keating wiped his mouth.

"Toby could help the situation if he stays put for a while. You could come out of this thing smelling like a rose. We all could."

One or both of them had cleaned the place up; the smell of bleach was so strong it stung her nose. Keating eyed Jamie and motioned to Loyal to keep talking. There seemed to be a code between them that she couldn't follow.

"Everything points to a theft gone wrong," Loyal said. "Toby got caught with Bangor's wallet, the cops can't quite figure out exactly where or how that happened but they got enough to suspect the boy. And Toby will never be able to explain it to their satisfaction because he's got no alibi. He was home alone most of that night, watching TV."

Keating nodded contemplatively and pushed away from the table. "Might work. But where *did* he get the credit card?"

"Doesn't matter. He was found with it and we can make it work."

It was true. Over the years these two men had learned how to make a lot of things work. Toby might be reckless and wild but he feared Loyal too much to tell the cops where he'd gotten that wallet. At least, until he realized he was facing a murder charge, and by then he'd have changed his story so many times that no one would believe him if Loyal and Keating backed each other up.

Keating drank a glass of milk and belched. "So, there's nothing to trace?"

Loyal leaned back and crossed his arms at his chest. "Not much. Not enough."

"What about the girl?" Keating asked, pointing at her with his chin. "Squashing a crazy girl is one thing, but a girl with a crazy little brother? That's an altogether different bug."

"That's why she's here. She needs to hear it from you."

"Huh," Keating said, and cleared his throat, a long and windy noise. He straightened his back and pushed his empty plate to the center of the table where, Jamie supposed, a maid would find it later. He smoothed the arms of his red cashmere sweater. When he stiffened and turned to face her, she saw a transformed man and something inside her shrank.

This was Circuit Court Judge Jefferson William Keating, a man who'd been reelected virtually unopposed in Blind River for thirty years. In this town he decided who was a criminal and who was not. He handed down sentences. He shattered families in the interest of the public good. He decided which companies would drown in taxes and penalties and red tape and which ones would flourish. He might've grown foolish over the years but he never suffered fools—and foolish young Toby meant nothing to him.

"Your brother was arrested yesterday for assaulting a public servant. The court was lenient when it shouldn't have been and allowed bail. Not a day later he was caught making purchases using the stolen credit cards of a missing man, virtually impersonating the victim of his crime."

Jamie said, "He never even met that man."

"No!" He slammed his palm on the table. "No, you don't speak here. You don't interrupt me when I'm talking."

Loyal crossed his arms over his chest and gave Jamie a look meant to shut her up.

"But Toby didn't do anything," she said. "Doesn't that matter? What about the law?"

"I am the law!" Keating yelled. "In this town, I am the law." He sneered at Jamie. "You don't understand that yet, but you are about to. What I say goes and you don't get to say anything. That boy used a stolen credit card from a missing man. That gives the law reason to hold him indefinitely. He did that and no one made him." He hit the table hard again and his plate bounced.

"You mean to go along with this?" She asked Loyal. "He's your blood. Aren't you going to say something?"

"This is how I see it," Loyal said. "Toby is out of control. He's turning into a drunk troublemaker. He needs to cool off for a few years. Once he's in the system, the judge can get him into a program where he'll learn a trade. After a while, he'll get out and have a chance at a real job."

The back of Jamie's head went cold. When had incarceration become the best option for a troubled kid?

Loyal and Keating watched her. They'd said all they had to say.

"There's got to be a better way," she said, moving toward the door.

Loyal moved fast. He grabbed her jacket collar and pushed her against the wall. "This is how it plays. Saves me lot of trouble, so wrap your head around it."

"Is that what we are? A lot of trouble?"

He shook his head, his eyes suddenly hopeless. "You know what I mean." She tried to get loose but he had her pinned with his big forearm. "Toby's always in trouble.

You're always fishing him out. This way you're done; you get to have your own life." He had that faraway look in his eyes that he got when he'd made up his mind and nothing was going to change it.

"You got trouble in your house," Keating said. "First your mother, now your brother. And you? Sleeping with a married man."

Her face burned.

He waved the air like it was foul. "What's in store for you? A life of ratty babies, meaningless jobs, waiting tables like your mother, or living off welfare and the taxes of hardworking people. Or worse? That's all there is for girls like you. No one expects a thing better from your kind."

She leaned against the wall feeling a twist in her gut. She'd been so stupid. What kind of future would she have with a man like Jack? All her decent choices were behind her, college, the lousy but steady job. Now she was in debt to her uncle and this man.

Loyal stood there nodding and letting the old fool rant about her, her brother, her mother. He said nothing to stop Keating. Silently she begged him to make the bastard shut up, but Loyal shook a cigarette from his pack and fumbled with his lighter. He took a drag off it and blew smoke toward the ceiling. "What's he saying that's not true?"

Something inside her gave.

Keating motioned at the air. "Let her go. We're done here."

Loyal stepped back. "You got it?"

She caught herself from falling, made it to the door. "I

got it." The brass doorknob in her hand was cold as hell. She yanked open the door and the freezing air hit her hard.

"Where you going?" Loyal asked.

"Where you're afraid to go." She needed to see him. The idea of Toby alone in a concrete cell would keep her up all night. Someone needed to visit him and no one else could be bothered.

"Good. Then you tell him."

She looked back inside at her uncle but he stared at the floor like he was looking right through it, like he could see all the way to hell.

"Me?"

"Yes, you. Go on," he said. "Get it over with quick."

28

JAMIE LEFT KEATING and Loyal sitting in the kitchen in smug agreement undoubtedly toasting each other with a bottle of Hennessy. She walked by Keating's Cadillac sitting unlocked in the driveway behind his house, his cell phone in the passenger seat. *Unbelievable.* The man thought he was so untouchable he didn't even have to lock things up. She took the phone just because.

There was a trailhead at the back of Keating's yard, and Jamie decided to take it rather than walking the streets and taking the chance of running into Garcia. The path ran alongside a shallow creek cluttered with muck and debris, ruining her boots. It was worth it if only for a little privacy and a chance to think through this shitstorm. It was colder in the shadows by the creek. Icicles formed on roots where the water stood nearly motionless. She pulled her cap down over her ears and tugged her cuffs over her half-frozen fingertips. Some of the bandages were coming undone and a finger was bleeding again. She sucked at it and wrapped the strip tighter, hoping it would stick another few hours.

The creek forked beneath a single-lane bridge where the road veered south and led back to town. She stomped her boots and kicked at a metal post rail to get the muck off. Jamie stood in the center of the bridge and looked at the riverbed littered with soda cans and bottles. Water ran deep at the fork. So deep that in the summer, she and Toby would battle mosquitoes and hike through the woods just to jump off the bridge into the cool water. The impulse to jump now, to feel the ground disappear beneath her and leave all this shit behind, was strong. Everything felt edgy and tight, balanced on a knife-edge.

She threw rocks off the bridge, watched them smack the water and sink. She pulled Keating's phone out of her pocket. It would serve him right if she threw it, but before she did she hit the home button. *What the hell?* It wasn't even locked. It was worth at least two hundred bucks online. She stuck it back in her pocket and found more rocks to throw instead.

Overhead, exhaust from the single remaining stack at the fertilizer plant swirled upward into a band of weather coming in from the west. When they were little, she and Toby had often lain on their backs in the field behind the trailer and stared at that plume, watching the exhaust just lift and vanish like a cheap magic show. Inside that jail cell, Toby probably couldn't even see the sky. The creek ran south toward a greater river, but staring at it now was just wasting time. She had to see Toby and somehow convince him to hang on and give her time to figure out this mess.

She walked across the bridge and caught the road toward town.

The courthouse at the town center faced west. Its high columns and large oak doors appeared majestic compared to the plain three-story hospital next door or the police station across the street and its low, squatty jailhouse—a single-story building of steel doors and surrounded by electrified cyclone fencing.

The only time Jamie had been inside the jail was the day her mother had pled guilty and been sentenced to a prison upstate. Phoebe had wanted to see her children one last time and Loyal had dragged them here on the morning of her transfer. More than anything, Jamie remembered the doors—loud, heavy doors. Phoebe had dropped to her knees to hug them but the guard had refused to take the handcuffs off and when Toby saw them on his mother he'd come undone. He'd run straight back to the door and hunkered there, trembling and inconsolable. When the guard finally let them out, Jamie vowed she'd never enter that building again. But here she was.

Standing in front of it now, Jamie tried to imagine Toby inside, but all she could conjure up was the memory of him cowering at the foot of that steel door, screaming, not so much for his mother but to get outside its walls.

There was a three-bay garage in the parking lot between the police station entrance and the jail. Outside, two men stood smoking cigarettes while another made notes on a clipboard. They were going over Loyal's old truck. Garcia emerged from inside the garage, squinting in the sunlight. She started walking faster, but he raised his arm and pointed in her direction.

"Just who I'm looking for," he said. He peeled off a pair of latex gloves as he approached. It came together abruptly. The truck inside the garage. The detectives and their latex gloves. Garcia constantly dogging her.

Jamie tried to quiet the impulse to run from him. She waited as a car passed, trying to separate exactly what she'd told him earlier from everything she knew and wondered what the hell she'd do if he'd found any hard evidence on the truck.

"That your truck in there?"

"Nope, not mine."

"But you were driving it, right?"

"Drove it some, yeah." Saying as little as possible seemed best.

"You loan it to your brother yesterday?"

"I didn't loan it because it's not mine."

"He just took it then?"

"He takes it when he needs it." Talking with him was like walking through a minefield. Anything she said could blow up in her face and he was trying to find a hole in her story.

"I thought it had a flat."

"Flats get fixed easy enough," she said, and turned toward the jail's entrance. She got a few steps away and began thinking she'd shaken him off when he called after her.

"You pick a side yet?"

She paused.

"Because, if not, we found something that makes me think you might slide in sideways."

A cruiser pulled into the lot. The cop driving it exchanged a two-finger salute with Garcia.

Jamie could barely breathe. It had been so cold that morning, and that man had been wrapped up so tight in the tarp. She was almost positive that nothing, no blood anyway, had been in the flatbed of the truck. Loyal had said he'd hosed it down. She thought about running but her feet felt like blocks of ice.

"I'm going to ask you one more time and you need to think hard on the answer. Do you know where TJ Bangor is?"

He'd framed the question in the only way she could answer honestly. She knew the man was dead and lying somewhere beneath a pile of rocks and tree limbs, but no, she couldn't say where he was.

"No," she said, keeping her back to him.

She forced her feet to move, first one crablike step to the side and then another, just aiming each foot at the sidewalk and trying not to trip. He didn't stop her but she felt him watching. She counted her steps in sets of three and made it to the jailhouse entrance without falling down.

The waiting room was stark and smelled of disinfectant. Dingy green walls, a white metal door, pale and scarred metal chairs lining the room. She yanked off her stocking cap and checked in at the clerk's window. A heavyset woman in a uniform took her name, glanced absently at her face, and waved her toward the chairs.

Fluorescent lights shined a bluish tint. The only window was a square foot of wire mesh on the main door. Somehow, that made sense. It was cold. She kept her hands in her pockets and stood near the door, telling herself it wasn't much worse than the high school guidance counselor's office. She'd mention that to Toby. But doors were constantly slamming from deep inside the building.

An hour later, her nose was running and she was shivering. In all that time no one had entered the room. She checked with the woman, who told her she'd have to wait her turn. When Jamie pointed out there was no one else there, the woman left the window and didn't return.

Jamie pushed a chair away from the wall with her boot and sat down.

Fifteen minutes later an overhead buzzer screeched, the locks on the white metal door clacked, and the door began to open with a sucking hydraulic noise. Jamie would have to walk into that hallway on her own free will and trust they had nothing to hold her on.

"I ain't got all day." The clerk stared at her clipboard and motioned from inside the doorway. As they walked deeper into the maze of hallways, she opened each consecutive door with a separate key, all the doors closing loudly behind them. It grew warmer near the interior of the jailhouse and Jamie unbuttoned her jacket. The woman left her in a small room with two chairs and a table bolted to the floor.

A vent in the ceiling blew heat straight down over her chair. In minutes, sweat soaked her back and she peeled off her jacket. She tried not to think of what might happen if there was a fire, or a nuclear attack, or the fertilizer plant blew up again. She was at the mercy of the woman with the keys who might or might not feel compelled to come find her in an emergency. She wiped the sweat off her lip and fought for a rational thought, tried to think of Toby. She would be leaving here within the hour. He might never.

The door opened and bounced against the back wall. Toby and two guards filled the opening. Ankle and hand cuffs stopped him from moving forward until the smaller guard wedged through the door. Toby's nose and eyes were red.

The guard pushed him forward awkwardly so he could latch the chain to the table.

"This is a little overkill, don't you think?" Jamie asked.

"Not really. I'll be outside," he said, and slammed the door.

Toby leaned on his elbows. "I hate it in here. You gotta get me out."

The bruise over his eye was turning purple. His face was damp from crying and she didn't even have a tissue to give him. She fought the image of him trying to get out that prison door all those years ago. "Is that bruise from this morning or did the cops hit you?"

"No, they didn't hit me. Maybe I should say they did though. Does it look bad?" He dipped his head toward her, his eyebrows repeating the question. "When will Loyal get here? I can't stay here another night. It's so fucking loud." He pulled his hair. "The guys in here, they're mean fuckers and big. Three of them ganged up on me, pushed me around like I'm some kind of faggot." He clenched his fists, gingerly testing the swollen knuckles. "Now they got me in my own cell and no one talks to me. It's freezing in there."

"You need to stay calm, you hear? Don't let them scare some bogus confession out of you."

He lurched forward, hissing, "This is not cool. It's horrible in here. You know this place is filled with rapists, right?" He started crying. "I've been here for hours. Where's Loyal?"

She needed a joint, a beer, something to stop her heart from pounding in her throat.

"All I did was use someone else's credit card. Loyal probably stole them. And so what? I bought some gas. All I did was go out for a ride, and they're acting like I killed someone or something."

That weird numbness hit her spine again and she shivered.

Toby stared hard at her. "What is it?"

"You need to be patient. This might take time."

"Don't tell me to be patient. Every time you say that I want to punch something. Tell me what's going on."

She pushed away from the table and braced against the wall. Toby's face was turning red. She couldn't think.

He yanked the chains that locked him to the table and screamed, "Tell me what's happening!"

She faced him square on. The least she could do was look him in the eye. "He's not coming."

He ducked his head low. "Goddamn."

She watched him sorting things out, tried to think of something that would soothe him, came up empty.

In the distance, another door slammed. Jamie jumped, but Toby didn't flinch. When he raised his head, his eyes were dry, the splotches gone from his face. His eyes flitted around the room, then locked on Jamie with a stare that made her cringe.

"Where did you and Loyal go that night?" he asked.

She had no idea how much to reveal and stared at her hands to buy time.

"Hey," he said. "You know more than I do and I'm the one sitting in jail. I got a right to know."

"Keep your voice down." Jamie leaned forward to whisper, "All I know is something happened at Keating's. That guy? The football player? He's missing."

"What? Is that what this is about? He's the guy whose credit card I used?" Toby's mouth fell open. "Fucking hell." He cupped his face with his fingers and pushed at his temples. "That was TJ Bangor?"

"I think it had something to do with that game at Keating's." It was the wrong approach and she wanted to take it back.

"What? Is everyone in this family insane?"

It occurred to her that might be true. That all along he'd been the sane one stuck in a family of nutjobs. Toby was breathing hard again.

"Keep it together, Toby. Don't break now." Her words sounded stupid and hollow.

"What happened?"

"I don't know." She had crossed the line where speculation was starting to blur the facts.

"What do you mean you don't know?"

She didn't know how far to go, how much she could tell him and expect him to keep it together, how much she needed to say to give him hope. "There's more," she said, struggling to think through every angle.

"Don't fuck with me, Jamie. Are they going to pin something on me?"

"It's complicated, Toby."

He slammed his fist on the table. "Jesus Christ. Tell me what you fucking know."

"I can't prove anything yet. Just keep quiet and give me a few days to figure things out."

"A few days? Just tell mc the rest. What else?"

She stared at the wall behind his head. "You know, Mom was at that game."

"So what? Was she—ugh . . ." He rubbed his head. "With Keating?"

"Yeah. It's gross."

"Do you think she loves him?"

"I think she'll do or say anything to stay out of prison." She didn't mean it the way it came out.

"And all this has to do with Bangor going missing? You think she's capable of something that bad?"

"How would I know?" The poison in her tone surprised her.

"But, do you think Keating makes her happy?"

"You're handcuffed and you're wondering if she's happy?" Jamie shook her head. "What does it matter if she's happy?"

"It matters to me. This is so fucked." His eyes unfocused slowly as he lay the side of his head on the table like a schoolboy napping at his desk, whispering softly to himself.

She wanted to say something more, something hopeful, but everything had come out wrong, so she shut up.

Toby raised his head but his eyes were still distant. "You remember that day we went to the river?"

"What day?"

"That day. The preacher was baptizing people."

"You made me wait so you could take a turn." He'd been so stubborn about it and she'd sat there sweating in the sun for an hour.

"That river was cold. I always thought that's what it'd be like to die, you know? Everything just goes cold." He pushed up from the table.

"Toby, don't go there. Don't do that."

But he was already yelling for the guard. The guard opened the door, unlocked the chains, and grabbed Toby's arm. She tried to grab his sleeve, but the guard blocked her hand.

"Give me a little time, Toby," she said, but he didn't turn back. His metal anklets clanged against the concrete floor as he disappeared into the sound of a dozen slamming doors.

CHAPTER

29

Garcia's phone buzzed. Over at the jailhouse entrance the girl, head down and shoulders hunched, stepped out of the darkened doorway into the bright light of the snow-lined street. Just like he'd instructed her, the clerk had texted him when Jamie had finished visiting with her brother.

She glanced toward the middle bay where the truck sat and made a U-turn when she spotted him walking her direction, but the sidewalk was closed off due to a broken pipe the utilities department hadn't yet fixed. When he called her name, she stopped walking and spun around to face him.

"What is it this time?" she asked.

It was exactly the kind of frustration he wanted. He worried about the instinct to go easy on her, knew he should've taken her in for questioning by now. "How's your brother holding up?"

"Looking forward to getting out." She couldn't seem to help but look toward the garage.

"You worried about that?" He pointed at the truck parked in the center bay. In the last hour they'd found a small bit of deer skin and a tiny blood smear on the tailgate latch. Almost everyone in Blind River put meat on the table with deer, but hunting season had ended months ago. It wasn't enough to drum up any charges, but he could still use it to apply pressure in an interview with a boy like Toby.

"Nope. Just want it back."

"That's good. I got something you want, you got something I want. See how it works? I learned a long time ago that nobody talks to a cop unless there's something they want. Think of it like chess. I got your queen and your rook but you still have your knight. You can still make some moves."

"I just want the truck. Doesn't mean I can't get by without it."

"I thought it wasn't yours."

"It's not, but I drive it some." She squared her shoulders and scanned his face, then just as quickly turned away.

He'd seen a question in her eyes and wanted to keep her talking. "It's a matter of time, you know. Facts are starting to surface."

She chewed a thumbnail. In the garage the sound of a saw ripped the air.

He pointed over his shoulder. "You know what's going on over there?" Thinking she was probably getting scared by now, he tried the tone he used with battered women: authentic, official, sliding toward sympathetic.

"Looks like a scene from a movie," she said.

"Yep. We'll tear up that truck to find what we need. And if we come up empty, we'll give it back in a thousand little pieces, let you put it back together."

She wiped at her nose and put her stocking cap on. "Doesn't seem fair."

"A man is missing, Jamie. This isn't a game. Whatever they find on the truck is information that didn't come from you. You don't get points if you don't contribute. And if they find anything that leads them to a body on or in a truck that is connected to your family? Well, you can see the obvious problems there." He watched to see her reaction to the word *body* and saw her cringe a little. He pressed a little harder.

"Folks are wound up about this guy. Football hero goes missing in Blind River? That's not good. This thing isn't going to blow over. Really bad timing considering your uncle's poker tournament. From what I heard, Bangor was going to play in that."

"Well, maybe he'll show up then."

"His family's worried. Can you imagine what that's like? His car's been found, his credit card was used. By your brother. If there's any DNA on that truck, like blood for instance, we'll find it and then the FBI will be all over this town. In cases like this we usually get a confession in about a day."

"You won't find anything because there isn't anything to find. Toby won't confess to something he didn't do."

"Did you ever consider he might actually have had a hand in this? Do you know for sure he didn't? People confess when they get scared. They do it all the time. Break down, bargain for a lesser sentence. Whatever we find, Toby's the one we'll look at first. I'm sure your fingerprints will be in there, too, though. That alone is enough for me to hold you here until they finish up."

She flinched at that. Or he imagined she did. He sensed an opening and leaned his shoulder into hers, making the kind of nonthreatening physical contact that helped break down resistance.

"But listen, I arrest people all the time. And the one thing I've noticed is that once someone's arrested, their life kind of gets off track. I'm actually tired of throwing people in jail, especially if they haven't done anything wrong. Lawyers cost money, public defenders are slow to respond. Jail is no place for a girl like you." He lowered his voice. "I've got some advice for you. Do what you can to stay out of there. I know all about Loyal and his buddies. Keating, the old fart, throwing his weight around, skimming off the top. And your boyfriend, taking money from the hardworking people in this town."

"That's got nothing to do with me."

"We both know that's not true. You get a piece of that, don't you? A roof over your head. A truck. Who's going to come up with bail money for Jamie Elders? Your uncle? I don't think so. Your mom? Maybe, if she could. But you know she's broke."

"I thought you were worried about TJ Bangor."

He pulled out a pack of cigarettes and offered her one but she shook her head.

"Of course I'm thinking about Mr. Bangor, but I hate to see an innocent kid take the rap for something they didn't do. It might be time for you to stop worrying so much about your brother and stand up for yourself. My gut tells me it isn't you, but someone close to you, who is responsible for this thing."

He watched her closely for any sort of reaction, but the girl might've been made of wood. He put the cigarettes back in his pocket, let his words sink in, hoping he'd said enough to unnerve her. The temperature was dropping, the sun slipping toward the tree line.

She squinted at the bright horizon. "I could snoop around if you want, but what's in it for you?"

That was exactly what he wanted to hear. Now he needed to let her figure out her next move. "I get to be good at my job." He flipped the latch on the gate and walked inside. "Get back to me quick, Jamie. Time's running short."

JAMIE TURNED HER collar up and walked with her back to the freezing wind blowing down Main Street. That cop was starting to get to her. Maybe he was on the level. Or maybe he was just good at getting to people, but he knew she was involved and denying it any longer was beginning to feel useless. He was doing that thing counselors do, looking in her eyes, talking low and slow. It was probably all technique and psychological training but it made her feel weirdly safe, like that day she and Angel had smoked some super-chill weed and baked brownies all afternoon.

When she got to the diner, Mike Tuckahoe and old Mrs. Tuckahoe were coming out, rattling the bells on the front door. The woman smiled at her son as though he were still a Little League star with a big future. He stuck close to his mom, glancing once at Jamie. She resisted the familiar urge to kick him in the knee.

The lights went out in the pawnshop and Mack Dyson stepped onto the sidewalk. Jamie paused for a moment before following him into the diner, waited as he stood near the cash register and ordered a coffee to go, then she sat at the far end of the counter. Phoebe saw her, wiped at the bangs that had fallen out of her hair clip, and brought over a bowl of beef stew. Her hands were thin-skinned and veined, chapped from cleaning fluids and hot plates. It was impossible to imagine this frail woman pointing a gun at any breathing creature.

Jamie blew on her soup, picked out a hunk of meat, and set it on a napkin.

"You always were a picky eater," Phoebe said.

Mack poured cream into his coffee and set a dollar and a napkin on the counter.

Phoebe rang up his coffee, swept the napkin into a garbage bin, and said, "Have a good night."

He hesitated.

Phoebe stared a question at him.

He tapped the counter with his finger.

Phoebe said, "Oh," and grabbed the napkin out of the garbage. As she stuffed the napkin into her pocket, Jamie noticed it had been written on. She blew on a spoonful of soup wondering just how close Phoebe and Mack had become and if her mom was making up for lost time by screwing every man in town.

As Jamie ate, her mother bussed the remaining plates, dirty glasses, and cups. Then for a moment the woman stopped moving and stared into space, fingering the string around her neck.

Jamie thought about what Garcia had said. Her brother, the truck being dismantled by the cops, her fucked-up family. Her choices were getting complicated. The diner was emptying out. She asked for the check.

Phoebe waved at the air. "Oh, for God's sake, Jamie. It was just soup."

"Then how about I walk you home?"

"Walk me home? I live two blocks from here."

"I've never seen your place."

Phoebe untied her apron. "Ha. Okay, but there's not much to see." She gathered the tips she'd collected in her apron pocket and laid them on the counter. "Count this for me while I clock out."

Jamie counted the bills, all singles, twenty-four dollars and change. Her mother had been born to wait on others, a one-woman delivery system for blue-plate dinners. Never mind that she could never collect enough three-dollar tips to get ahead or that one week with the flu or a sprained ankle was likely to put her on the street.

Phoebe returned from the kitchen, picked up the cash, and brought it to her nose. She took a deep breath and her face relaxed. "Don't you love the smell of cold hard cash?"

"I guess," Jamie said, remembering how her science teacher had said almost all paper money contained cocaine residue.

They left through the back door and entered the damp alley.

"Wouldn't you feel safer taking the street?" Jamie asked.

Phoebe walked quickly, said nothing.

"Because I would."

"What did you really come for tonight? What do you want?"

Jamie slipped on a patch of black ice and caught herself. Phoebe reached for her arm, but Jamie bristled. "I didn't come for myself."

"What then?"

"Toby."

Phoebe slowed her pace, glanced sideways at Jamie. "I thought Loyal took care of that."

"He did."

"So, what do you need me for?"

Jamie reached out to touch Phoebe's arm, to stop her so they could talk, but she couldn't remember the last time she'd touched her mother and pulled back her hand. "Could we stop walking for a minute?"

Phoebe spun around. Overhead, sleet fell like tinsel in the alley lights.

"He got caught using stolen credit cards."

"What? For God's sake." Phoebe lifted her face to the sky. "What the hell? Where did he get them?"

"Probably found them in Loyal's room."

A rat scampered out from behind a dumpster and Jamie moved closer to her mother.

Phoebe stamped her foot. "They don't come at you unless they're rabid." The thing disappeared and she started walking again. "I guess it runs in the family."

Jamie followed behind. *That and a persistent disregard for the law.* But she needed to get to the point. "Loyal won't post bail for him again."

"Let me guess. The first bail money was forfeited with the second arrest, right?"

Jamie hung back. "Mom," she said, trying out a word she hadn't spoken for the last eight years. She was surprised at how easily it rolled out of her mouth—and just how lonely she felt saying it.

Phoebe stopped walking again and raised her head. "What?"

"They were TJ Bangor's cards."

Phoebe shook her head. Sleet wet her eyelashes. A bone-thin cat crossed the street where the alley ended. Something small and dark twisted in its mouth. The sleet was thickening and turning to snow.

"Put your cap on, Jamie," Phoebe said, and turned down the alley. "God, it's cold."

Iced-over metal steps led to her apartment on the second floor. At the top of the landing, Phoebe unlocked the door and flipped the switch for the overhead bulb. They stepped inside. There wasn't a kitchen, just a cabinet with a sink and a hot plate, cracked plaster walls, a linoleum floor, a couch with a blanket and a pillow. Remnants of breakfast sat on the coffee table.

A suitcase, filled with thrift store clothes, lay open on the floor. Phoebe pushed it with her foot and sat on the edge of the couch, squeezing the back of her neck.

Jamie said, "We could go to the jail and see him in the morning. Get him a lawyer. He's going to need a lawyer."

Phoebe bent her head forward, stretching it from side to side. "Public defender. They've probably already assigned him one."

"He deserves better than that."

"Deserves? What's that ever had to do with anything? Besides, there's no money for that. A public defender will have to do."

"What about that?" She nodded at the string around her mother's neck. It seemed an obvious solution.

Phoebe fingered it. "That would be ironic, wouldn't it?"

"No one else is going to help him."

Phoebe pulled the ring from beneath her blouse and studied it. "If I get caught fencing this, it all comes down on me."

Jamie took a breath and said, "It looks to me like it's all coming down on Toby."

Phoebe took the clip out of her hair and shook her bangs loose. "Is that what it looks like to you? Because to me it looks like an ex-con with stolen property who was present during the commission of all kinds of felonies. That adds up to parole violations and one very convenient scape-goat." Her voice got tighter with each word. "It looks like the rest of my life behind bars." She rubbed her eyes, her fingers digging into her temples.

How many times had Toby made that same gesture? Jamie remembered him sitting at the kitchen table just before he'd given up on algebra, rubbing his forehead that same way. She went to the window, opened it, and stuck her head outside, hoping the cold air would clear her mind. "You could go see him."

Phoebe slumped against the couch. "No, I can't. I can't go there. You can't ask that of me. You have to understand that."

"If none of you speak up, they'll pin this on him. You know that, right?"

"What do you want me to do? He's just like his father. He used stolen credit cards, Jamie. I mean, it *is* against the law."

Jamie brought her head back inside and sat on the window ledge. "Loyal's given up on him."

"He's just letting him cool off. They'll get him for the credit cards but there's just not enough evidence for anything else."

"Do you really believe Keating can't frame him for this?"

"I really believe you and I are no match for that man."

"So, what are you going to do?"

Phoebe pulled Mack's note from her pocket, read it silently, and put it back in her pocket. "You could come with me. There'll be enough for the two of us. Mack found a buyer. A guy on the Jersey coast."

"How much?"

"Plenty."

Toby was sitting in a jail cell right now enduring what his mother could not face. "And leave Toby?"

"He's going to do some time, despite your good intentions. He used a stolen credit card. There's no way around it." Phoebe folded a blouse and tossed it in the suitcase.

What she was really saying was that they shouldn't both go down for it.

"Don't you want a new start, Jamie? We could get a little apartment near the water, have a real kitchen. You could have your own room. We could sew some curtains.

Something yellow. Someplace sunny. This is a real chance. Jamie, think about it."

"There's nothing to think about. I can't just leave him in there." She stepped over the suitcase on her way to the door.

"Your father," Phoebe said, stopping Jamie when she was halfway across the room. "He had good intentions, too."

"My father? You mean the guy who died in a barroom fight?" She grabbed the doorknob, her skin whitening over her knuckles. "Why would you bring him up? I barely remember the man."

"He died trying to protect his little brother, but it wasn't exactly a fight. It was stupid. He and Loyal weren't even that close and the fight hadn't even started. A couple of them went outside to settle things and your father tripped on the curb, fell and hit his head. Died on the sidewalk before the ambulance even got there. He was a handsome man. You favor him. You'd remember him if you tried."

She remembered more than she wanted. Jamie and Toby had walked into the funeral home and seen the coffin but Toby had stayed at the back. Jamie had walked right up to it. The wood was shiny and glossy. Someone had put a small step stool by its side. She realized years later that it had been meant as a place to kneel and pray, but on that day she'd stepped on it and hoisted herself up to see inside the coffin, to see her father's face. Up until that point she'd never seen death up close, not a dead bird, not even roadkill. Her father's face appeared to be smiling or maybe grimacing, but he was dead and it was impossible that he could smile at a time like this, at this departure that she realized was completely irreversible, and at that moment, at ten years of age, she had decided that death was a permanent state of pain. She'd lowered herself off the stool, turned to see her mother sobbing in the first row, and Loyal, with his vacant face, sitting on the opposite side and swaying slightly, the smell of whiskey hovering in the air around him. Toby had stayed at the back, his face as white as his button-down shirt, his hands clenching and unclenching, breathing through his slightly parted lips. She'd walked up the aisle, grabbed his wrist, and taken him out of there.

Her mother's voice seemed an echo from the future. "He would've been proud of you. He would've wanted you to leave Blind River."

After the funeral, she and Toby had hidden in the back seat of the car until suppertime and only come into the house after everyone had gone home. But there'd been no need to hide. No one had come looking for them. Loyal was drunk and snoring on the couch. Their mother was being tended to by a neighbor who, when she saw them in the kitchen, made them each a plate of food, clumps of unrecognizable brown casseroles. Toby had swallowed mouthfuls, belched, and finished Jamie's plate.

But it seemed to Jamie like she'd fallen off the earth. Her father's voice, his face, his good-night hug. Everything that had meant anything was gone. Grief was like air, everywhere and invisible, unavoidable, filling every breath she took.

Remembering only left her gutted.

She watched her mother on all fours reaching for something under the couch. Jamie asked her, "Did you even notice that we weren't at the funeral that day?"

"What?" Phoebe threw a pair of sneakers into the suitcase. "At the funeral? I hardly remember a thing from that day but I would've sworn you were there, both of you."

"We were, for a few minutes." Jamie watched her mother fold another blouse.

Snow was blowing sideways, sticking in inches, despite gravity, to the metal staircase, the side of the power pole. A few snowflakes blew in through the open window, across the room, settled on the arm of the couch, and started melting. The draft made Jamie shiver.

Phoebe said, "Close that window."

"I like the cold." But she went to the window and closed it. "When are you leaving?"

"Loyal asked me to deal at that tournament tomorrow and I need to get him off my back. Acts like I owe him my life. I leave after that." She found a clean sweatshirt and pulled her work blouse off. A tattoo was on her shoulder blade. Prison quality.

"You got a tattoo?"

Phoebe glanced at it in the mirror. "Stupid, is what I got. Another six months when they found the needle hidden inside my mattress."

Jamie looked closer. The queen of spades. "You should get it touched up."

"Supposed to be the card of wisdom. Huh. Whatever."

"You always said, 'Follow your heart—'"

" '—but bet your spades.' You remember that?"

"Toby says it all the time."

Phoebe froze and for a moment Jamie thought she'd finally gotten through to her. Then she picked up the necklace Toby had shown her that day on the sidewalk, still in its box, and handed it to Jamie. "You should find the receipt and return it. I'm pretty sure he paid cash."

Jamie took the box, wishing it would bring enough to retain a lawyer but knowing it wouldn't. "Mom. I was there. I saw you in that upstairs window."

Phoebe didn't react. She picked up and folded a towel. "The less you know about that night, the better."

"I saw him."

"What did you see? A tarp wrapped around something big. A shadow in a window. That's all you saw."

"I saw his face."

Phoebe held the towel to her chest, looked at Jamie. "What are you talking about?"

"The tarp fell off when we pulled him out of the truck. I saw his face." She braced herself in the doorway, waited for her mother to say something, childishly hoping she could make it better.

Phoebe tossed the towel on top of the clothes and turned back to packing. "What can I tell you, Jamie? The best thing is to wipe that out of your mind." She closed the suitcase lid.

31

A BLAST OF wind followed Jamie inside the trailer. It rustled the papers spread out on the kitchen table where Loyal was adding up columns in his ledger and working to empty a quart of Jack Daniels. He said, "God-damn," and she hurried to shut the door.

He picked up a postcard that had blown on the floor, folded it in half, and stuck it in his shirt pocket. The map he liked to look at sometimes—creased to show the eastern coast—sat next to the ledger.

"Get another postcard from Mr. Bobby?"

"Not your business." He folded the map and stuck it in the back of the ledger.

She turned away to hide her smile. Over the years that guy had probably sent a hundred postcards and Jamie had read them all. They had their own language, nicknames, a bunch of code words that hinted at their old days together. Inside the fridge she found bologna and a tub of mac 'n' cheese, made a roll-up with it, and ate it over the sink. "Why don't you have friends that live in town?"

"I got plenty of friends."

"No, you don't. You got the judge, the guy in Key West, and that lady friend." She rarely mentioned the woman from the Piggly Wiggly, but she and Toby always joked about how Loyal had been screwing her in the back seat of his truck for God knows how many years. She didn't understand this man and it nagged at her. How had her life come to such shit in just nineteen years? She had gained nothing by keeping quiet.

He stared at the ledger, wrote down some numbers.

"I'm just saying. You've lived in this town your whole life. I got more friends than you."

He looked up from the ledger. "Maybe I been busy. You ever think of that? Huh? Maybe I been raising two kids weren't my own. Maybe I been working real hard for ten years to keep the two of you out of foster care."

Foster care. Whenever Jamie heard those words she remembered the couple that had wanted them, but when she tried to conjure their image all she saw was a green lawn, a white picket fence, and the vague shape of two adults. "What's so bad about foster care?"

"What's so bad about it? Kids get fucked in foster care. Literally. Don't you know that? They get separated, farmed out for labor, not fed right."

"What are you talking about? That shit doesn't happen anymore."

"The hell it doesn't."

"But there were people who wanted to adopt us."

He pointed at her. "You, Goddamnit, were raised by family. Not strangers! Do you know how much I gave up to stay here and keep the two of you? No, you don't. You have no idea."

"Staying here? You grew up here. Your life was here way before me and Toby."

"I was moving down to Key West. Had it all planned out. Instead your mother goes to jail and leaves the two of you to me. Drug-stealing bitch. And whatever you think you know you can be sure you're wrong. You know nothing about the whole thing."

"I know you got a lot of stupid pride. Probably why you run so low on friends."

This seemed to hurt him and she felt a little good about that. He rubbed his eyes like his vision was blurring, like he did when he'd had too much whiskey. It could go either way now; she'd get another backhand or he'd stumble to his bedroom and sleep it off. Not for the first time she imagined ducking the slap, catching him off balance, and her coming around with a blow to the back of his head. He started to stand and she flinched, but then he leaned back in his chair and shook his head.

"Keating is not my friend. I paid him a great deal of money to keep the two of you out of the system. A great deal. And I never took a dime of that welfare."

"What? We sleep on camping cots in a storage room!" He was deluded, telling himself he'd done a good job, being so damn proud. "We could've used some welfare."

"You had enough and you were raised by family." He pointed at her. "And you know where you came from."

She should've run when she'd had the chance. What was the good of knowing where you came from if you came from shit? Not knowing had to be better. "Yeah. I know where I come from. My father's dead and my mother's a thief." *And my uncle's a con man.*

"Welcome to the real world. It's about time you grew up."

He offered her the bottle of whiskey and she drank from it.

"Did you see Toby?" he asked.

"Yeah. I saw him."

"How'd he take it?"

"What the hell do you care?"

He stared at the bottle for a moment. "Huh. Maybe I don't. What I do care about is tomorrow. Make sure you get some sleep, be sharp for the game."

He started to stand but a car turned into the driveway out front, its lights shining briefly on the wall behind him. The lights went off and a woman stepped out of the car and into the porch light.

"Goddamn." Jamie said, "What's Jilkins want?"

The only reason the woman would show up unannounced at this hour was if Toby was in trouble. Opening the front door, Jamie had the urge to flee down the street. Instead she met Jilkins's eyes and asked, "What happened?"

"Toby's been moved to medical detention." Jilkins climbed the last step and stomped the sludge off her shoes.

"Why, was there a fight?" The bologna turned inside Jamie's stomach.

Jilkins came inside. "No. It wasn't like that. No one thought he was a danger to himself, so the guards left him alone. I'm sorry to have to put it so bluntly, but he tried to hang himself."

Jamie's mind flashed with a vision of her brother dangling from metal bars, loose-limbed and dead. She braced herself against the wall. "Is he dead?"

"No. He's not dead, but he's hurt."

Loyal sat at the kitchen table, mute and seemingly unfazed. Jamie knew by the look in his eye that he wasn't just done with Toby—he was done with both of them. He pushed himself to his feet and thudded down the hallway to his room.

Ms. Jilkins led Jamie to the couch and got her a glass of water. It was a small act but the woman's kindness was almost too much to handle. She swallowed some water, felt the sting of tears. The burnt hole on the couch, the one Toby had picked at until it had grown to the size of a fist, was right there at her fingertips. She picked up a loose thread, felt the room begin to fall away, heard a warm buzz in her ear and realized Jilkins was talking.

"I see it all the time. Kids like Toby are like a tidal wave that just rolls over you. Parents think they're creating something better than themselves, something beautiful and wondrous, but it isn't like that. Kids are their own form of grief—if they don't pull you under, they show you what you're made of."

In his bedroom, Loyal dropped his boots, one after the other, on the floor. She heard the clunk of the lid of his lockbox drop to the floor. He'd be snoring soon and Jamie hated him even more for that.

"How? What did he use?" Jamie asked.

Jilkins sank into the couch. The movement rippled Jamie's brain and the room spun. She looked at the woman's face, needing the steady sound of her voice, but lamplight fell across her face, making it look like a skull.

"I don't—" Jilkins halted. "I don't have all the details."

What did it matter anyway? Shoestrings, sheets, his ripped-up T-shirt—there were only so many possibilities. "How bad is he?"

"His windpipe is crushed. It isn't good, but he'll recover."

Her thoughts spun out as if she had no control over them. Toby in that jail cell, his face red, his eyes distant and vacant. Why hadn't she just taken his hand? "Can I see him?"

Jilkins seemed so far away, but when Jamie tried, she was able to focus on the shadows falling on her face, the familiar sound of her voice.

"No. He's an injured minor in custody. I'm sorry, but the only people the police will allow in will be a parent or a guardian." The woman exhaled. She seemed deflated. Her lips trembled slightly, and Jamie wondered how much of this she felt. She'd known them going on eight years.

"He's heavily sedated, anyway, and on a breathing machine. And he's going to need months of rehab." Jilkins looked at the ceiling. "I always worried something like this might happen. Don't get me wrong. Toby is a beautiful kid, but he was always in motion, never at peace, and the cards were always stacked against him."

Were they? No, not always, but it would seem that way to Ms. Jilkins, someone who had only seen the hard years.

"I wanted better for you two," Ms. Jilkins said. "But all I could do was keep an eye on you. I never understood why the judge decided to leave you here when there was that family waiting for a boy and girl." She glanced darkly down the hallway. "I mean, look at this place. Your uncle was clearly unprepared to raise children. Even with all that government assistance. It seems like that money would have gone further than this."

Jamie had never thought of Jilkins as having kept an eye on them. She only seemed to come around to cause problems, but now Jamie wondered if she'd had it wrong. Maybe Jilkins had come around only when problems came up. Jamie had never told Toby about the couple who had wanted them. Foster care might've made the difference. Maybe he wouldn't have been such a bully if they'd gone to live with a real family. Maybe they would've gotten adopted, gotten a different name, grown up without the Elders curse.

"I mean, why didn't he go all the way and grant Loyal custody?" Ms. Jilkins continued. "Why keep Family Services involved?"

"Loyal would never have accepted a dime of welfare."

"It wasn't welfare. It was Social Security benefits for your father's dependents. Once your mother went to, uh . . .

away, your uncle got those payments. I filed the forms for you and Toby myself. That's why I wanted you to get in college right away. Those benefits run out at twenty-one if you aren't in school."

Jamie stared at her hands as the pieces slid together in her brain. *I paid him a great deal of money to keep the two of you out of the system.* Their benefits had been funneled straight to Keating's reelection campaigns while she'd lived most of her life feeling like a burden, like a criminal for needing Pop-Tarts and pencils. Loyal was deluded saying it was family duty and pride. It wasn't. He protected his gambling operations by bribing the judge and Keating kept Family Services involved to keep Loyal in line. To keep the donations coming in. She thought the word out loud. "Donations."

Ms. Jilkins looked at Jamie blankly. "What donations?"

"Never mind." Jamie looked around the trailer at the broken windows, the ruined couch. She'd been a fool. He'd been so enraged when he found out she'd flunked that first semester and now she understood why. The benefits. Pride had nothing to do with it.

"You poor kids." Ms. Jilkins picked up a framed photo of Toby off the coffee table, his high school portrait, and ran her fingers over his face. "None of this would've happened if your mother hadn't taken that prescription."

Jamie was tired of hearing how her mother was a thief. She took the photo from Jilkins and wiped the glass with her sleeve. Another smaller photo sat in front of the portrait. Toby and Jamie about the time of their dad's funeral,

her arm draped over his shoulders, his eyes shut, wearing
a goofy smile.

She'd never meant to leave him on his own but she had.
All those nights she'd spent with Jack, ignoring Toby, thinking he was finally big enough to take care of himself. Without knowing when she'd done it, she had taken on the
responsibility to see him grow up. But Jack had come along
and she'd gotten distracted. She tried to remember her last
conversation with Toby. Was she the last person to have
talked to him or seen him? Why hadn't she been kinder?

Jilkins pulled a tissue out of her pocket, blew her nose.
"He must have been desperate to rob that man."

The words banged inside Jamie's head. "He didn't rob
anyone."

"The police think he did."

"And you believe them?"

"Why else would he try to take his own life, Jamie?
People get hurt in robberies. For all we know, that man is
dead."

"It didn't happen that way."

Goddamn. Had Toby confessed? He'd been so worried about Phoebe's happiness after Jamie told him about
Keating. It had been stupid to implicate Phoebe while
Toby was locked up. He might have tried to take the rap
for this thing just to close down the investigation. But Jamie
couldn't tell Jilkins any of that.

"The man's been missing for days." Jilkins rubbed the
back of her head and sighed. "But, of course, you know
your brother best."

Ms. Jilkins yawned and Jamie saw the dark circles beneath her eyes. "It's late. You should go."

"Will you be okay? I hate to leave you like this."

"I'll be fine," she said. "Really. I'll call if I need anything."

"Try and get some sleep." Ms. Jilkins picked up her keys and purse. At the door, she said, "I'm just a phone call away."

The lights of her car flicked over the walls as she backed out of the driveway. Jamie sat for a while staring at the hole in the couch, the dismal walls, her brother's picture.

She couldn't settle. She walked to the front door and then back to the kitchen, where she poured some water over the dried-up potted ivy on the windowsill. Every noise spooked her: the fridge compressor kicking on, a squirrel scuttling across the roof, a pinecone falling on the front porch. This place could never be her home again. She texted Jack hoping he was still at the store, turned on the TV to drown out the silence.

In the back room she saw that Toby had left in a rage. The window over his cot had been kicked out. Shards of glass were on the floor and his pillowcase. A draft blew in through the opening.

Diesel engines idled in the street outside. Yellow utility truck lights pulsed against the night. The neighborhood dogs barked in their kennels. A worker climbed into a cherry picker as three men watched, their faces lit by intermittent lights, their hard hats casting long shadows on the road. The generator kicked on as the truck lifted a worker up to repair the streetlight.

Toby's muddy sneakers, laces broken, stuck out from under the bed where she made him keep them because they stank. His clothes were where he'd left them—thrown on the floor, slung over the metal footboard, half jammed under his pillow. His science book was sticking out from under his cot, gathering dust. His Game Boy sat on the dresser, grimed with Doritos cheese muck. She ripped the Army poster off the wall and tore it in half. She untied the length of rope he used to practice knots and stuffed it under his bed.

Inside the dresser, she found the wallet she'd given him for Christmas, the one he didn't use because he loved the one Phoebe had given him for his eighth birthday. He used the new one to save things in, the one letter his mother had written from prison, pictures he loved. Jamie knew them all by heart: Toby on his first day of school, his skinny arms wrapped around a gigantic book bag, refusing to smile for the camera; the pocket-sized version of his seventh-grade portrait. He looked just like their uncle with his hair slicked and combed back, though Jamie would never mention that to his face. A snapshot of him blowing out birthday candles at the kitchen table, Phoebe sitting next to him smoking a cigarette. Probably the last cake she ever baked.

A square of plastic fell out of the wallet. A condom, the kind the science teachers handed out on AIDS awareness days. She almost wanted to cry, wondering if he'd ever had the chance to use one, if he would have even bothered, or if he just liked the possibilities that came with keeping one in his wallet.

The last photo was of her and Toby. He was laughing maniacally while her mouth gaped and she looked wildly at the space above the camera. Phoebe had taken the picture just after he'd poured ice water down the back of Jamie's shirt. She'd hated him in that moment, hated Phoebe, too, because it had been her idea. It was always like that with the two of them.

The Elders clan time bomb ticked in his DNA, and Phoebe had done nothing to keep him safe. Always in on it, always encouraging his pranks. Like she didn't know all that would lead a boy like Toby straight to juvie or the ICU.

On the TV in the outer room, Lena Bangor was on the local news. The newscaster said charges were pending against a juvenile suspect, already in custody. Lena held up a photograph of her father, announcing a reward for information leading to his whereabouts.

How basic was it, this need to bury the dead?

She picked up Loyal's empty whiskey bottle and started to throw it in the garbage, then set it back on the table. If she didn't get out of here now, her future was more of this, more of this place, more cleaning up after him. She sat in his chair at the kitchen table, opened the ledger. On the front pages he'd written the locations of every coin pusher, slot machine, and fake lottery ticket dispenser. Thirty-seven locations.

There was another set of numbers in the back. A column with her name and one with Toby's along with monthly deposits into a checking account. Over one hundred entries. Enough money to have hired a team of lawyers for Toby.

A bank statement sat on top of the stack of mail she'd brought in. She opened it, read the balance. Twenty cents. There were only two transactions. The day after the state's deposit had come there was a corresponding withdrawal. The bastard had given every cent of it to Keating and, according to what Jilkins had told her, he'd been giving Keating that money every month for eight years. All that money, while she and Toby had nothing.

She went into Loyal's room. He was passed out face-down, one arm dangling off the side of the bed, the latest postcard from Bobby showing under his pillow. The street-light blinked on and lit the room in a yellow haze. His pack of cigarettes and an overflowing ashtray sat near where his hand rested on the floor. He'd tossed his belt on a chair.

His shotgun stood in the corner next to a box of shells. She kicked over the box and the shells scattered across the floor. He didn't budge. She picked up one, loaded the shotgun, and felt the weight of it in her hands. A sweat broke out on the back of her neck. His sleeping head fit neatly in the shotgun's sights. Jamie stood there panting.

This was exactly what the world expected from her, the Elders girl gone bad. She wavered. A plan began taking shape. A new idea. She decided on it. Lowered the gun. He snored and mumbled something in his sleep.

She laid the gun down on the bed next to him where he would wake up next to it in the morning. In the outer room, she found Keating's cell phone in the bottom of her backpack, did what she needed to do, and packed up.

CHAPTER

32

A FIRE TRUCK idled loudly in the emergency drive out-side the hospital where Toby and Jamie had been born. From the sidewalk, she looked up at the darkened windows wondering which room he was in and if he would be able to see the sky when he opened his eyes. She hoped he was warm. The memory of their last conversation haunted her; his slumped shoulders and the defeat in his eyes when she'd carried on about Phoebe.

She crossed to the sidewalk beside the courthouse. Keating's Cadillac was parked in a reserved space and she fought the urge to key it because security cameras were bolted every fifty feet on the buildings and utility poles. Men like Keating ran this town by keeping an eye on people like her. But if Toby knew what she knew now, he wouldn't have cared about those cameras. He'd have keyed the entire car and slit the tires. He was fearless that way.

Jack finally texted back saying he would wait for her at the store.

She walked down Main under streetlights turned hazy by an evening fog. Her nose started to run again. What she really needed was to curl up under a blanket on the futon. But when she turned the corner, she stopped short. *Shit.* Billy's truck was outside Jack's store. She went inside anyway. The store smelled like cinnamon from the can of room deodorizer he used whenever he smoked pot.

Jack came out of the back room with bloodshot eyes.

"What's Billy doing here?" she asked.

"He's got some good shit. Come to the back and try it."

She wanted to be alone with him, to slide up next to him and thaw. Now she'd have to wait until Billy left.

He took her hand and led her into the office. "Want one?" he asked, popping a beer.

Billy sat on the futon happily sucking on a pipe. He offered it to her.

She waved off the pipe but took the beer. Billy Wages hadn't smiled at her since his wedding day and she wondered if he'd scored some of the medicinal "happy weed" he always bragged about. He blew smoke at the ceiling.

Jack took the pipe from him and slid into the chair behind the desk. "What's up, Jamie?"

She hated the cool tone he used when other people were around. Like Billy didn't know they were sleeping together. *What's up?* It was hard to know where to begin. It would take an hour to catch them up on everything that had happened and another hour to repeat it once the pot wore off. The light from the laptop lit Jack's face. He glanced at Billy, who smiled at Jamie again. It had to be the weed. Their mood was not right for this kind of news and it made her feel weird when she blurted out, "It's Toby."

Jack closed the laptop and took a deep draw on the
pipe. He tried to hold it in and coughed. "Of course it is.
It's always Toby."

"Dude's cray." Billy's eyes were bright and watery.

"Yeah, and you aren't? The guy who knocked up his
girlfriend at the prom, then had to get a job at a fertilizer
plant working the graveyard shift and selling pot on the
side to pay for the kid?"

"Fuck off," Billy said, laughing because it was true.

Someone came in the front door and rang the service
bell.

"No fighting, you two," Jack said, and went out front.

Jamie slid behind the desk, silently willing Billy to
leave, hoping Jack would let her spend the night in the
office even if he couldn't stay. Light from the small window
lit Billy's face with an eerie green glow. The bottle of sleeping pills Jack sometimes gave her was next to the laptop.
Once she took one, though, she'd be out. Billy was still
smiling at her even though she'd just insulted him.

"The fuck is it with you?" she asked.

He reached over, his hand passing too close to her
breast, and opened the laptop. The screen came to life and
he hit the play button. "You're *the fuck* it is," he said. He
dropped back onto the futon and stretched, crossing his
arms behind his head.

The image didn't make sense. Not at first anyway.
Something about the scene was familiar but strange. The
guy in the video was getting blown. Billy and Jack had
been watching porn, like they always did when they hung
out. A creepy habit, but that was what dudes did, watch
porn and smoke dope.

The picture was blurry. Then the guy smiled at the camera, and Jamie recognized Jack. He held the girl by the back of the head, then pushed her off him and yanked off her jeans. For a moment Jamie didn't recognize herself. This had to be some other girl.

But in the video she saw Jack's desk, an open bottle of wine, the futon, and a girl flat on her back. Jack was biting her nipples, stopping once more to turn and smile at the camera. Then he slid down her body, his face between her legs.

"You are the bomb," Billy laughed, holding his crotch, and that's when Jamie knew for sure. She stared at the screen unable to move, her heart stomping in her chest, white heat exploding in her throat.

She didn't remember any of it but she recognized herself, moaning, flailing, orgasmic. He'd given her a pill two nights ago and she'd been sore the whole next day. She grabbed the laptop and threw it at the wall. The lid busted halfway off and the screen went dead. She picked it up again and threw it at Billy. He'd seen her at her most vulnerable and he couldn't stop laughing. He blocked it with his knee and kept laughing.

Nothing in her life had prepared her for this much rage. She felt the room sway and the edges of her vision blur. She grabbed the bottle of pills, dumped them into her hand. Billy laughed as he followed her to the front room.

"What's the problem?" Jack was counting out bills to an old woman. Her eyes widened behind her glasses. She grabbed her cash and stuffed it in her purse.

"Hold on," Jack said.

"How could you?"

He held his hand up. "It isn't what you think."

"Fuck you," she screamed.

She fought to breathe. Her brain leaped wildly from shame to fury and back to shame.

Billy leaned against the doorjamb, giggling.

The woman clutched her purse to her chest. "Ooh, she mad," she said, and turned to Jack. "Boy, what you gone done?"

Jamie leaped at Jack.

"What are you doing?" He grabbed her, but rage made her stronger than she'd ever been.

She jammed the pills into his mouth, but he clamped his mouth shut, grabbed her wrist, and squeezed. Most of the pills fell on the floor. Then his hand was in her face.

He spit out the ones that had slipped through, swore at her.

The woman backed away. "Girl, you make him pay."

"You're a fucking asshole." She tried to shout, but there was no air in her lungs and it came out as a whisper. "Did you put this online?"

"What? No!"

Billy was bent over and laughing, trying to catch his breath. Jamie lunged at him and landed an elbow on his chin. He smacked the counter on his way down and landed at the woman's feet.

Jamie grabbed the keys to Jack's car from under the counter, said, "Goddamn you," and kicked open the front door.

*F*UCK HIM. THE words looped maniacally in her brain. *Fuck them all.*

Her mind replayed the image of herself in the video—on her knees, on her back, naked and writhing—and Billy laughing in her face, laughing so hard he couldn't breathe, and she felt filthy. Her face burned as though on fire. Rage liquefied her muscles, made her want to hit things, brought forth involuntary tears, buzzed inside her ears. It would take a lake, a river, an ocean of water to ever feel clean again. Fury funneled into a kind of lucidity that she recognized as fate, as though the next twenty-four hours were already history.

It was clear what she needed to do, where she had to go. She aimed Jack's car north and gunned it up Main Street.

Betrayal wasn't a state of mind where her brain could rest. It wasn't static like death or defeat and already its alchemy began to change her. Already, she felt the heat inside her chest cooling into something new, something wary and wild. Something that could stand flat-footed in the middle of a burning house and calculate the next move.

She passed the courthouse and the jail, Keating's Cadillac and Garcia's crappy sedan, the hospital. The streetlights ended at the edge of town. She gunned it on the highway. She rolled down the windows. Cold air was life and she breathed it in, screamed it out, "Fuck you all!" If she survived the next day she'd get those words tattooed on her arm.

The first billboard for Mimawa lit her windshield with a yellow glow and she passed it going eighty. The next billboard was a neon rainbow and she eased up on the gas. The last one was a pot of gold and she let the car slow. She cruised past the exit and took the underpass where the road narrowed and turned to gravel.

The shoulder dropped off to the right, but she remembered how her weight had shifted to the left that night on the floorboard of Loyal's truck. She found a flashlight in the console and shined it out the window as she drove slowly, hoping to see a bend in the road, a crook in a tree, something to trigger the memory of this place. The pavement ended and turned into a dirt road. She remembered potholes and weeds slapping at the fenders. The county didn't maintain roads this far outside of town, or on private land.

A black silhouette stepped onto the road and Jamie braked. Her heart banged in her throat. Anyone could be out here. A hunter, a lunatic, an escapee from the penitentiary one county over.

A massive head swiveled on a giant gray torso. A stag stared unblinking into the headlights. Her throat turned to ice. Insanely she thought of the stag from all those years ago, but it couldn't be the same one. They'd eaten venison that whole summer. And this one was even bigger than the one she'd killed.

He was unfazed by the headlights, his gaze coming straight at her through the windshield. He lifted his head, sniffed the air, and blew a moist spray out his nose.

She cut the engine. The animal ignored her and continued across the road.

Jamie turned off the lights to let her eyes adjust to the dark. A half-moon sat over the field, its light shining along the length of the stag's back as he walked through the grass and disappeared at the edge of the woods.

Farther up was a broken gate, rusted and off its hinges. Old fence posts sagged under ancient wisteria vines. A washed-out path dropped left where a single pine tree stood in the center of the field. She got her backpack and walked.

The sky was black and silky, the ground soft beneath her boots. An owl called out and she froze as though caught in a childhood nightmare. The way she pitched between fear and anger was exhausting. Nothing worse could happen. Nothing more could be lost. She could be afraid for the rest of her life, but now, she knew, fear had never kept her safe. It was time to get some damn courage. Whatever happened tomorrow, this night belonged to her.

The pine glowed silver in the moonlight. Ladder rungs were nailed to its trunk, one slat every few feet. The floor of what looked like a tree house hovered midway up the tree. She recalled her thirteenth birthday, more than five years ago. The contour of the branches extending from the trunk, the low walls surrounding the hidden platform— nothing had changed. This wasn't a tree house. This was the old hunter's blind.

She tested her weight on the first rung. It held and she climbed another. There were seven in all. The floor of the blind was a grid of two-by-fours covered by plywood with a hole cut in the bottom for access. She banged the flashlight against the floorboards to flush out any animal that might have nested there. Claws scratched against the floor and she ducked, raising her arm protectively against a rustle of wings. A large bird leapt up and flew from the tree, gliding out over the field.

Holding the flashlight up, she looked into the opening. A short wall surrounded the blind, tall enough that when she climbed through and sat down she could see out over the top. The floor was covered with pine needles and twigs, the remnants of a nest. She shined the flashlight into the overhead branches, checked the floors for bugs and the corners for snakes. She cleared a space and leaned against a wall that was the exact height needed to steady a rifle.

Her phone startled her when it blinged and lit up with a text from Jack demanding to know where she was and that she bring his car back. She turned the phone off. Even if she could tell him where she was, she wouldn't. Somewhere in a field outside of town where no one would ever find her. The realization calmed her: no one knew where she was.

All around her, the typical graffiti was carved into the walls. Initials scratched with penknives, some set inside the shape of a heart. She imagined lovers coming up here. Jack might have taken her someplace like this if he hadn't had that futon in his office. If only he hadn't had that office. When she closed her eyes, the images from the sex tape played in her mind, a torture that would last a lifetime. She opened her eyes and stared at the tree trying not to see what had been burned into her memory.

She searched the walls closely. On the opposite wall she found a *T*, the one Toby had scratched that cold morning when Loyal had dragged them out of their beds to hunt. In the blind, they'd been bored, cold, but alert. Toby had taken Loyal's field knife to scratch his name and gotten as far as the *T* before the stag appeared and all hell broke loose.

As she traced the letter with her fingertip, she felt a grief for the emptiness of Toby's small life as sharply as the grief she felt for her father. Toby wasn't even full-grown and he'd already been arrested. Twice. Toby's initial, a simple mark on a tree, might be all the boy ever left behind.

She dug through her backpack for a Sharpie and used it to ink the *T* with a vine that curled and blossomed with ivy leaves. Nothing would be the same after tonight. It was clear what her life would be if she stayed in Blind River and let Loyal boss her around. Maybe she'd end up slightly better-off than her mother. Maybe she'd manage to stay out of prison. The future was set unless she found her own way, unless she got out of here. When she was done with his initial, it filled an area as big as a tombstone, and she was calmer.

She wanted to say a prayer for her brother, but all she could think of was "Our Father" and she didn't know the rest, so she stared at the moon and thought through what she'd do in the morning. She used her backpack as a pillow and lay down for the night, doubting sleep would come, but taking comfort in solitude and the empty field glowing silver under the moon.

34

JAMIE SHIVERED AWAKE when light began to brighten the eastern sky. She rubbed her hands and cheeks, turned to watch the sun lift beyond the tree line, surprised at how hard she'd slept under nothing but pine canopy and sky. She scanned the area. The car sat on the dirt road where she'd left it, near the broken gate. A ravine dropped off a hundred yards to the east.

Sunlight spread over the field and she shielded her eyes from the reflection off the barn's tin roof. She climbed down from the blind and walked in the direction of the sun. The slope of the ravine was steeper than she remembered, the funeral mound smaller than it had seemed that night. The air smelled sour. She pulled the brush and the tree limbs away until the stones were exposed. They were so purposefully placed it could never have been confused with a rock slide. It was wrong to be here, standing over this man's body when his family didn't even know he was dead.

She looked around until she was sure she had her bearings, then headed back to the car to let the engine run and get warm. She turned on her phone. The first of fifteen messages from Jack demanded that she return his car. She wanted to set it on fire. She skipped to the last one offering an apology and deleted the ones in between. In a few minutes the car was warm and her body began to thaw. It had to be eight o'clock. By now, folks would be heading to the veterans' hall for the tournament. Loyal would be there setting up chairs and tables, putting the coffee on, setting out bags of pretzels.

She backed the car through the weeds to the dirt road and drove to the highway, south toward the 7-Eleven. She resisted the impulse to drive Jack's car through the glass storefront and instead went inside and bought a cup of coffee and a jug of bleach. Then she parked on the bend around the corner from a stand of pine trees and looked through the pictures she'd taken of Loyal's ledger one more time, hit the send button, and waited for the bling that told her the message had gone through. Then she drove to the bridge.

Icicles hung off its railings. She pulled to the center and got out, Keating's cell phone heavy in her hand. Runoff from the fertilizer plant upstream smelled foul but earthy. Debris caught on the frozen ice and swirled in foamed eddies. She threw the phone as far as she could. It splashed and floated downstream for a moment, hit a fallen tree trunk and sank. She drove to the veterans' hall.

A hundred or more cars were parked on side streets and in the surrounding vacant lots. Men milled around outside the hall, smoking their last cigarettes before the kickoff. She parked the car on the street and poured the gallon of bleach into Jack's gas tank. When she saw Loyal's truck, she wished she'd bought two jugs.

A handwritten poster taped to the front door listed the tournament jackpot. She did some quick calculations. There had to be over a hundred entries. She hated that she'd agreed to collude with Phoebe, Jack, and Tuckahoe. The thought of collaborating with any of them on anything put a vile taste in her mouth, but spending the day in her uncle's presence was her best cover. She swallowed hard and went inside.

A picture of TJ was taped to the wall behind the check-in table along with a note about a reward for information leading to his whereabouts. It made her sick to see that man's face. Maybe he'd been a kind man, a good father. Her mind went to Toby. He'd never graduate from high school now or join the Army and become a soldier. She'd never have to worry about him getting blown up in a tank or getting shot in combat. Blind River would never forgive him for his part in this thing. They'd already labeled him as one more troubled boy and any argument against that was futile.

Eddie from Crowley's Pub was collecting tournament entry fees. He closed the lockbox and slid it under his chair. "You're Loyal's girl, right?" The smirk on his face told her he knew exactly who she was.

"Niece."

"Got here in the nick of time," he said. "He waived your buy-in."

As a juvenile, Toby's identity should have been protected, but that smirk said something different. By now the whole town would be talking about the missing-persons investigation and everyone would see her as the sister of the guy who'd been arrested. But that smirk also told her that word of the attempted suicide hadn't got out.

Eddie gave her a card with her table and seat number on it. "Over there," he said, pointing.

The hall was dingy and gray, filled with round folding tables and metal chairs. Flags from various armed services were tacked on the walls. There was a coffee station in the back near a small stage with a microphone. Her seat was at a table near the back and she snaked through the room to find it.

Judging by the size of the crowd, she guessed the tournament would run until late afternoon. Most of the players had already found their seats and sat eyeing their opponents, trying to gauge the level of competition. Loyal meandered through the crowd greeting players. One day a year, Loyal Elders was elevated from the redneck country boy they knew him to be to the man who ran the annual veterans' fund-raiser. Over the years those days had amounted to a bond of sorts, and even though he'd never even considered joining the military, and even though he tore his parking tickets up, and even though the money raised from this tournament never quite made it into anything tangible for the veterans' hall, the fact that he ran it every year and that the men had a good time earned him their admiration, if only for a day.

The average age, she guessed by the gray hair and beer

bellies and the flasks hanging out their back pockets, was sixty-something. These men had been playing cards their whole lives and they'd be tricky. Once they saw her they'd come gunning because no one here wanted to get beat by the only girl in the tournament.

It seemed her eyes had a will of their own because the first person they landed on was Jack, sitting at a table near the front. She swerved toward him. His slumping posture and sunken eyes and scraggly beard suggested he'd had a rough night. She slung the keys at him fast. When he caught them from smacking his face, she was disappointed but kept moving.

Phoebe, dressed in her starched white shirt and black vest, sat in the dealer's position at a table in the center of the room. When she looked up and smiled, Jamie's heart felt like a stone wedged between her lungs. Jilkins despised Phoebe and wouldn't have told her about Toby. Loyal wouldn't have said anything that might mess up the tournament. There was nothing anyone could do for Toby anyway, and Jamie decided not to tell her until the end of the day.

She passed Tuckahoe and her fists clenched. He rolled a chip in between his fingers like a magician, but when he saw her he touched his nose in a stupid signal of their collaboration. Chip dumping with a pervert, an unfaithful husband, and an ex-con. The *fuck you all* mantra started looping through her brain again as she found her seat.

Loyal went to the front of the room and tapped the microphone with his finger, sending a screech through the speakers. The crowd quieted. A young guy and a middle-aged woman sat in folding chairs by the stage. They seemed removed, like they didn't really want to be in this room. Loyal handed the microphone to Keating, who wanted to make an announcement before the game started because he could never pass up cheap publicity for his reelection campaign.

When the girl stepped out from behind Keating, Jamie's mind iced over. The girl looked exhausted and worn out, even smaller than Jamie remembered from that afternoon in Crowley's Pub.

Keating said, "You all know that TJ Bangor wanted to play in this tournament. And you probably all know that he, uh, hasn't been seen for a couple of days."

A murmur went through the crowd. Phoebe's face turned as pale as marble.

Keating put his arm around the girl's shoulders. "But his daughter, Lena, is here in his stead." He gave Lena a crushing squeeze. She stumbled against his bulk but his hold on her kept her from falling. The crowd made a low, approving noise. He looked at the girl with a tenderness that made Jamie scream inside. She slipped lower into her chair, wanting to disappear.

"We want you to know," he said, "that we're praying for your father's safe return."

The girl seemed to shrink beneath the weight of his arm.

Keating wiped a nonexistent tear. "And we're going to play this tournament in his honor."

The sham was unbearable.

"Now do us a favor, um . . . honey." The bastard

had already forgotten her name. "Start the tournament for us?"

He lowered the microphone to her and the girl said softly, "Shuffle up and deal."

There was some scattered applause before the room went quiet and the cards started flying. Keating took his seat at a table near the front.

Lena stood there alone for a moment—her shoulders narrow, her eyes wide and brown—glancing around the room until the guy and woman came to her side. They had to be her brother, or maybe a cousin, and Mrs. Bangor. They looked so broken. Jamie mucked the first round of cards without even looking at them and watched them walk to the entrance and out the front doors. Jamie gripped the edge of her chair. What was she waiting for? Better timing? For who? Herself? There was only one right thing to do. She stood, about to follow after them, just as Loyal walked up behind Jamie and gripped her shoulder with his hand. She collapsed back into her chair, felt him move in closer, smelled the whiskey on his breath when he leaned over and whispered in her ear, "Don't even think about it."

35

THINKING ABOUT BOMBING out on that first hand at Mimawa still stung enough that Jamie folded every hand for the first thirty minutes, but once she'd settled in enough and got a read on the other players, she decided it was time to play. An hour later, she'd doubled the size of her stack by making a few key bluffs. Now it was time to turn up the heat.

She peeked at her hole cards, saw a suited king/nine, and tossed a couple of chips into the pot. The action went clockwise around the table and everyone folded except the old guy to her right. He played tight, but in the last thirty minutes Jamie had taken a giant pot from him with a bluff too big for any sane person to call. He called her bet now and the dealer spread the first of the community cards on the table. A king, ten, and a nine. The old guy checked, and Jamie bet out hard.

"Why so much?" he asked.

"Guess I'm scared you hit something on the flop," she said.

Her stomach growled, but all she found in the bottom of her backpack was the remnants of a spilled bag of trail mix and a roll of Tums. It would have to do.

The old guy looked at his cards for a full minute. She knew he would fold, and tanking on his decision like this was just his way of saving face. He didn't fold until the other players started complaining, then mucked his cards faceup—a king/jack—and Jamie almost laughed. Old guys hated folding paint and they showed their hand every time as though to prove some point.

He smirked and said, "Nice hand, little lady."

She hated the word *lady* but said nothing.

Her next hand was a pair of jacks and she made the same play against him, knowing there was no way he'd let her keep stealing pots. He called her bet. They flipped their cards and he had a pair of eights. Her jacks held up and he was out.

"A girl like you," he said, letting his eyes drift from her face to her chest and back, "steamrolls like you got nothing to lose. Maybe you should slow down once in a while."

She said, "Yes, sir. I'll pull up a little if it's better for you." She meant for her style to annoy other players, stayed unpredictable in order to throw them off balance, but hated when she won a hand and the loser told her how to play.

His buddies chuckled and one of them said, "Watch yourself. That's Loyal's niece. You can bet she knows a thing or two."

She folded the next few hands, trying to stay under the radar. What she needed was to sit tight as long as possible and let things play out, give herself a solid alibi. A couple of small hands went her way and she built her stack a little more.

Thirty minutes later, the dealers rotated and Phoebe landed at Tuckahoe's table. Jamie glanced over and saw he was holding his own, but with the first hand Phoebe dealt him he shoved all his chips to the center. One other player called him and they turned their cards over. His pair of nines were up against a pair of queens. When another nine hit the river, Tuckahoe won and his opponent was out.

Tuckahoe caught Jamie looking at him, smiled, and tapped his nose. She stared at his stupid face, caught up in remembering the satisfying smack of her elbow against Billy's face last night.

*   *   *

Two hours later, Jamie had knocked out two more players and built her stack to fifty thousand chips, enough to coast for another hour or two. There were twenty-six players and three tables left in the game. When they got down to twenty players, Loyal moved Tuckahoe to her table. He sat down and touched his nose, and Jamie had to dig her fingernails into her wrist to keep herself from leaping across the table and punching him in the throat.

An hour later they were down to sixteen players. If she kept her end of the bargain, she'd go up against Jack and then Keating. She hated this, hated the idea of losing a single chip to any of these men. When the dealers rotated for the last time, Phoebe landed at her table and dealt Jamie some big cards.

She never knew who had taught her mother the mechanics of card manipulation, but the woman was a magician when it came to sticking aces. Sitting at the same table with her now brought the memories back: all those days and nights spent around their kitchen table when she was little. Phoebe's fingers quick as lightning, Jamie soaking up the odds of making various hands, the thrill of catching her mother pulling an ace off the bottom of the deck for the first time.

Everything had baffled Toby. He could never do the simplest trick, was always stunned when his mom pulled the jack of hearts from behind his ear. Jamie was thrilled when her fingers were finally long and strong enough to impose her will on the cards. Soon she was the one surprising Toby, like on his ninth birthday, when she had him shuffle the cards and then randomly counted out the date in diamonds.

Three more players busted out and they got down to the final table. Tuckahoe was on her right and Jack was three players to her left, which was a good distance because she didn't want to see his big sad eyes, the fake innocence on his face. Keating sat smug and calm across the table from her like he was holding court. Phoebe was still wearing that string around her neck and had yet to look directly at Jamie. Her mother was a pro and a pro would never give anything away through eye contact. But she would deal pocket kings to her own daughter on the very first hand.

Jamie raised the blind by four, and Jack raised her.

She let herself glance at him for the first time since he'd sat down, his sad fucking apologetic face. Fuck him and his stupid fucking designer scruff. Heat rose in her throat. If she looked into his eyes, she would burst into flames.

She pushed all her chips to the middle.

Phoebe told them to turn the cards over, but Jack refused when he saw Jamie's kings. He tossed his cards into the muck and stood up. "Good game."

Asshole. She was just doing her job, and when good cards came her way she was going to play them hard.

Her next three hands were crap and she knew Phoebe was cooling her off. It worked. Her gut calmed as she watched Keating take Tuckahoe's entire stack by hitting a full house on the river. Keating took out the last two players in consecutive hands and it was down to her versus him in a winner-take-all final match.

Loyal announced a fifteen-minute break to arrange the chairs on opposite ends of the table. Keating had about three hundred thousand in chips—twice her stack. She was supposed to lose to this man. The man who sentenced her mother and jailed her brother. He stood to stretch and saw her glaring at him. He winked and she'd never hated anyone more.

Jamie went for a soda while Phoebe sat at the table watching over the cards and chip stacks. The crowd mulled around the table, speculating loudly about the two remaining players. Everybody had an opinion. Keating had the advantage. The girl, a child barely out of high school, was a rookie even if she was Loyal Elders's niece. Walking through the crowd, Jamie watched as men exchanged cash. The

side-bet odds were ten to one that the judge would take
her out in two hands, no more than five.

They could be right.

Jack was sitting near the stage next to Lena Bangor and
the two people who had been with her earlier. Jamie was
surprised to see they'd come back, but this tournament was
the only thing happening in town and it had been dedi-
cated to Bangor. Mrs. Bangor, blondish-gray and gaunt,
looked about fifty. She clutched a handful of tissues and sat
tilted on her chair. The guy hovered over her as though he
expected her to fall. Jack had already zeroed in on Lena.
It was no surprise. The charming seducer with the stupid
bouncy hair falling in his eyes. He stared at the floor, listening attentively to the girl, shaking his head. It made
Jamie sick that she'd fallen for his act.

When she got back to the table, Phoebe was counting
out the deck and Loyal was hanging up his phone. He
glared at Jamie as though he knew exactly what she'd done
and it made the skin on the back of her neck prickle. His
eyes stayed on her a little too long; it wasn't her imagination. He knew what the cops were up to and suspected
she was to blame. Her breath felt shallow and her heart
beat too fast. She tried to feel the floor beneath her boots
and guessed at how far Garcia might have taken things
by now.

Just then, Garcia and two uniformed officers slipped
inside the front door. Jamie sat in the chair designated for
her. Phoebe froze, staring at her hands, seemingly not
even breathing.

"Mom, chill out, okay?"

Phoebe inhaled a sharp breath. "What're they doing here?"

"It's no big deal."

"I can't do this." Phoebe's eyes widened as she scanned the perimeter of the room. She put her hand on her stomach and motioned toward Loyal, who was hanging up from yet another phone call. He came to the table and Phoebe whispered in his ear.

He checked his watch and held up two fingers. "You got two minutes."

Phoebe grabbed her bag and went off toward the restroom.

Loyal narrowed his eyes at the entrance. "What's he doing here?" he said, motioning with his chin toward Garcia and the cops.

"No idea," Jamie said. She picked up a small stack of chips and shuffled them to stop her hands from trembling.

"I'm serious," Loyal said.

Jamie recognized his tone. She stared at the far wall to calm her nerves, trying to appear thoughtful. "Not much happens in this town. They probably just want to see the game play out."

The break was over. Keating pried himself away from his admirers and took his seat. Two minutes passed, then three. Loyal checked his watch. "Where is she?"

"It's her stomach," Jamie said.

"Go check on her," Loyal said.

Jamie walked down the hallway to the restroom. She saw her mother's clunky work shoes beneath a stall door. "What's going on, Mom? Everyone's waiting."

The toilet flushed, and Phoebe stepped out, glancing toward the door, her bag hanging off her shoulder. "Why is that cop here?"

"It's not about you." Jamie hesitated, trying to piece out what to tell the woman and what to keep from her until later.

"How do you know? He's been sniffing around all week. He's got something on one of us."

"Okay, relax. Something did happen last night. But listen to me. You gotta keep your cool and play this out. We got to make it look like we got nothing to hide."

Phoebe turned white and leaned against the sink. "I knew it. I felt it all morning. What happened?"

It was just like Phoebe to come unglued at the most crucial moment, but Jamie suspected the woman's instinct was more survival than maternal. "Toby's hurt, but he's okay."

"What do you mean, hurt? Where is he?"

"The hospital."

"Why the hell didn't you tell me?"

"Why tell you? There was nothing you could do."

"Nothing I could do?"

"He's still in custody. You can't just walk in." The lie came out like poison. Jilkins had told her a parent would be allowed to visit, but Phoebe had done nothing to earn that right.

"I can't believe you didn't tell me this. I know how the system works. I'm his mother. They'll let me in."

"You're my mother, too, and I need you to keep it together."

"Come on, Jamie. You never needed anyone, least of

all me." Phoebe pulled the ring out from beneath her blouse, took the string from around her neck. "I can't be near a cop with this thing."

It was bigger than Jamie remembered, as big as a golf ball, blinding with gold and diamonds. "That's the least of our worries."

"Not the least of mine." Phoebe pushed the ring at Jamie. "Get this away from me. Throw it in the river. I don't care. Just get rid of it." Her eyes darted around the room.

"Okay, okay. I'll figure it out." Jamie slipped the ring into her pocket. "Just come back out to the table. Keep it cool or you'll draw more attention."

Phoebe opened the bathroom window. "Someone else can deal the rest of that game. I'm his mother, Jamie." Phoebe pointed at her chest. "I'm the only one they'll let visit." She threw her bag out the window into the alley behind the building.

"Now you're his mother? I fed him and sent him to school every morning for years but *now* you're his mother. Scared is all you are. If you take off now, it makes all of us look guilty."

"Yeah, I'm scared. Scared that if I get locked up I'll never see him again." Phoebe crawled out the window. "Tell Loyal I got sick and went home."

"I knew this would happen, damn it. I knew you would leave like this," Jamie said, but Phoebe kept walking.

The alley was empty except for an overflowing dumpster. A plastic garbage bag caught in the wind and tumbled around the corner. Jamie watched as Phoebe neared the corner, pulled a card from her cuff, and threw it on the ground.

Shit. The last thing Jamie needed was to have that deck of cards come up one card short. She crawled through the window and ran to get the card. The queen of spades. She slipped it into her cuff and climbed back inside.

Jamie ran water in the sink, splashed some on her face. She should've seen this coming, should've known it would go down like this, that her mother would leave her to finish things on her own. Like always. She dried her face with paper towels, stared, pissed off at the mirror, hated that her eyes were the same grayish-blue as her mother's, set too far apart with that same slope of eyebrow. A cleaning roster and a pen hung on a nail over the sink. She took the pen and scribbled ink on her finger, smudged it over one eyelid. She liked the effect it had and did the other side. Jamie stood back and checked her image in the mirror. Here was a new creature. One with the eyes of a warrior.

CHAPTER

36

A CROWD HAD gathered around the final table when Jamie returned.

"Where is she?" Loyal asked.

Jamie sat down. "Dunno. It looks like she left."

"What the fuck?" There was a moment of chaos as his chair thumped backward and he went down the hall to the restroom to see for himself, as though Phoebe might have left a trail. By the time he came back he was angry and grumbling about a new plan. Lena Bangor would deal the final match.

The girl refused to get up from her chair. "No, I don't know how."

"Don't worry." Loyal pulled her to her feet. "I'll tell you exactly what to do."

"But I've never even played." She flicked her eyes at Jamie, who dropped her gaze and pretended to count her chips. Instead, she was quietly speculating about allowing herself to lose, how much it would piss off Loyal if she didn't take the beating, and how the cards might fall without her mother's interference. Fades and bluffs. Regardless of the cards, she had to play to the man's weakness, his ego.

"It's easy." Loyal led Lena to Phoebe's empty chair. He pulled his own chair up behind her and said, "In fact, it's even better this way."

Keating said, "Your dad would be proud," and the girl picked up the deck.

The crowd pushed in closer. There was no pretense here. No one expected Jamie, the strange-looking girl, the contender with the weirdly dramatic eyes, to bring much game. Jack leaned against a wall across the room and stared at Jamie. He pointed at his eyes with a perplexed expression but Jamie didn't care. *Fuck you all* resumed in her head, drowning out everything else.

"Shuffle up and deal," Loyal said, but Lena spilled the cards on the table.

It was better than a shuffle. Even if her uncle had stacked the cards while she was in the bathroom, Jamie knew he couldn't plant a card in this situation if his life depended on it.

She folded the first hand and Keating folded the second, trading chips and staying even. On the third hand, Keating made a big bet and Jamie raised it by three. She propped her elbows on the table and leaned her chin on her fists. He tapped the shirt pocket holding his cigarettes, his eyes darting sideways and then back to center, and called her bet. Two jacks came on the flop. She bet again, hoping he'd fold. She guessed he had face cards, maybe a king and a queen. He hesitated, then called her bet. She pushed all in when a nine came on the turn.

Loyal sat with his arm stretched possessively across the back of Lena's chair, cleared his throat, and glared straight-faced at Jamie. He'd be pissed if she made Keating look foolish, but if the crowd of men betting against her wanted a show, she'd give it to them.

Keating folded. "I'll give you this one, little lady." He turned over an ace and threw his other card into the muck.

Jamie slid her cards facedown across the table and said nothing.

Keating smiled his campaign smile. "Be a sport and show one."

"No, sir. I never show my cards," Jamie said.

"Oh, come on. This is a friendly game." He reached for her cards and flipped the first one he touched, the ten. She gestured *whatever*, hoping he'd flip the other card, too. He did.

When he saw the deuce he glanced hotly at Loyal.

Jamie stacked her chips and willed a straight face. She'd pulled off a classic bluff with a ten/two and someone in the back of the crowd laughed. Keating couldn't have expected a move like that in a game that was supposed to have been rigged in his favor. His face reddened, but the embarrassment was his own fault. He shouldn't have turned her cards over when she'd said no. He drummed his fingers on the table, tapped his shirt pocket again.

Loyal shuffled the deck and handed the cards to Lena, who dealt the next hand.

Their stacks were even now and any hand could end the game. Keating leaned back and stretched his arms over his head, smiled at Lena. It was pathetic. The old guy sucking up to a grief-stricken girl. He might appear to be consoling and fatherly, but Jamie saw how his eyes lingered over the girl's breasts.

"The action's on the judge," Loyal said.

Keating peeked at his hole cards and tossed a few chips in the pot.

Jamie checked.

Lena turned over the first three community cards, two tens and a king.

Keating fired a huge bet and Jamie folded her lousy pocket threes.

On the next hand, Jamie turned the corners up on her cards and saw a good hand, the ten of diamonds and nine of spades. Her vision narrowed but her mind expanded with an odd but familiar awareness. This was the hand it would all come down to.

Lena spread the community cards, the king of hearts, the ten and three of spades. A pair of tens was good in a heads-up match, but Keating was too calm.

A murmur went through the crowd. Someone whistled, someone said, "We might get some fireworks now."

Keating bet half his stack and the crowd hushed. He might have big cards, but she was still in it with her pair of tens and the spades. She could hit a legitimate spade flush, but right now he was beating her and he knew it. She made her hands tremble slightly.

Toby never folded spades. He'd always bet them, always believed they'd come through. *This one's for you, brother.* She made her hands tremble a little more, fumbled the chips as she counted them out. Keating watched her closely, tried not to smile at what he would have to presume were nerves.

Her mind was quiet except for the ticking of her heart. It had been so cold that day at the jail, Toby's fingers nearly blue. She imagined his hands, cold and numb while he tied the hangman's knot. He was so damn good at knots. She wondered how many times he'd changed his mind, tied it and untied it, before deciding to go through with it. How long had he spent trying to get the rope the right length?

The turn was the ace of diamonds. Loyal tapped a knuckle on the table. "Earth to Jamie."

Keating fired a big bet.

It would take half her stack to make the call. Keating looked smug. She guessed at what he might be holding, maybe ace/queen. In that case, his aces would beat her tens, and if the last card was a jack, he'd have a straight. He leaned back in his chair, linked his fingers over his belly, breathed deeply as though he was struggling not to smile. He didn't, she noticed, look her in the eye or pat the pack of cigarettes in his shirt pocket. She felt sure he had the aces and a straight draw.

Had there been a pipe overhead or a high, barred window? Toby's last lonely wish must have vanished as the chair went out from under his feet and his neck snapped in the noose. Had he hoped that someone—his mother, uncle, or sister, someone, anyone—would step in and pull him back from the edge? Had he changed his mind in that last second? How long had he suffered before the guard came back on his round? Thank God they'd found him in time.

Loyal rapped impatiently on the table.

She bent up the corners of her hole cards again. She was supposed to fold here, let Keating take half her stack and move him one step closer to the win. Chances were his aces would hold up and then this whole stupid charade would be over. But no one could blame her for staying in it with a pair of tens. They would say it was a good call. But if she won—then everyone would come unglued.

The crowd moved in tighter to watch the last hand. Garcia pushed through to stand behind Loyal. When he put his hands into his pockets, Jamie saw the flash of metal cuffs hooked to his belt. She decided to go for it. When she made the call, the top of her head turned cold.

Loyal hunkered over the table and flicked a warning at her with his eyes. She ignored him. What could he do in front of all these people?

Lena held the deck with both hands. Loyal said, "Burn one." She placed the next card facedown in the muck and then turned over the fifth card.

A blur passed in front of Jamie's eyes. The jack of spades. If she'd read him right, Keating had made his straight. There were only three spades on the board. That queen was in her cuff, but her pulse was beating wildly and her hands jittered like moths in a streetlight.

It was Keating's move. His eyes were dead still on her, practically gloating. Her water bottle sat on the floor beside her chair. As she reached for it, she moved the queen to her palm.

Keating said, "All in."

Her heart banged in her throat. She picked up her hole cards again, switched the ten for the queen, coughed and moved the ten to her jacket pocket. She straightened and counted to three. Anyone who'd seen what she'd done would speak up immediately. But no one did.

"I call," she said.

He turned over the queen of diamonds and the ace of hearts. Just as she thought, he'd made an ace-high straight. The crowd buzzed and whooped. Keating punched the air with his fist and high-fived Eddie. Loyal's shoulders gave a little and the tension in his jaw relaxed. He pushed Keating's cards forward to show the straight and let it sit there.

Jamie turned over her queen/nine and waited.

Keating read the board.

A hum rustled through the crowd. "Goddamn," Eddie said. "She's got spades."

JAMIE COUNTED THE spades again, two in her hand, three on the board.

"My straight is best, right?" Keating asked. His mouth gaped like he needed air, his hopeful tone fading as comprehension sharpened in his eyes.

Loyal let the straight stand as the winner for a beat until someone said, "A flush beats a straight."

Lena set down the deck and put her hands in her lap as though she'd done something wrong.

"Goddamn it to hell," Keating said. His hands gripped the edge of the table as though he might turn it over. He looked at Loyal and mumbled something about getting even.

Loyal studied the board, swiped Keating's straight to the side, and pushed the spade flush forward.

Jamie had never experienced a thrill like the one bouncing in her belly now, making her feel like she would burst if she didn't vomit first. But she waited to see what Loyal would say. He leaned across the table and whispered, "Where'd that queen come from?"

"From that deck." It wasn't exactly a lie because that's where Phoebe had taken it from. No one had seen Jamie pull that queen out of her sleeve, but he knew as well as she did: Elders kids were rarely innocent. And they never, ever, won that easy.

Keating's eyes went flat. He stared at the cards as though they were evil, as though in a moment they would correct themselves and line up in his favor. There was a lot of cursing as the spectators started paying out side bets. Eddie slapped Jamie's shoulder and set a tiny wooden plaque trophy on the table in front of her.

Jamie felt an impulse to run and tell Toby—he would be so psyched—then remembered he was laying half-conscious in a hospital bed.

Loyal said, "Pull up your sleeves."

"Whatever," she said and showed her wrists.

Loyal grabbed her wrists and yanked at her cuffs, but she'd tucked the card into her jacket pocket, so he turned her loose.

Garcia stepped closer.

Loyal picked up the lockbox he'd been keeping under his chair and stood as if to leave. If he didn't give her the prize money in front of this crowd, she'd never see it.

"You're not going until you award the prize," Eddie said. "You always pay out the money at the end of the game." Loyal shook his head, but Eddie persisted. "She won it; give it to her."

The crowd pressed closer to the table. Eddie started chanting, "Show her the money!" A few other men joined in.

"All right, all right." Loyal set the lockbox on the table and opened the lid, said low enough that only she could hear, "You're giving this back to me before you leave this building."

A few men clapped. The wad of hundred-dollar bills in her hands was heavy and wonderful and intoxicating. She jammed it in her pocket, wondering how she could get out of the building before Loyal cornered her and demanded she give it back.

Across the table, Garcia motioned to a uniformed officer. The man took Lena's arm and walked the Bangor family out the front door. Two more uniformed cops stepped inside.

Loyal pulled on his coat and stood up, but Garcia stepped in front of him and wheeled him around. Loyal slapped Garcia's hand away. "Jesus Christ, Garcia. What the hell do you want?"

Garcia took the handcuffs off his belt. "I have a warrant for your arrest."

"The fuck you do." Loyal pushed Garcia and lunged at Jamie. "Girl, what the hell did you do?"

She tripped backward, but Eddie and another man caught her from falling. Loyal hit the ground hard, though, and Garcia swiftly cuffed him. He and a cop helped Loyal to his feet as Jamie got her balance and righted herself. She'd never expected to see cops manhandle her uncle, and now she noticed just how much his belly protruded over his belt, how his pants sagged at his ass, how gauzy and washed-out his eyes were, the amount of gray in the scruff on his jowls. She'd never expected to feel such pity for the man.

Garcia held a document in Loyal's face. "This doesn't have anything to do with her. We confiscated thirty-seven illegal gambling machines purported to be owned by you."

"What? Are you kidding me? What are you talking about? Those machines raise money for charities."

"That's bullshit and everyone knows it."

"You're taking food out of the mouths of children!" Loyal yelled.

"You're being charged with operating illegal gambling equipment," Garcia continued. "The information came from a highly reputable source."

Jamie bet no one would take her as the reputable source but still wanted to run from the room. She fought the urge and stared hard at Keating because everything hinged on Loyal believing he'd been sold out by his buddy.

"A reputable source?" Loyal wheeled around and looked at Keating. "You? What did you do?"

Keating's face shifted to recognition.

Loyal pulled out of Garcia's grip. "Don't do this, Keating. Don't you do this!"

Keating cleared his throat and held up his hand. For the first time in his life he was outnumbered. He took the safe route and rolled on Loyal. "It seems like it's already been done. It's time to clean up Blind River. Certain things . . ." He stopped and glanced at Loyal. "Certain things have been going on unnoticed in this county for too long. I'm promising right here and now that a vote for my reelection is a vote for a more decent town. You can count on that."

Loyal stood dumbfounded, flanked by Garcia and the cop.

Garcia faced Keating and said, "Maybe it's time we called it a day. What do you say, boss? Isn't it time for some whiskey?"

Keating's face relaxed. He gathered his things with the same dignity Jamie imagined he displayed in his courtroom and began moving through the crowd. Garcia and the cop guided him toward the door. Someone mentioned Crowley's Pub and the crowd began to disperse and follow them outside.

Loyal glared at Keating as the man walked out the door, and something inside Jamie shifted in reaction to the defeat on her uncle's face. It surprised her how calm she felt. He stood alone behind the table, his hands cuffed across his waist.

Part one of her plan was complete. Jamie walked up to him, hoping to set the last part in motion. She needed Loyal to believe Keating had ratted out the gambling operation. "What are you going to do?"

He seemed stunned. "This is bullshit. What the fuck just happened?"

She shook her head sympathetically. "Looks to me like things got too hot for Keating and he sold you out. He used your operation to throw the law's attention off that missing man, so if things start surfacing, he'll look innocent and you'll get pegged as Toby's accomplice."

"I don't know. He's never let me down before." He looked her in the eye. "How do I know it wasn't you?"

A good bluff, her mother had always said, starts and ends with a blank face. She made her face unreadable, realizing it was her only weapon. "Wasn't me."

She saw a flicker of doubt cloud his face and held his gaze until his eyes dropped and he shook his head.

"I got to think. Get the flask out of my back pocket."

"He could've pulled the plug whenever he wanted. But he waited till right now, till that man's goes missing, till right before the election. You going to let him get away with that? Who do you think is going to walk away from this thing? You or the man these people elected?"

She got out the flask and unscrewed the top. It would be his last taste of whiskey and she knew he'd miss that more than anything.

"All you ever needed was the location of that man's body. You said as much yourself that night."

He lifted the flask to his lips.

"You think about that when they book you, when they take your belt and shoes. Think about how Keating sold you out same as he did Toby."

He drained the whiskey. "You're right, little girl. That fucker will regret this. You figured that out fast, though, didn't you?"

"I always heard that apples don't fall far from the tree."

"Maybe. Maybe that's true." His eyes turned to her and she read suspicion there. "You be careful now. Sometimes you get what you want in this world, but what's more often true is you get what you deserve."

Jamie took a step back. He was cuffed but he was still a big man. "You're not threatening me, are you, uncle?"

"It's not a threat, it's a prediction. Every Elders gets their due."

She tried to shrug it off, but that wicked chill ran up her spine again. Was that true? Didn't her father die stupidly, her mother spend years in prison? Wasn't her brother lying half dead in a hospital bed this very minute? Wasn't she trying to outsmart a lifelong con man? She lowered her voice, but her words still came out shaky. "The way I see it, you got one chance to settle the score. Go for the man who came for you."

Garcia brought another cop over and told him to take Loyal downtown.

She figured she had an hour or two before Loyal met with a public defender and spilled the details on Bangor.

The cards and the lockbox sat on the table. Jamie brought the missing card out of her jacket pocket and slipped it back in the deck.

"I didn't see that," Garcia said. He gathered the deck and put it inside the lockbox, which he opened and held out in front of her. "In here."

"What?"

"All money associated with Loyal Elders's operation is considered evidence while he's under investigation by the state commission."

"This is my money. I won it. Everyone saw."

He held the box up and shook his head. "You can't have it both ways, Jamie. Nothing Loyal Elders touched is legit."

She pulled the wad out of her pocket and put it in

the box. Garcia closed the lid and handed it to another cop, who bagged and sealed it with the date as Jamie watched her last hope at getting the hell out of Blind River disappear.

Garcia had done exactly what she'd wanted. He'd used the photographs of the ledger off Keating's phone to find Loyal's gambling sites and bust the whole operation. And Loyal's only retaliation would be to give up the location of the Bangor's body. The two men would likely never speak to each other again and, even if they did, they'd never figure out how she'd set them against each other.

Soon enough Loyal would be sitting in the same jail where Toby had been just yesterday. It was hard to imagine her uncle confined to a small cell, the guards laughing when he asked for a cigarette and some whiskey or demanded an aspirin and a cup of coffee.

She scanned the room for a soda or a bag of pretzels, but the players had wiped the refreshments table clean. She dug through her backpack for leftover crumbs from the trail mix, anything to stop the grumbling in her stomach. Something sharp in the bottom of the bag jabbed her finger and she pulled out a Greyhound bus ticket. Departure time: 8:30 PM, destination: Atlantic City. There was a message written on it: *Follow your heart but always bet your spades.*

"THERE'S ONE MORE thing I need from you," Garcia said once they were inside his car.

"I need to stop by the hospital and see my brother first," Jamie said.

Garcia gave a glacial sigh and shook his head no. "There's a family waiting for their father and husband."

"I just gave you the biggest arrest this town has ever seen and you just took my last dollar."

"What you gave me was a list of illegal gambling sites. Your uncle just got arrested and if he has any information on Bangor he'll play it right away. I'm guessing you have a very short window of time to get out from under whatever part you played in this."

"All I need is ten minutes."

Garcia turned south on Main and pulled into the hospital's emergency drive. He got a letter out of his jacket pocket and held it open for Jamie to see. "Sign this right now or I can't help you." The car doors clicked locked.

She pushed the paper away and tried the handle. "I'll be right back."

"You aren't getting out of this car without signing this first." He handed her a pen.

"Christ, Garcia. What is this?" Jamie took the form and saw her name on the first line.

"This makes you an official informant in your uncle's illegal activities and lets me give you protection and keep you anonymous in an investigation. Whatever your involvement was, I know you were a pawn to these people. Sign this form and I got your back."

There was that word again: *protection*.

"But Keating would never agree to something that helps me. Where'd you get this?"

"He has no influence with the state's gaming commission, and Bangor's disappearance seems connected. It's too suspicious. This is their jurisdiction now."

Jamie sank in her seat. "This makes me an official snitch?"

"That form puts you on the right side of things and is likely to keep you out of jail. The courts tend to take illegal gambling operations seriously. Sign the bottom line."

"Is this how you deal with your own daughter? Because it probably pisses her off."

"Not that it's any of your business, but I never had children."

She didn't see another option. He was offering protection and, real or not, no one else seemed to even care. It was her only play. She took the pen and signed her name.

He unlocked the doors and pulled a lighter from his pocket. "You got till I finish this cigarette."

A cop was stationed outside the ICU and told her she wasn't allowed inside. Through the glass wall she saw Phoebe sitting next to Toby's bed, holding his hand, her clunky white sneakers sticking out beneath her ridiculous high-water jeans. Except for the single tube protruding from his mouth, Toby looked like he was sleeping off an all-nighter. Jamie tapped on the window and Phoebe came outside.

"How is he?"

"His eyes opened when I took his hand. I think he might've smiled at me." Phoebe's eyes glistened. "The doctor is optimistic, but the nurse said he'll be in county rehab and it will be weeks before he'll be able to talk." She lowered her voice. "Come on, let's get away from this cop."

The two of them went to the vending area for whatever the snack machine had in it. Jamie sank onto a plastic chair near the window, stared at the dingy hospital walls while Phoebe dropped coins into the coffee machine.

"Interesting thing you've done with your eye makeup," Phoebe said, and Jamie bristled.

What did she have in common with this woman? Love for a self-destructive boy? DNA? A mutual fate? Neither of them had ever had the freedom to make their own choices in life, and they'd fought back as best they could, with a tendency toward theft. That's what they had in common. That's what she'd inherited. She didn't want to be near her mother, the source of her dark side, but she wanted answers.

"Why did you steal back then? How was that so much more important than playing it straight, staying out of jail so you could take care of your kids?" The question came out angry and she hated how it made her sound like a child.

"That was a long time ago."

"Seems like nothing's changed."

"That's not fair."

"You're leaving here without explaining anything. I might never even see you again."

Phoebe tilted her head and turned away. "It was hard to make ends meet, you know. Your dad didn't leave any insurance and I was broke. Toby got a bad fever and I took him to a walk-in clinic. It was six months after your dad died and I hadn't filled out the paperwork for Medicaid yet. When the nurse found out I had left you home alone, she threatened to call Family Services. They handed me a bottle of antibiotics for Toby and I snuck past the front desk without paying. They wanted two-hundred and eighty dollars for one bottle of antibiotics! Next day a cop comes knocking on my door with an arrest warrant. There were other misdemeanors, bad checks, petty stuff. Back then I made one mistake after another. I was already on probation. The DA worked out a deal to get me a reduced sentence if I pled guilty and saved the town the cost of a trial. I knew Loyal would take you two in until I got out, so I took the deal."

It took a moment for that to register, and when it did, Jamie's voice was not much more than a whisper. "Antibiotics? That's what you stole? A bottle of pills for Toby?"

It had never occurred to her that Phoebe might have stolen drugs to help one of her kids. Jamie had just assumed oxy, and in eight years no one had said a thing that made her think differently. "No one told me."

"Yeah, well. I'm sure Loyal spun it to make me look like a bitch. But you were a kid, and people? People believe what they hear."

Jamie and Toby had never talked about their mother stealing drugs. Despite small-town rumors, she'd hoped to keep that one thing from him so he'd grow up believing in his mother's innocence and see himself in that same light. She'd hoped to get that one thing right. But it had been a stupid plan because she herself had never believed. All she knew was that she'd been abandoned and that made her angry. Angry enough to assume the worst and never question it.

Phoebe handed Jamie a cup of coffee. "You hungry? They got chocolate chip." She dropped more coins in the machine.

"But eight years? That doesn't make sense."

"Well, prison was rough. I made the wrong friends, got punished for things I did and framed for things I didn't. Got into fights. Pissed off the guards. They added months, years, before I figured out how to keep out of trouble. Some people get along inside, some don't." She reached down to retie a shoelace. "It took me a long time to learn. Strange, though, I almost miss it. It's not so different outside. I work hard all day, six days a week, but all I got either place is a meal and a cot. Except one thing. Out here I got at least one kid that needs me."

Phoebe's smile seemed defeated. "It's okay, Jamie. We're family. We don't have to be friends."

Jamie thought about that night she and Toby had gotten picked up as runaways—the steel grid in the back seat of the police cruiser, the tidal wave of anxiety. The sight of those bars still left her breathless. She couldn't imagine living inside them. She handed the coffee back to her mother. Her mother stared out the window, her reflection stark and plain. It was frustrating, this anger, and never being able to place blame.

"But, that man—"

"It was self-defense. Jesus. He was angry, drunk. He recognized me from the poker game. He lunged at me and, I don't know. I jumped and my gun went off. Then there was a bloody hole in his stomach and he was dead. You could tell from his eyes, the way he stared at the ceiling. It was horrible. Keating went ballistic and I knew right then I was screwed. So, I took the ring, because I knew I would need money if ran. But it was Keating who started the whole thing, getting him to bet that stupid ring."

Phoebe shivered and took the chair opposite the window. Neither of them would ever be completely free of the images from that night.

"Do you know what it's like? To think your life has taken a turn for the better, that you might have a future? And then watch it fall apart because two men get into a pissing contest? Keating's a powerful man in this town. Do you really think I could tell him no? He changed my life completely once and he could have done it again. He'd been nice to me, gentlemanly. I let myself hope that maybe I'd found a home, a real home. I let myself think that for a whole day and half of one night. I wanted to get back a little bit of what I'd had with your father. Is that so much to ask?"

Jamie's memory of those days existed in the form of snapshots. Her mother and dad and Toby at a picnic. Her parents sitting together on the couch watching reruns. Briefly, they'd had it all. Jamie put her hand on her mother's arm, surprised by how thin it was. It startled them both, this sudden intimacy, the small bones of the woman's forearm feeling like a wing Jamie could twist and break. She pulled her hand back. "I don't know what to believe anymore."

Phoebe shook a cigarette out of her pack, said nothing.

"You can't smoke in here."

Phoebe lit it anyway. Silence hung between them, thick as the smoke clouding her mother's face.

"I never lied to you. Your whole life, I never told you one lie." Phoebe pocketed the lighter. "I've done a lot of bad things, but the one thing I never did was lie to you. That's what happened that night. You decide to believe it or not."

An aide pushed an empty gurney around the corner and Phoebe crushed the cigarette under her sneaker. "Doesn't matter," she said. "I'm not leaving, not now, anyway."

"You're staying?"

Her mother stared at the floor, her face stern and gaunt with something it took a moment to recognize. Determination. Between the bad luck and the bad choices, the woman was down to nothing but her own free will.

"The cop said they'll let me visit him for fifteen

minutes, twice a day. I'm broke but I still have my job, my apartment. When I got out of prison I thought I was getting a second chance to get things right. But I was wrong. This is my chance. My only chance."

"I thought you were afraid to stay."

Phoebe stood up and stretched her back. "What I am is tired. There's not enough to pin it on me unless Keating testifies, and what's for sure is that he doesn't want anyone to know he was screwing an ex-con."

"But once the body is found, some other piece of the puzzle will give." Jamie searched her mother's face for some evidence of truth and saw it, right there, in the steady way she held her gaze.

"It was Keating's house that got broken into. He picked a fight with that man when he swindled him out of the ring. That cop saw it. And Keating's the one who got Loyal to cover everything up."

Jamie squared that with what she already knew. Keating had gotten rid of the guns because the gun Phoebe used was registered to him.

Her ten minutes were almost up and Garcia was waiting.

Jamie handed Phoebe the necklace from Toby along with the bus ticket. "You should keep this and get a refund on the ticket."

"You never even thought about coming with me, did you?"

Jamie shrugged. "Not really."

"I guess it was silly to hope. You've been a good sister to him, you know? But this is my time to try and be a half decent mother." She lowered her voice. "Did you get rid of that ring?"

"Not yet, but I got a plan." She made a zipping motion over her mouth. It was the only thing linking Phoebe to Bangor, but Jamie knew exactly what she needed to do with it.

"Fair enough. How did the tournament end?"

"I found that queen of spades you tossed down in the alley and played it against Keating."

"Ha! I was going to slip that to you just to keep things interesting. Don't tell me you won with it."

Jamie laughed darkly. "I hit a flush."

"And won?"

"I won, but Garcia busted Loyal's operation and confiscated the prize money."

"Loyal got busted and you're broke? Jesus, kid. The curse lives on."

CHAPTER

39

GARCIA WAS WHERE she'd left him in the ER driveway. When Jamie closed the car door, he put it in drive and asked, "Which way?"

"Straight up Main. Keep north on the county road."

He cracked the window and clenched a cigarette between his lips, offered her the pack. She waved it off.

"Put your safety belt on."

She tugged the thing over her chest, hating the way it cut into the side of her neck.

They passed the three billboards for Mimawa, the neon lights still pulsing but pale against the sky.

They approached the interstate and he asked, "East or west?"

"Straight." She pointed. "Take the underpass."

"Huh," he said, and slowed the car a bit. "People don't come out this way much unless they're hunting."

At the end of the tunnel, the road dipped and turned

to gravel. The sedan bounced and bottomed out briefly, and Garcia swerved around a pothole. Another hundred yards and the gate appeared off to the left. Everything was how she'd left it. He would still be there, under all those rocks. It made her queasy to think of decomposing flesh, worms, maggots. A flash of heat hit her stomach and she fought it off by rolling down her window and letting the cold air hit her face.

"Right there," she said, and he stopped the car in front of the broken gate.

He threw his cigarette out the window. "I remember that gate. I came hunting here once, with some guys from vice. This is Keating's land. Are you telling me TJ Bangor is here?"

"Follow me." She grabbed her backpack.

"Christ. Is your uncle in on this?"

Jamie got out of the car. "You could call him the cleanup man."

"This is enough to get a warrant for Keating's house." He cut her off in front of the car. "You know you're about to cross the most powerful man in this county."

"As far as he'll ever know, Loyal gave him up for revenge."

"Okay, but you need to be clear. A move like this will affect the rest of your life."

"I know that. I already made my decision. I know exactly how this plays out if I keep quiet. I've seen it with my own two eyes. From now on I take my chances."

The ground was squishy and wet, weeds bending beneath her boots. The deer blind in the pine tree was to the left and beyond that the ground sloped away to the right. Garcia followed her awkwardly, his shoes already caking with mud. They stopped at the top of the rise just before the gully. The rock mound covering TJ's body lay untouched at the bottom of the slope. Stones piled in the shape of a coffin.

Garcia caught up and stopped next to her. "Oh, man," he said. Wind blew across the field and he turned up his lapels.

Jamie said nothing. The mound of rocks had caved in a little in the middle and it made her uneasy to think of the weight of them pressing against the man's soft middle. Jamie shut her eyes, pushing down the queasiness, telling herself it was almost over.

"How long has he been here?"

The days were a blur. It seemed like a year. "Five days, maybe." He could piece it together himself.

"Was he killed here? Do you know what happened?"

"No and no. You should ask Keating, though. He's the man with all the answers."

Garcia shook his head. "I figured, what with the game that night and the ring. How did you get dragged into it?"

She told him about that night, how Loyal had woken her up after a call from Keating, how her uncle had made her sit on the floorboard so she wouldn't know where they were going, how just last night she'd put the pieces together on her own and found her way here. She didn't mention seeing Phoebe in the second-story window that night at Keating's, but added, "It's not surprising. Loyal and Keating go back years."

"Nothing surprises me anymore." He shook loose another cigarette.

Jamie fingered the ring inside her pocket, thinking it through. The diamonds alone might be worth more than fifty thousand. But if the Elders curse was real, she had this one chance to break it.

"I'm going to have to talk to your mother, you know? There's a lot of unanswered questions."

"No, you don't need to talk to her. But, if you go looking, you'll find her where she's been all along. Working in a little diner on Main Street, dishing out blue-plate specials to the good people of Blind River." Jamie held her hand out, opened it palm up. "You should give this back to Lena Bangor and her mother." What was left of the day's sunlight caught in the facets of the diamonds and bounced off the gold.

He took it, turned it over in his palm. "Where'd you get this?"

"It's everything you wanted, right?" She shrugged. "Here's what I think. TJ Bangor went back to Keating's house and got shot during an argument over that ring. It was between the two of them. Maybe it was self-defense, maybe he'll say that he wished he'd handled it better. Nobody else pays for this. Not my mother, not my brother."

"That's what you think?" He wiped the ring with a handkerchief.

She'd just handed over a fortune, yet she felt like she'd dropped the weight of a hundred lies.

"It's a fair deal, don't you think?" She adjusted her backpack, caught herself when the horizon tilted.

"It's homicide, Jamie. If your mother's involved, it will come out."

Sweat began to bead on her forehead. "Keating would never let it come out if he had an ex-felon in his house, much less if he'd slept with one. He'd be ruined. All his convictions from the last twenty years would get thrown out and throw this town into chaos. He'll claim innocence or self-defense, but his career will be over. He'll retire early and spend more time at his country club. That's the way things work in this town, right? And you'll be rid of a dirty judge." A sweet decaying smell came at them on the wind. She rubbed her forehead, wincing at the bruise Loyal had left with the back of his hand.

"It's freezing out here and you're sweating. You okay?"

"There's a dead man under that pile of rocks. No, I'm not okay."

He pulled a roll of peppermints out of his pocket and handed them to her. "Sometimes, sugar helps."

She moved away from the smell and sucked on the candy. Her stomach settled a little.

"Here." He handed her a slip of paper with a phone number on it. "Give me a password."

She took the paper. "What's this?"

"Text that number, type in the password, and the funds will be transferred to the bank account number you give it."

"The reward? I don't want it. That family? No, I can't take that." Another little part of her died right there, having to pass on that money.

"It isn't just the family's money. Half of it came from Keating." He turned the ring over in his palm.

"What? Why would he do that?"

"Probably wants to look innocent. Look, I had to take that prize money, but isn't it better this way? The reward money is free and clear. Yours because you earned it."

She thought it through. This money wasn't tied to Loyal, and she *had* found the body on her own. Still, wasn't it blood money? "I don't know."

"Listen, kid. You've been through a lot. Maybe it's time you let go of everybody else's business and started building a life. This money is a result of doing the right thing. It's twenty thousand, not enough for you to feel guilty about but enough to give you a start in life. Maybe somewhere new. Take it."

The unexpected kindness caused her eyes to burn and a hard knot to form at the back of her throat. For once she'd have enough money not to worry about food or clothes. She could have a place of her own, somewhere far away with a door and a lock. A feeling of warmth settled about her shoulders. *It would be enough.*

"It can't be traced if you use a burner cell phone. Give me a password."

It might even be enough for her to play the professional circuit for half a year, if she kept the buy-ins low and lived cheap. She said the first thing that came to mind. "The Odds."

"I'll set it up as soon as I get a positive ID on the body."

"What about the ring?"

He hesitated. "Forget you ever saw it. But don't be surprised if you read in the paper that it turned up when we searched Keating's game room. As far as anyone can recall, it was the last place it was seen. Eventually it will get back to the family."

Family. She thought of Phoebe sitting by Toby's bed, holding his hand, wanting this last chance to get things right. All Jamie had to do was step out of the way.

Garcia brushed his fingers on his trousers and climbed back up the ridge. "Stay in touch. I might need to get a statement from you. Down the road."

"I thought all I had to do was locate the body. I thought it would all be anonymous."

"I'll do everything I can. You've been instrumental in two big cases and you got no priors. That should go a long way. I'd say, as things stand, you'll be okay. Who knows? You might even be the first Elders to avoid seeing the inside of a jail cell. But you should lay low. You got some-place to go?"

She thought about Florida, where the legal age for gam-bling in the Indian casinos was eighteen. "I was thinking about heading south."

"Where?"

"Florida."

"Florida? What the hell's in Florida?"

"Casinos. Big tournaments." *Warm weather and orange trees.*

"Huh. All right. Just make sure I know how to find you." He flipped open his cell phone. "You got to go now. Once I call this in, this area will be swarming with a forensic team."

She pulled an envelope out of her backpack and handed it to him. "Can you get this to my uncle?"

Garcia opened the envelope, looked through the stack of postcards. "What's this?"

"They're from a guy who used to be his friend. He likes to look through them at night." She imagined Loyal sitting in a small cell thumbing through the cards, maybe trading them one by one for a pack of smokes or a bar of soap.

Garcia stuffed them into his coat pocket. "I'll get them to him, Little Miss Sunshine."

She walked toward the woods.

"You're not like them, you know. Your mother or your uncle," he yelled as she walked away. "Be your own girl, Jamie Elders."

A plume of smoke snaked above the tree line where the tracks ran through the woods and she headed toward it. She'd follow the tracks back to Blind River to catch the late train. By midnight she'd be on her way. Over to the coast then south, all the way to Florida, to Jacksonville, and further. Tampa, then Fort Lauderdale.

She looked back once. Across the open space, Garcia was talking into his phone. Imagining the distance she could travel in a few days caused an unexpected lightness in her chest. What if she was different than them? What if she could shed the past? What if she had her own fate, separate and unknowable?

Low on the blue horizon, wild geese flew across the sun. What if there really was something better waiting for her; what if she was moving toward it right now? Pines swayed in the breeze overhead and sunlight slipped through the branches. In the distance, the southbound train approached with a gathering rumble. Soon it would come booming around the bend, shattering the afternoon with its inevitable thunder, oblivious and unyielding, harsh and exciting. Charging the air with hope.

ACKNOWLEDGMENTS

If writing a first novel requires determination and solitude, getting one published takes a village of generous people willing to suspend disbelief and give their time and energy to an unproven writer. I am enormously grateful for the support I've been given by those who first believed.

Chelsey Emmelhainz is a remarkable editor. This book is a result of her vision and her confidence in this story. It is a privilege to work with Chelsey and the fantastic team at Crooked Lane Books: Matt Martz, Sarah Poppe, Jenny Chen, Melanie Sun, and all the rest.

Mark Gottlieb and Trident Media Group provide excellent guidance and direction. Thanks for betting on Jamie and Blind River.

Sterling Watson was unfailing in his support, friendship, and guidance.

When I ran low on confidence, Steve Yarbrough leant

me his and told me not to give up on this book. I'm so proud to call you my friend.

My earliest readers were Gerry Wilson and Barbara Nicolazzo. Thank you for the gift of your time and energy. Thanks to Tom Bernardo, who taught me everything I needed to know to start this book. Thanks to Lori Roy, who read an early draft, offered crucial feedback, and answered dozens of questions.

Three conferences provided scholarships and fellowships and gave me opportunities to develop as a writer: the Writers in Paradise Conference, the Vermont College of Fine Arts Novel Retreat, and the Sewanee Writers' Conference. Thank you.

Over the years I've had the privilege to study with many exceptional teachers: Connie May Fowler, Andre Dubus III, Ann Hood, Parneshia Jones, Jill McCorkle, Margot Livesey, and Stewart O'Nan. Thank you for your patience with those rough drafts and the vision to see what might come.

Eternal gratitude goes to my friends and family who kept me company on the journey: Nick White, Maggie Mitchell, Mary Henry-Marcus, Tricia Booker, Juanita Thompson, Pat Spears, Paulette Boudreaux, Amina Gautier, Kate LeSar, Meg Harris, Sheila Stewe, Louise Marburg, Nancy Levine, Leigh Muller, Dahlma Llanos Figueroa, Glenda Bailey-Mershon, Brenda Lewis, Karin Cecile Davidson, David Eye, Joan Leggitt, Karen Becker, Andrea Greenbaum, Lisa Schuchmann (for the excellent website), and Kris Radish. A special heartfelt thanks to my St. Petersburg friends for cheering this book along its way.

Thanks to the booksellers, librarians, book clubs, and readers. Your dedication and hard work keeps the reading world vibrant.

The biggest thanks of all goes to Lyra. You are the kindest and most generous person I've ever known, and your very presence in my life convinces me that anything is possible. You are my best luck and this book is for you.